PRAISE FOR
HELL OF HOSANNA

....

"Kip Langton is a writer to watch."

—Fiona Davis, *New York Times* Bestselling Author

"*Citizen Kane* meets *Brave New World*—as enthralling as it is devastating. Kip has envisioned a near future that feels perhaps too near for comfort."

—Pierce Berolzheimer, Director of *Crabs!*

"Images elevate, emerge, submerge, and break out like light from behind a distant cloud in Kip Langton's debut novel, *Hell of Hosanna*, an exuberantly imagined whirl of all-too-human relationships and radically unexpected visions. It is a novel that can easily transport the Empire State Building and the Seagram's Building from Manhattan to a private 'pleasure' reserve and move the reader to an oddly familiar fire-new land, where the luxury goods of our civilization have become mute curios in an elite museum. Langton's narrative touches science fiction, family dynamics, social satire, the richness of metaphor, and cultural overload, all with the precision of a well-oiled time machine. It's Tom Wolfe meeting Thomas Pynchon over drinks with Kurt Vonnegut in a low bar furnished with the jagged detritus of the past one-hundred years of the American Dream."

—Kevin Lane Dearinger, Author of *Bad Sex in Kentucky* and *On Stage with Bette Davis: Inside the Fabulous Flop of Miss Moffat*

"Once in a great while, a writer comes along whose words and ideas are so mind-bendingly original and compelling that they inhabit a category all their own. This is that writer. And this is his first book."

"In a twisted tale of the 1 percent, Kip Langton's imagination takes us on a fast-paced young man's journey to a visionary future which feels like it could be upon us tomorrow."

"Propulsive and imaginative writing keep the reader turning the pages of this compelling debut novel about a young man's self-discovery set in a dystopian future."

"New York re-imagined. The narrative drive through the vignettes of this story is historical yet apocalyptic. I enjoyed taking a dip into the imagination behind a new New York style. Breathtaking and unforgettable."

"Kip Langton is an exceptionally talented writer. His look into the future is fascinating and all too possible."

Hell of Hosanna

by Kip Langton

ISBN 978-1-64663-742-3

Published by

◀ köehlerbooks™

3705 Shore Drive
Virginia Beach, VA 23455
800-435-4811
www.koehlerbooks.com

Hope you enjoy the read!!! Kip

HELL OF HOSANNA

A NOVEL

KIP LANGTON

VIRGINIA BEACH
CAPE CHARLES

For Jeanne Quigan Scott.

CHAPTER ONE

Our Father, Who Art in . . .

My father pulled the butterfly door shut and the exhaust popped like a firecracker, the sound of the pistons no different than dragonfly wings shuddering the air in sequence next to your ears. This racecar was stripped down and eggshell light. It had a hollow porcelain-plastic weightlessness superimposed with stiff, seemingly Martian-made, aerospace strength. The licorice-black candy-cane weave of the carbon fiber traveled along the pointed nose, and the abuse from the sun faded its protective gloss layer into what looked like a dirty and rusted mustard-colored casing. This piece of engineering, friction-fought down to its raw framework, performing its whole life at its highest and most self-destructive level. Ultimate, ceaseless output, until its eventual end. A vessel of automotive creativity in its most refined and potent state.

Its nitrogen oxide discharge, the brass melody from *Star Wars*.

Its WD-40-lathered gear shift, the strings from *Jurassic Park*.

Its ascending speed, the horns from *Indiana Jones*.

Theatrics in mechanical form. And my father, Fep Stubb Anglish, in the central driving position of this kinetic opera house. Controlling and guiding these iconic sounds. And me, without any control or guidance, in that "bitch seat," as he called it.

I, his bitch. *He*, my master. *I*, in this sweaty gray Mickey Mouse shirt.

The look he possessed would be different on a weekly, sometimes hourly, basis. At this moment, he had hair full of Einstein madness. The thick sugar-white dreads went out in all directions away from his ever-expanding forehead exposing his receding hairline. A sculpted and pointed white beard and a mustache with a few black threads still left in it covered his chin. His angered eyes were hidden behind the brown lenses of his carbon-fiber Tom Ford sunglasses and his gamy, tense body grew fiercer underneath the fashionable shell of his deep brown Horween leather jacket. He was hatred draped with style. And he'd cut through the turns with that hatred, too close to the edge, teasing death with a catlike pitter-patter precision of gentle and deliberate paws scanning along the corners of a wall in search of a mouse.

The grip, always there.

He knew where it was before he even turned into the corner.

On the straights, playfully searching for that grip.

The machine, dancing with him, handling like a go-kart.

The gold foil lining the exhaust to reflect heat.

The exposed green goo crudely holding pieces of the dashboard together.

The plastic twisty knobs jittering in reaction to the pumping pistons from behind.

That smell and feel and tactility of a very long-gone analog age.

"James, pull your door shut," he barked at me from the center seat before we could move. I was in the seat to the left of him. The seat to the right of him was always empty.

"Now!" he demanded, trying to sweep away my lethargy.

Then the door knifed down in vertical motion and the thudded interior sound had shaking notes of carbon and plastic, held together by that green goo.

"James, there's nothing more beautiful than a machine like this, broken in for the very purpose for which it was made."

The pistons pumped and the gears and the exhaust and the whole working system moaned in one low, drawn-out warning. Feminine in its high-pitched rev, the engine sent waves through the rest of the chassis, rattling and reverberating until we rolled off onto the track and sliced by the solar-paneled lampposts lining the snaking outline of the rubber-streaked tarmac.

Those climbing speeds.

That titanium throttle pedal straight to the floor.

Constant acceleration. Hand-machined needles going up and down, and left to right, and right to left. Heat blistering out of the dashboard. Burning plastic. Burning rubber. Carbon fiber, disintegrating. My Mechanix automotive racing gloves, smoldering. My father, with one hand on the wheel, taking a swig of his Laphroaig to substitute his urge to prematurely shift, drinking that whiskey to shift his own gears.

"Amateurs see emotion as performance," he said, the Laphroaig splattering from his mouth. "Professionals see performance as emotion," he splattered again.

The dawn light of such early morning hours spilled into the end of night and muted and dulled the solar-pumped light. Dawn fueled the adrenaline that remedied my juvenile morning tiredness, which my father so, so hated.

But, god, those continuous climbing speeds.

That titanium throttle pedal still to the floor.

Those needles still in a fever behind the thin plastic of the instrument panel.

The rhythm of this theatric rattling catching up with itself in angered fleeting resonance.

Then . . . a calm.

Weightlessness.

Like we were exiting the atmosphere into smooth outer space. All the while the Goodyear tires melted beneath us, shredding against the dry heat of the tarmac. That friction forcing the pistons to cry as my father upshifted and downshifted, careless of the machine's breaking point. The centrifugal, g-force-ridden hold of the sticky and melted tires making you feel there was just too much grip to be had.

Turn One: Empire Corner.

We wouldn't slow down.

No anticipated squeaking and whistling from the Brembo brakes.

My eyes locked onto the wooden emergency handbrake lever.

"Dad!" I screamed.

He's gonna brake too late, I thought.

"The turn," I cried. "Dad, the turn!"

"Oh, god!" I howled.

Then—that sudden reversal of force.

Deceleration.

Finally.

Thank God.

The brakes whistled and went up in flames and these flames whipped around the sides of the car. He was so hard on these brakes, but he matched the oppressive downward force to avoid wheel lock and wasted grip. It resulted in the car boomeranging out of the turn, grabbing its own momentum to go further into this unknown of ultimate performance. My father's focused cathedral glass green eyes would now emerge from behind the brown lenses and his cigar-skinned face, and it showed his total control in this wild chaos of hellish speed.

"The exit of a corner," he preached, "is more important than the entry to the corner."

"Yes, father," I answered.

"James," he carried on, "don't focus too much on what you're doing right then and there on the track—rather, use that energy to focus on what's coming next."

"Yes, Father."

"And don't ever press the gas pedal until you know you never have to take your foot off it. That'll help you avoid the amateur mistake of braking and pumping the gas because the speed is uncontrollable."

"Yes, Father."

The Empire State Building now came into view.

This building had been disassembled in Manhattan and reassembled here in my father's very private, very grand, and very elusive pleasure palace. This pleasure palace of his was locked away in the middle of nowhere in the most eastern province of Canada. It was called Fogo Island. My father's helicopter pilot told me once it was right off the mainland of Newfoundland and Labrador, and it was now the new home for many of the world's most iconic landmarks. They weren't stolen, as my father would publicly defend. They were, instead, pieces of architecture saved from "the total liquification of real estate into a zombie graveyard of spatial financial assets." (As he put it.)

The Empire State Building stood tall and gothic against the burnt marshmallow fog oozing under the low-sitting clouds. The clouds absorbed the purple-and-gold blaring lights emitted from the Art Deco cliffside-edged peaks, which travelled up into these deepening levels of darkening sky. Like the purple luminescent skin of a jellyfish, these glowing puffs would move along in a thoughtless current to nowhere, it seemed.

Fogo Island, a ghost paradise, a state of mind, really. I felt I was stuck in a still-life painting, my stiff and lifeless body positioned against a piece of fruit next to a colorful vase with a flower in it. I felt so useless in Fogo Island, this angular and hard-edged landscape. This place made you sink into yourself. Because you meant nothing to it. Because this was the ultimate of opulence. The ultra-modern in its most barren form. A Martian existence for no one else but the super wealthy. This was the flagship of trillionaire minimalism at its purest. So distilled with wealth it went beyond the decorative into some type of gilded blandness. Between that, and the cragged granite hills and the snow so white it looked like frozen milk against the oil-black racetrack, it was enough to make you scream out of boredom and self-hatred.

Turn Two: Metropolitan Corner.

My father downshifted as fast as someone running their hands across piano keys. The BMW V12 engine hummed along in reactionary pleasure and the exhaust sounded like a tea kettle.

Passing by the planted Beaux-Arts architecture of the Metropolitan Museum of Art—once in Manhattan, now in Fogo Island—numbed my nerves and the building's sallow lights came through the fog.

This, too, was disassembled and reassembled only for my father's selfish enjoyment.

The French neoclassicism, mixed with cruder components of iron and glass, and the bone-dry gothic flair, only for Him.

He'd turned the Metropolitan Museum of Art into his treasure chest, filled to the brim with objects he had taken from the public. These objects symbolized the peak of man. That analog age he stole from the rest of the world.

When you entered The Great Hall, you saw a black titanium beast. Long and sharp, it appeared to be moving in its stillness, with the delicate red *WATCH STEP* warning lines tattooed on its lightweight, curved skin. Attached to the widened rear of this beast were the two Pratt & Whitney J58 turbojet engines. Their prominence in the back reminded me of the bulbous butt of a hornet, its whole skeleton like a perfectly fossilized space insect. Some weird bug, it was, stolen from its home at the Intrepid Sea, Air & Space Museum.

"Lockheed SR-71 Blackbird," my father would say whenever we entered The Great Hall. "Used to be the fastest aircraft in the world."

I would follow him past its stinger into the other rooms. These rooms—once containing invaluable Greek and Roman art, modern and contemporary art, European sculpture and decorative art, medieval art, the Robert Lehman Collection, etc.—now housed what he called his "forgotten analog objects."

The Robert Lehman Collection became a warehouse for very high-end leather goods, footwear, handbags, and jewelry. The luxury French brand, Chanel, had its own spot. Gucci had another. There was also Hermes, Louis Vuitton, Fendi, Givenchy, Valentino, Dolce & Gabbana, Burberry, Balenciaga, Yves Saint Laurent, Prada, Dior, Harry Winston, Van Cleef & Arpels, Tiffany & Co., Piaget, Bvlgari, Chopard, Mikimoto, Graff, Buccellati, and Cartier.

The objects were placed behind protective glass and never worn by anyone besides my mother—but only sometimes. Unless she wore them, occasionally, within the borderlines of the property, they were untouched museum pieces to my father. They were artifacts from a hyper-capitalistic period that he, so proudly, had ended. My father told a reporter once: "When Bentley produces a car as shitty as a Kia and Kia produces a car as shitty as a Bentley, that's when I've won."

And he did win.

Many years ago.

Purpose without Pretension was his slogan for ultimate democratization.

Because it was about *you*. Not *them*.

YOU. NOT THEM—that's the philosophy every company he consumed would follow. That's what would create his mega company known as U.

U was formed from the unnatural compression of all forms of industry into one entity, producing sameness out of the pursuit of common need. It became the largest holding company in history, owning over 60,000 companies worldwide. My father became the first trillionaire and the gap between him and the rest of the world would grow at an exponential rate.

Such a simple letter like U. Amazing how something like that would become more iconic to the public than the McDonald's arches or those Coca-Cola script letters.

Purpose without Pretension; what a formula. More than a tagline. Rather, a world-dominating mantra. And that mantra would echo through the halls of the Metropolitan Museum of Art and everything else my father touched.

Purpose without Pretension.

Purpose without Pretension.

Purpose without Pretension.

Echoing into that space where the medieval art used to be, now festooned with the analog age. Ferrari, Porsche, McLaren, BMW, Mercedes, Alfa Romeo, Jaguar, Range Rover, Bentley, Rolls-Royce, Lamborghini, Maserati, Audi, Bugatti, Tesla, Koenigsegg, Pagani—trappings of the archaic, the inefficient, and the elite. None of which Fep Anglish had any use for anymore. Unless he could have it all for himself by hiding it in the middle of nowhere, like he did now. This analog age could only have use here and nowhere else. These objects were his and not for others to enjoy.

Purpose without Pretension.

Purpose without Pretension.

Purpose without Pretension.

Echoing onward into the room where the Temple of Dendur used to be. Replaced with the Space Shuttle Atlantis, taken from the Kennedy Space Center, along with a lot of other NASA-related objects from many centers across the country. This came to be known as the NASA Room.

One big recording of the past, this modern life became. Nothing happening because it had already happened and would never happen again. Besides musicals, and a few other strange things that were left in place, there were no public gatherings of any kind anymore. No baseball. No basketball. No football. No soccer. No tennis. No hockey. No golf. And on this list went. You could watch a rerun of Michael Jordan leading the charge for the Bulls in his 1996 NBA final victory over the SuperSonics and pretend it was unfolding in real time. You could trick yourself that way. My father did it very well. You could ignore the fact that nothing would ever happen again, that organized human contact was classified under *biohazard activities* via the Clean Up Act, better known as CUA Rules.

The meds also helped you forget reality. You could pump yourself full of them, daily, hourly. This beautiful cocktail of sedatives and pain blockers and antidepressants and SSRIs and anxiolytics and whatever else was floating around in your system. You did it to carry on. Because we were all active participants in something that'd already passed. With the added kick of cocaine and amphetamine and crack and meth, those things would really bring the shock value. "Jordan does it again," you'd holler after the buzzer-beater from your own buzz. You'd react to it with the same enthusiasm every single year. Because the stimulants did that for you. They brought that shock and awe. And they were advertised well that way. Pharmaceutical marketing gorged on the corpse of general advertising. It was the only thing that could thrive in the decay of today. The resilience of its drug-dealing public platform and the way it repackaged serious chemical combinations under the consumer supervision of Coca-Cola's Santa Claus and Polar Bears, McDonald's' Ronald McDonald, Kellogg's Tony the Tiger, Energizer Batteries' Energizer Bunny, KFC's Colonel Sanders, and even GEICO's Gecko. The Pillsbury Doughboy, brought back to life by Clowde & Clowde Wellness (CCW), had already sold me on an array of inhibitors, which I snacked on daily. CCW was the last creative shop in the world, and it was smart enough to plagiarize the advertising archive before my father absorbed and swallowed up all the creative agencies, obliterating the rest of the industry. Santa Claus and those polar bears and Ronald McDonald and all the rest were now demoted mascots selling you over-the-counter inflammation inhibitors for your self-diagnosed uveitis, psoriasis, ulcerative colitis, rheumatoid arthritis, psoriatic arthritis, Crohn's disease, juvenile idiopathic arthritis, and your hidradenitis suppurativa. They sold chemical products like candy. And we all loved them so very much. I loved them so very much indeed. My father loved them even more, though. And my mother—well, she loved them even more than my father. That says something. And, in consequence, the division between fact and fiction became a very fluid thing. "They're Gr-r-reat!" Tony the Tiger told us. And they were great, let me tell you. They were really Gr-r-reat! And we loved them just so damn much. Just loved them to pieces. What a beautifully original slogan from a wonderful and honest place like CCW.

Turn Three: Dakota Corner.

The Dakota—removed from the Upper West Side of Manhattan—came into view with its satanic, aged French architecture with the drooping roofs and the balustrades and the niches and the terracotta spandrels and the balconies and the gables and the dormers. That mustard-colored mausoleum of some dead past. Once the oldest standing apartment building in all of Manhattan, John Lennon had lived there. We slashed by it like a cheese grater against burnt toast.

Turn Four: Seagram Corner.

The Seagram Building—removed from Midtown Manhattan—came into view. My father would always drill into me the critical importance of this building. How the structural necessity of the bronze and steel gave the skyscraper aesthetic appeal. No need for forced and pointless formal additives. "Stripped down to the bones," he'd say. "And the bones look good." We slashed by this building, too.

Turn Five: Chrysler Corner.

The Chrysler Building came into view. "Art Deco at its best," he'd say. And on and on the lecture would go, thereafter. I won't get into it, but this was one of his favorite skyscrapers.

Turn Six: Freedom Corner.

The Freedom Tower came into view. He'd say something else about that. By this time, I simply couldn't listen to it anymore. I would completely turn off. God, my father was such a prick.

Turn Seven: Liberty Corner.

You wouldn't believe it. But he managed to do it. The Statue of Liberty came into view. My father would be quiet for this one. It spoke for itself. He owned the symbol of America.

And on and on and on it went with these misplaced landmarks. Fourteen miles of tarmac display tucked away in ninety-one square miles of my father's private property. The whole island, *his*.

He'd visited Fogo Island way back and then decided he had to own the entire thing. He had to possess it and harness it. He talked to my mother about it like he talked about all his obsessions. Every day. Every hour. Every minute. Every second. All for his own inner growth and the total rejection of the indigenous people of Fogo Island. He let a few live there. I really doubted they were indigenous, though. He made them out to be. But I'm pretty sure they just worked for my father and took on the lifestyle of the Beothuk. I had no idea what the Beothuk was. Or even if I was saying it right. But I overheard my father calling them the "Butt-fuck" a few times. Shows you how much he cared. Respect for heritage and culture was by no means high priority. To give you an idea, I didn't even know my father's father was from the Congo, until my mother told me. When I asked him about the Congo, he punched me hard in the side and said, "Not the Congo—The Republic of the Congo." This correction gave him the moral advantage over me. He sounded worldly and I sounded like a domestic ignorant. That would be enough to shut me up. Then I asked about his mother. He was very transparent about his mother. His mother and my mother happened to both be from Shoreham, England.

He screeched to a sudden stop. The engine clinked in the motionless heat. It sounded like pellets were being bounced around in a metal box.

"Drive!" he barked at me. Before I could resist, he got out of the driver's seat and buckled himself into the always vacant right seat. "James, play pilot now."

I stayed strapped in.

"James!" he barked. "You. Fucking. Fool."

"I can't," I whimpered.

"This world asks little from you," he spat. "Never a driver, always a passenger, I guess."

"I'm sorry," I abdicated.

"Stop your *sorry* crap. You're always sorry with that sorry crap of yours."

"Father, I am failure."

"Success is simply overcompensating for failure, my boy."

"Father, I am failure—I am sorry," I repeated like an animal unable to communicate anything else. In the face of his hatred, I could have no substantive reply. It took the life out of you. That rhetoric. He would teach, and I would learn. My generation wading through heavy, unanswerable, but very ponderable, existential questions, each carefully planted to waste our time as he thought up the setting for our existence. But like an author of a book, he could make us his characters and think up our reality and permanently bond us to it. Reality was his creation, and he didn't have to be a part of it. He invented it and left it alone. And he would only come to visit when he spat out this sermonized gibberish. This "car talk" of his. This conditioning. To teach us to act like him. To fade away in his whiskey talk. The dam of subtlety and restraint had broken, and he flooded our culture with criticism, and he turned us into directionless self-righteous opinion pieces. My life, his life, everyone's life; we were all telling, never showing.

"You sack of afterbirth," he hissed, his face close to mine, initiating this man-to-man mental wreckage. How Hemingway of Him.

"I can't," I repeated in that youthful and stubborn and very thick way of mine.

"This bitch gives you nothing," he went on.

(A swig of Laphroaig.)

"No traction control."

(A swig of Laphroaig.)

"No power steering."

(A swig of Laphroaig.)

"Nothing to guide you."

(A swig of Laphroaig.)

"You're on your own with it."

From this mental beating, I would always eventually fall apart, sobbing to myself as quietly as I could.

"Oh, shut up, you brat . . . you ass brat, you."

I cried harder.

"Go on, cry it out, boy oh little boy."

I cried it out.

"Be busy-being-busy, with nothing to show for. Water your plants and bitch about being too busy bitching. Your crying is too busy crying. Go on and cry it out, boy. Be busy crying and being busy . . ."

I went on crying as he would demand it.

"Be busy-being-busy, you cry-ass."

(A swig of Laphroaig.)

"You crying-cry-ass."

(A swig of Laphroaig.)

"Be busy-being-busy."

(A swig of Laphroaig.)

"Let the emotions flow, as they do for you. Follow them into whatever it is this is . . ."

(A swig of Laphroaig.)

"Be busy-being-busy."

(A swig of Laphroaig.)

"You know," he spat the rest of the scotch out, the whole cockpit reeking of that smoky peat, "if I killed you right now, the only thing that would suffer would be that stupid plant of yours. It would get no water. What would a plant do without you? With no water to be had."

As a nervous habit, I would push my hair back in these moments. There was so much in these gestures of mine. Such confusion and lack of will in them. This pushing back of the hair. These sweaty hands running through the gelled strands.

"You look the part," my father went on—and would go on, and on, and on—distancing his own worth from my worthlessness. "It's such a shame because you look like an athlete. You're pretty-looking, too, with that Al Pacino hair and that frame of yours. If I were a woman, I'd think you're something. But Halloween comes once a year, kiddo, and you can't pretend year-round. A great big game of pretend, you are. Smokescreen. All of you. Swarming places because a celebrity you dress like went there once. You're the Six Flags people. You know what this is—Six Flags . . . ? It's people like you who create crowds and lines and blind intrigue. You Six Flags the shit out of everything by just being there. You devalue. By just being there."

"Fine, Dad." I gave in.

I struggled to get into the center driver's seat, and I could hear my father sighing out of embarrassment.

I started the engine, and immediately stalled.

"That was fast," my father said in blunt cadence. "You don't last very long, do you?"

"I . . ."

"Move over, child. Move back to Bitch Land."

The real adult took center stage, once again, and pushed the clutch down, shifted the car into gear, and then pressed on the gas and released the clutch at the same time. He rode the clutch in a state of deliberate, pointless play.

Moving through the apex of the corner, we slalomed as the track moved from left to right. The exhaust, once again, popped, and coming out of that corner, my father opened the throttle and the stretch of pavement turned silver from the sun. The leafless lazy trees hung motionless and the muscles in my father's jaw protruded from the adrenaline.

We topped out at 240 mph.

The Last Turn: Fep Corner.

The sharpest turn of them all.

My father's house—called Fep House—came into view.

That Fogo Island barn loft. Akin to the local fishermen's homes, the house sat on stilts because everything on the island was built to be temporary. My father did that to carry out his façade of cultural respect and continuity. But this house wasn't going anywhere. It was landmarked by his brand name and his power—and everyone knew that.

Despite the timber construction and the whitewashed spruce interior and the rough-sawn pine exterior drizzled with solar panels, this house was a structure of ego, a trillionaire's New York City penthouse apartment wearing different clothes. It was a status symbol, disguised with that Edward Hopper moon-desert, Earth-walking feel and that Gatsby thought-provoking lonely singularity, both of which, when combined, mimicked everything that Fogo Island was.

This minimalist-surrealist feel was exemplified by those two opulent outdoor terraces. Each was furnished with a lady-leg lamp, verdigris-ridden copper and bronze trim moldings, and a humongous leather lips couch drowned in lipstick-red dye. Tim Burton black-and-white stripes, created from the variance of seams in the spruce strips, paralleled each other on the walls and the ceilings. The whole thing from afar, a monstrous black box floating above a sharp angular backdrop of rocks and mossy growth. Like a horizontal version of the monolith in Stanley Kubrick's *2001: A Space Odyssey*, it stood out. And whenever I saw it from afar, I imagined hearing Gyorgy Ligeti's swelling and unnerving build of *Requiem for Soprano* that accompanied its discovery by the apes. I would hear that music whenever I saw my father, too. Anything that reminded me of him made me think of it. That face of his so worn away by the weathering of his own ego and hatred for humanity.

240 mph—*no deceleration.*

Three more seconds.

240 mph—*no deceleration.*

Three more seconds.

240 mph—*no deceleration.*

"Jesus, Dad, please," I said, pushing my foot against a nonexistent brake pedal. "Brake. Please, for God's sake, brake!"

Smoke began to rise from the mid-mounted engine, pushed to a level of performance beyond the car's design capabilities. All the while, my father still had this casual grip-seeking dance with the machine, holding the wheel, and then letting it go, and then holding it again.

"Dad!" I belted.

He began to laugh, and I closed my eyes with utter obedience, anticipating a collision he so badly wanted.

But sadly, I wanted it, too.

More than my father had ever known.

More than anyone had ever known.

Because suicide is a quiet thing that only speaks up at the end.

So, my eyes closed, and my soul smiled. I wanted this. To get out of this Fep Anglish world. I wanted this death so very much. I wanted obliteration. Total self-destruction. I wanted the entire world to end with me. For all of us to be in the pile of gnarled metal and splintered carbon fiber. Everything in flames propelled by the severed gas tank blown out into the hellish air.

An end to the boredom and disappointment of this modern age of my father's. That jealousy I had of him. Born from my impotence, which created my boredom, and born from the boredom, which created my unfortunate upbringing. If Fep Anglish wanted to end it all right now, I'd wag my tail and follow him into the woods to be put down.

He was my maker.

He was my ender.

He is my father.

"Our Father," he said in soft notes, the engine behind us exploding, "who art in heaven, hallowed be thy name. Thy kingdom come, thy will be done, on earth as it is in heaven. Give us this day our—"

Three more seconds.

240 mph—*no deceleration.*

"James," he cried, "I am a slogan. A brand. A gimmick. Nothing."

Three more seconds.

240 mph—*no deceleration.*

"Brand recognition is creativity's tombstone. 'RIP: Mr. Shtick Gimmick,' my stone will read. Because, as with all true artists, six feet under lies the talent that made us."

I had that look children possess when they see something different.

But I was ready.

So very ready.

Because—life has no happy ending until you end it before it's over.

"My freedom of speech is my freedom of death," my father would say . . .

Right.
Before.

IMPACT.

CHAPTER TWO

Louis Vuitton–bagged Teacup Shih Tzu

"I don't think he's alive," a voice said.

"The *son*—is the son alive?" another asked.

"That's what I mean."

"Let me see."

A hand touched my neck.

"There's a pulse. Faint. But there's a pulse."

"Fep?"

"I'm pretty sure he's gone."

"Jesus Christ."

Echo. Echo. Echo. Gurgle. Gurgle. Gurgle. The sound seemed to travel underwater.

"James," the echo went. "James," it called again, drawing out the syllables that continued to echo in my head.

That static cotton dryness in my mouth, mixed with stale ginger ale bubbling out of the pain. The taste of wet wood, like that spoon from the Haagen-Dazs mini cups, with its harsh bark flavor strengthened by each lick. The ice cream now gone, though. I was left with just that chocolate-stained stick.

"James."

"*James!*" Again, the name stretched and pulled.

Echo. Echo. Echo. Gurgle. Gurgle. Gurgle.

"Pull him out."

"I can't."

He stretched his stiff body downward to hand me my toy pipe.

I saw a small planet.

It was white.

There were no oceans.

Nothing but white powder.

"Why, Dad?" I asked.

The man, silhouetted by some sun, looked down at me.

"Why, Dad?" I asked again.

The man wouldn't answer.

"Why did you try to kill me?"

Echo. Echo. Echo. Gurgle. Gurgle. Gurgle.

"He's breathing. He's speaking!"

"Why did you try to kill me?"

"He's saying something."

"Just pull him out."

"He's stuck."

The mint green light dematerialized and transitioned into different shades of green. From tea green to light green to neon green to aqua green to pistachio green and then into finer colorless images opening into recognizable forms. I could see the stiff shoulders of Rick's overly formal and very uncomfortable blazer, which always reminded me of a turtle shell because his head seemed to pop in and out of it.

"I got him," Rick said.

My body felt heavy and numb and light. And as he pulled me out, I felt like a spirit rising from the grave. There was no feeling. The weight of living, gone.

"Where's the chopper?" he yelled.

"It's coming!"

That U6 helicopter hovering above me. It was as quiet as an electric current running through a wire. It was based off the stealth-modified

Sikorsky UH-60 Black Hawks used in the top-secret Seal Team Six Bin Laden raid all those years ago. When U acquired more money than the federal government itself, my father gained what they called "platinum access" to a few of the military special-ops facilities, including the daddy of them all—Nebraska's nonexistent black site.

He would bring me along with him when he visited this black site. The board members were not allowed, per agreement. But his son, James Anglish, had clearance. My father was fun that way, sometimes, when he wanted to be. Though he did it to show his authority and power over his family. It was in no way intended to make me feel important. Because I was the Teacup Shih Tzu in the Louis Vuitton bag. He'd bring me to things like this as an unnecessary necessary accessory. And the people who worshipped Fep Anglish saw me as his annoying, yappy dog. To his followers, I was the pest my father had around. If you just put up with me, maybe you could become something worthwhile to the big man.

"Get him in," Rick said. "New York Presbyterian—*now*."

Splintering thunder.

"Honey, honey, come back to me," a woman whispered. "Come on, Jamie."

Artificial sterile laser-white light sourced from some globe in an off-white sky.

Masked faces looking down at me.

Commotion.

Panic.

A knifing lightning illuminating the memory of my mother standing in one of the streams running through the marshland.

"*Clear!*" I heard from beyond.

Thunder, only thunder, with no lightning to signal it.

"Great. See, honey, you're a swimmer," my mother said.

Swimming to her, I asked, "Can't Daddy swim?"

"No," she answered, "but he loves watching us."

"Can't he use his arms?"

"I don't think he wants to try."

"I would still swim."

"Well, let's see. Try to swim with just your arms."

I tried to swim and sank.

My mother laughed as I rose to the surface and up into the depths of some dreamy and hazy bar. The walls were filled with kinetic and vibrating sunburnt Fourth of July photos. They had turned a faint brown, which showed age but didn't muddy the image. Like a Hitchcock film, these photos cast an American Gothic blankness. That open grass, open ocean landscape of bland thought and indifferent, dim demeanor. The sun-bleached blondness of the bar, with the knotted wood walls, stained even further from the salt. It made you feel tired from the wear and tear, and those dark wood tables and chairs, caramelized by the beer and the whiskey, and the metalworking of the lamps and lanterns turned to that pistachio green and toothpaste blue from oxidation. And that smell of spice gone airborne into the bar's vaporization of body sweat, peat, and cigars. And the lingering hints of beef blood and forest floor and curry and old furniture and cherries in liquor and the very distant Mac Truck diesel stench coming from somewhere. A napkin left on a butt-squashed seahorse embroidered pillow by the corner window table. The dribbled notes listing random unknowns, each with a strikethrough, except for the last:

~~Inspector general~~

~~Black eagle~~

Where is Beashock Barnstormer?

For what reason?

For no reason.

There's another napkin I see.

A few doodles.

Wine ring stains.

A poem that reads:

The past is in debt.

The present, its collector.

The future, our revenge.

Wait, I knew where I was now.

I was in New York.

I had seen this place before. And now, cutting through this memory, a tall waiter came in close with those barbaric eyes of his, staring down at me, his tattoos flexing along his arms. That hellish song, "Machine Gun" by Jimi Hendrix, emerged from the hidden Bowers & Wilkins speakers, and those guitar solos, and that controlled feedback simulated the horrors of a war fought long ago. The sound of bombs being dropped, and machine gun fire, and men, and women screaming and crying, and the fierce sounds of helicopters chopping through the napalm air, and those distant notes from somewhere far off nowhere wrapping themselves around this cacophony of horror, tornado-tumbling together down into the dining room and, from there, into the sitting room and, from there, into the dancing area on the ground floor where hands turned dull yellow from decades of alcohol abuse hopped up and down pinching at the piano keys, invoking a soundlessness bleached-out by the wave-splashed night of this Rock Away, Long Island beach. I remembered. This was Rock Away. That familiarity of rattling of crystal and that thud of hollow eggshell Herend porcelain, and that subtle drum of a wristwatch against the musician's sweat-soaked skin. *Grand Seiko,* the watch read on its dial. *Spring Drive,* it said below. Not nearly a traditional quartz watch, it was one without a battery. How strange. That standard mainspring used to generate charge. And that magnet regulating the speed of the mainspring wind-down. A smooth sweep of this extra-long cathedral gong second hand. Its pace cleaner in microscopic movement than any pure mechanical device. This timepiece. What a thing. How much it meant beyond the man who wore it. The Japanese beating the Swiss at their own game. What a watchmaking feat. Such history in it. Such ingenuity. A beauty of a thing. The forty-one-millimeter titanium case. The caliber spring 9R65 movement. That engineering of another era. A 30 percent reduction in weight because it only used titanium. To the initiated, this was special. So bespoke. So useless. So pointless. The last of the past. A longing right on that musician's wrist. Such longing. In the form of a redundant piece of time-keeping machinery. Redundancies in so many forms. Like clothes. And shoes. Shoes. Yes, shoes. Antonio Meccariello. Norman Vilalta.

Gaziano & Girling. St. Crispin's. Stefano Bemer. Edward Green. The Newbury—the most beautiful shoe ever made, I think. Cut from a single piece of aubergine-colored calfskin tanned in mimosa barks, oak, and spruce for nine months. And John Lobb. Ah, John Lobb. One of the few shoemakers to never paint their shoes. With the best leather in the world, the patina of time was their paint. That's a philosophy. When people had principles. Those shoemakers. Those watchmakers. Those artists. *Gone.* Like this musician. *Gone.* His talents falling behind into his future. The tired hands forced to play the same tune, over and over, again and again, forever and forever, on and on and on. Bound by that *thing.* Lost to only be found, always right there just where he was supposed to be. Behind this piano, excreting hints of greatness from a time he hadn't ever been a part of. A period of free-flowing creativity (The Beatles, Queen, The Rolling Stones, The Band, Elton John, Bob Dylan, etc.) turned to a sterilized base concentrate for those seeking it. He could only now close his eyes to open them to the crowd gathering below. Somewhere, nowhere. Those fans. His art. That passion. The whistles. The cries. Echoing admiration. Off into somewhere, nowhere. Queen's "Bohemian Rhapsody" venting from that high-compression mind of his into his fingers on the piano. For a second it came and then it went, that rock and roll. The theatric, sugary-glazed slates of electric light zigging and zagging off the stage set of his mind into the open windows of the bar, the fans revealing themselves not as his fans but as hustling and bustling bartenders and waiters cutting through the dreamy light to take orders. That misty blue liquid dust not theatrical at all. No stage-set drama here. Rather the evaporation off the calm white-lined ripples of some illuminated Olympic-size swimming pool, snaking up to where I stood in this dream of mine. This oozing neon pool hidden in the oily darkness of an unattainable black-ink beach, which hemorrhaged into that boundless ocean. Those rows of cabanas. That splash of blue-and-white umbrellas, weather-torn and weakly adorned with the muted, faded, and very irrelevant RABC (Rock Away Beach Club) logos. RABC—there really was no future here. No present, either. Only a past powdered up with nostalgia so you couldn't see the decomposition. That destruction—everything my mother represented. Everything that my father had done to her. My mother here with me at this beach club.

Right there next to me. That dyed silver-blond hair of hers, hidden by her great big yellow sun hat. That over-the-top metallic lamé dress, festooned with glass beads and plastic sequins.

"I had a good cry before with Marlene," my mother said to me, shaking from her gradual withdrawal from alcohol. "It was a mistake they brought tennis back. Your father probably never told you Marlene and I were all-star doubles partners way back when. Marlene was the best in our age group. I was pretty good myself. Bet your father never told you I was good. Bet you he didn't. Well, anyway, they brought tennis back. And that young star: Angelina Monroe. That Angelina Monroe. Beautiful thing. Lost right in the finals. All that promise. All that hope. What she represented to us—to *all of us*. All that talent. Natural talent. Lost. Done. Like that. The match was over in two sets. We didn't expect that. Nobody did. How horrible. That cheat. What's her name? The opponent's name . . . ? Julia. Yes, Julia. Julia something. A nobody—a no-talent. She didn't deserve the win. It was supposed to be . . . it was always supposed to be . . . ahhh, Angelina Monroe . . . her beautiful start to a wonderfully historic career—the beginning of such a career. Stolen from her. In two sets. Barbaric. That monstrous Julia couldn't even give her a third set out of sympathy. It was stolen from us, that third set. How hateful. They really—*really, really, really*—made a mistake trying to bring this game back. They need to really get rid of it, *again*. Permanently. Gone for good. No return. Why? Why did they bring tennis back in the first place? They knew what would happen— how we would all feel about it . . . the misery in competition . . . a winner . . . a loser . . . sadness . . . disappointment. None of us wants to be jealous of each other. We just want to love each other. We want to be in harmony . . . to have equal opportunity, *always*. To live in hosanna. We just . . . we want to . . . I mean, all of us want to win, right? That's why. That simple. Right . . . ? We all want to win . . . that's why this poisonous game of tennis is very, very flawed, and very, very unfair. The corruption—it's happening all over again. And you know what? I'll tell you: Marlene and I are pioneering a revolutionary campaign to end, once and for all, the game of tennis. Great players like ourselves—and many other great players we also know—we . . . well, all of us don't want it back. We don't want it back. We don't want it back. We don't want it back. Get rid of it. Get rid of it. Get rid of it, we demand for ourselves and others."

The shaking quickened and the pitch of her voice was unstable in its resonance, and she looked very confused and now almost happily angry.

"I'm so sad," she cried and laughed. "I'm confused. I mean, I . . . I don't even know what year it is—none of us do. What season . . . ? It's been too long since we've had consistent weather . . . but what—sweetheart—what year are we in . . . ? My friend Andy goes by the Chinese calendar. Luna goes by the Ethiopian calendar. Ivy goes by the Hebrew calendar. Cora goes by the Islamic calendar. I think Rylee goes by the Balinese Pawukon calendar . . . I don't know . . . what do I go by . . . I don't even know what calendar you and your father use, if even the same one . . . ? Oh, honey, my sweetie pie, you're so lost. You can't even find the straight way. I'm so tired, you know."

"*Clear!*" I heard from somewhere far beyond the limits of this boundless ocean.

Rumbles off in the distance.

"Fep," my mother said to my father in their 1,300-square-foot-house in Lawrence, Long Island. I was ten years old. "You know as well as I, we can't get by."

"They'll make me manager, Samantha," my father confirmed with doubt.

"When?"

"Soon."

"When is soon?"

"Maybe next month . . ."

"You said that last month."

My father worked at the local Audi dealership, and he drove around a car he could never sell or afford. I don't think he was very good at his job.

"It takes time, Samantha."

"Well, I don't see it as a very complicated process—to get promoted."

"You know how my boss is."

"Why not work for Mercedes then? Why not?"

"There's no relationship there."

"My God, build one."

"I'm building one here."

"Slow build."

"Honey . . ."

"No, Fep, it's ridiculous."

"We got into the club—and you *love* the club."

"You know why we got into the club."

"That's how everyone gets into the club."

"A rich guy paying your dues? Because he wants only one—and *just one*, God forbid—nice-looking dark person there?"

"It's not like that."

"Oh, but it is. It very much is. Don't be so naïve, Fep."

"Either way, it got us in."

"I'm embarrassed to show my face there because everyone knows the truth."

"No one cares."

"Yes, they do."

"You're fucking nuts. How could you even think that?"

"You trust George . . . ?"

"He wouldn't say a thing. He *wants* us at RABC. He's always wanted us there. And ever since he got on the board, he's been pulling for us. And he finally got us in, in front of a lot of people who've been waiting a whole lot longer than us."

"Why don't you just work for George? Really."

"For George . . . ?"

"Fep!"

"I couldn't work for George."

"Why not?"

"He hasn't asked."

"You haven't asked either."

"That's not how it is with us."

"Mom," I finally said. When it came to my parents, I found myself listening to their arguments without realizing I even existed in their world. Then, somewhere deep within my nonexistence, I found myself, somehow, and this discovery resulted in something as simple as "Mom."

"Not now, James," she denied my significance. "Be quiet or go upstairs and be quiet."

I remained quiet.

"I will ask George for you," she went on bashing my father.

"No, you won't."

"What, you going to hit me, Fep?"

"Samantha!"

"Fep!" she mimicked.

"It isn't smart to mix friendship with work. It can only go bad."

"It isn't smart to mix this life of yours with mine."

"I'm trying, Samantha."

"Oh, come on, Fep. Who the hell cares about trying . . . ? Give me a break. You know, I had the sympathy you wanted many years ago. But you took it all away from me."

"I never asked for sympathy."

"You did, Fep. You asked for it the moment you saw I fell in love with you. Do you . . . do you even love me, Fep?"

She had made herself the victim now. It was impressive to make yourself the victim when you're the one in full attack. But she could do it when she wanted to. At times it was almost brilliant. And my father would learn from this manipulation and harden his hatred of impotence before that great success would take hold and greet him unlike it had ever greeted a human being before.

"Samantha," my father sympathized.

"Oh, you're such—"

"I wanted just you, not your sympathy."

"Fep, you're all talk—and I fell for that. And that's my fault, only. And, for that, I am sorry. But I'm not sorry for anything else. I won't be. And you won't make me."

"I'm not asking."

"Sure, you're not. You never ask. That's why we are where we are. Because you never ask. You wait, and never ask."

My father had nothing left to defend. She had gone full circle and hit him from an angle he never saw coming. She was too good and too quick. And, from the cheap seats, I could see this was very much over. But this defeat would teach my father more about power than anything. He would know what it was like to be on the vulnerable side. To know how it felt to flee or endure. Those were the only choices in the beginning for him. And he would pick to endure. Pick to watch his son witness his daily destruction. I, his son, the only person on the planet, besides my mother, who would ever know how vulnerable Fep Anglish once was. And he hated us for it. He would remember how I would just watch and do nothing. And he would remember how my mother used his status at work as a weapon for misguided and heavily projected anger. And, when it was time, and he became the man who changed humanity, my mother and I would become slaves to the story we started to write. My mother would get nice and disappear somewhere in herself, and I would get passive and disappear somewhere outside myself. I had to give up my identity after my father discovered his.

Our downfall and my father's rise all began when he left Audi.

"Samantha, sit," my father said on a Thursday night after returning home from work.

"What now?" my mother responded, surprised he had it in him to tell her to do something.

"I quit."

"You what?"

"I quit."

"Quit what? Your dreams? Thank God."

"No, my job."

"You're kidding."

"No."

"I hope you're kidding."

"No."

"A sick joke?"

"I quit."

"Fep . . ."

"I have something else. It's big."

"Jesus. *It's big.* I've heard this before."

"This is not before."

"Everything with you is before."

"I'm partnering with George."

"No . . ." She sounded incredulous.

"Yes. I met him at the club and told him about this idea I had. He went totally crazy about it and asked for a formal pitch deck, which he'll help me write. I've never written a pitch deck before."

My mother rolled her eyes. But she was still intrigued.

"So, you'll be working with George then?"

"I have to write this pitch . . ."

"Will he pay you?"

"Not exactly."

"So, this is just an idea he thought was fun?"

"No."

"How are you earning?"

"Audi was in the way. I need to focus on this pitch."

"What is this pitch exactly?"

My father paused to collect his thoughts and my mother rolled her eyes again. Never had I seen such concentration in my father's face and this eye rolling wouldn't faze him. My mother took note of this and exhaled heavily for maximum derailment of his new sense of confidence.

"It's a car company that helps elevate lower-end brands and helps democratize higher-end brands. Bottom line. Let's say . . . well, let's say Ferrari wants to broaden their consumer base to the taxicab companies . . . well, we, ahhh . . . we can think like Ford . . . think like Ford for Ferrari and produce taxicabs with the Ferrari badge. It's 100 percent badge recognition but we will have the cues needed to hint to the consumer that it is indeed a Ferrari. Mainstream reaction will receive these subliminal cues and accept them. The result, a subconscious acknowledgment that this Ferrari taxicab is a Ferrari. Success. Now, we all understand, the more *in the know* people will always be a problem because they're, you know, *in the know.* These are the Ferrari people. The guys who collect F40s. These guys will reject the Ferrari taxicab and say it's Ferrari's downfall—the end. That's fine. Expected, even. But what's unexpected is Ferrari's sudden influx in budget. Revenue is now touching the stars and this newfound money can be used to manufacture even more impressive elite cars. Ferrari's mainstream taxicab division can now fund their halo models. And that's all they really care about: making the next Ferrari F40. Right? I mean, Samantha, think about what this could do for these struggling car brands. And we will follow this business plan for companies like Ford and Honda and the likes of them . . . but just inversely. We'll take the learnings, and the partnership, and the friendship built from a company, like let's say Ferrari, and provide Ford an unparalleled service to produce a whole new range of halo cars they've never produced before. Ford can be *in the know* just like Ferrari. And they have the money to do it. They just need us to get them there. And we can—because of our new relationship with the best of the best (Ferrari), we can help mediocrity become fantastic and we can help fantastic become a little bit more, well, normal. We saw hints of this with the famous 1964 GT40 racing car and a few road cars built after that. But I want to do it on a more massive scale. Could you imagine that?"

My mother needed time to think this over and he would give her the time.

"And . . ." she finally blurted, "George is backing this?"

"We have a few more meetings set up at the club. But, yes, from our initial meeting, he is over the moon about this. I'm sure, with George, there's something bigger in this for him. Something he's not letting on. But it makes all the sense in the world to both of us. Audi taught me a few things about the car market—expensive is getting too expensive and cheap is getting too cheap. Why can't we have everything meet at the middle? That simple."

"Okay, okay," my mother hissed, "Gosh, I get your salesman talk, Fep. If George likes it, well . . . you know . . ."

CHAPTER THREE

Mr. Clean

Five and a half years after my father made his pitch, I took an entry level position at one of his companies. By then, he had fully become the prick everyone talked about but could never see for themselves. But I was the lucky one who could see this prick almost every day. Good for me, they all thought. How cool it was. James's father, Fep Anglish.

My first day at Porsche was a nightmare. I worked for their public relations department, and it was tasked to me to promote their new Porsche scooter. The Porsche scooter was a big thing for my father, and he exhaustively told me it was his ticket into Porsche. Too bad none of these companies knew what he would do to them once he got in. It wasn't until later I found out his master plan. That it was his agenda to coerce massive redundancies in the car industry so he could pave the way for the largest holding company in history. My guess—George saw this potential from the very beginning. Too bad he died just about three years into its unprecedented success. And too bad my father didn't talk very much about him really, ever. But George always talked about my father. Fep Anglish was his masterpiece, my mother would tell me on one of her drunk days. Those were the days my father would vanish from existence for weeks at a time. This travel became too much for George and my father dumped him with us to relax. My mother treated George like her father, and I could only feel bad for him. It was all his money my father used, and he was at the age where he didn't care much about it. I could tell he accepted he could no longer keep up with my father and it was time for him to eat the food my mother served him. A few times he forgot who she was and that wasn't a good sign. Then he just died, and my father came home early from a meeting and buried him and moved on. All of George's money was left to us and it was more money than anyone could imagine. At the time, George was one of the wealthiest people in New York. And he had no wife, no kids—the rest of his family dead or off somewhere else. Now, everything George made could finally be burned like coal for the future destruction of the car industry—and so much more.

"Welcome to Porsche," the extremely attractive blond-haired and blue-eyed representative said to me at the entrance. Porsche people were engineered like their cars, balanced and symmetrical. They looked like proper Ralph Lauren Polo models, and you couldn't find a blemish.

"Happy to be here," I answered—such a clever response.

"Now, your father said you will be helping us with our new electric scooter, yes?"

I followed her into the PR pits, farther and farther into those cubicle trenches.

"Yes," I responded, "that's what I was told."

"Okay," she laughed, "we're on the same page—that's a good start."

I nodded my head and we stopped at a little cubicle tucked away in a corner. The lighting was out of hell.

"Good?" she asked.

I nodded my head again.

"Your computer is here and all the papers you need to set up are right here, too."

She spread her perfect-cuticle hands across the orientation papers. In the packet was a list of company benefits and other things my mind went blank on. It was easy to not pay attention to pretty people when they were talking. You couldn't get bored because you liked what you saw. This woman could talk about the weather for the whole day, and I would be fine with that.

"And a gift for you on your first day," she smiled with too much sincerity.

I nodded my head yet again and opened this gift. It was a one-eighteenth scale model of a Porsche Carrera GT. I only knew this because it said it was a Porsche Carrera GT on the outside of the box. It also said it was a one-eighteenth scale representation. I'm not that good with space and sizing, trust me. I wasn't very much good at anything, and my father would make sure I knew that. To be the son of one who bears great success can be no different than Alice stuck in Wonderland; you take the mushroom to get through the keyhole to then find yourself too small for the world behind the door. I had to be a certain size to enter my father's world and that's how he would diminish me. Just like he would diminish my mother and most of the people around him.

"That's nice," I said, putting the model down.

"From Porsche to you." She grinned so symmetrically, her face seemingly unable to contort in an unattractive way. Had she practiced giving this gift to new hires a hundred times over? I bet she did. And since I was the son of Fep Anglish, I'm sure it was a lot more than that.

"What time is it?" she asked, without looking at the time.

"It's—"

"9:00 am," she interrupted. "Perfect."

She knew what time it was. That was her way of not seeming so scripted. But it all was. She was too perfect—even with the cadence of her words—for it not to be. I really liked her, though. But I liked everyone. Even if I didn't like them. I always felt bad being me, so liking people was a form of self-defense and acceptance. It came off as being nice, but it really was all self-serving. But everyone was.

"You can meet with our HR department at ten o'clock," she continued. "You can use this hour to get acquainted with Porsche. If you have any questions, please don't hesitate to ask. My office is through those glass doors."

She had a nicer office than I did because it was an office. I'm not a brat, but I sound like one when I complain about things like this. Sorry.

"*Clear!*" I heard from beyond.

Rumbles off in the distance.

Ten years went by at Porsche. Like my father at Audi, I found no relief through upward mobility. I was still sitting in that same cubicle doing the same PR nothingness for new dumpy products my father made Porsche produce. The electric scooter was a success, and my father gave all the credit to my boss. His name was Rex Potts. Yes, and he was as annoying as his name. And he did nothing, too. He could drink with my father and that was about it. But the Porsche scooter business was Rex's neglected baby, and I was the babysitter who fed it and cleaned it without any credit. I voiced this dissatisfaction to my father, and he told me to hop back on some metaphorical vibrating saddle so I would calm the hell down. That's how crude he would become as the wealth bled through him. And certain people knew how to react to it and others would find themselves fired the next day if they couldn't react to it. But Rex. Wow, Rex. He knew how to play the game well. I would overhear him once shooting the shit with my father. He would tell him a joke that only Rex knew could work. He knew everything about him—how much he hated me and my mother, how superior he felt to the common man, how reality had to warp around him and no one else. If he could make a funny joke about the downfall of marriage, it meant another two solid years of job security.

"So, here it goes," he began, walking beside my father, this joke timed out perfectly so it could be told before the doors opened to the office of Porsche's CEO. "A guy takes his wife out to dinner for their anniversary. He gets her a nice bottle of wine . . . multiple courses of food . . . the whole shebang. They have a great, great time."

Rex laughed to himself to push some humor into it and keep my father interested.

"At the end of this great meal," Rex continued between bouts of self-aggrandizing giggling, "at the end of dinner, the man says, 'honey, if you weren't around, I'd be screwed.' His wife then leans over to kiss him, saying: 'oh, that's so sweet.' The husband suddenly pulls away from her in shock and replies angrily, 'that wasn't meant to be a compliment.'"

That stupid joke bought Rex another two years at Porsche. He would later hear that my father could barely make it through the meeting with the CEO without laughing. This would make Rex's month, maybe even year. It would also buy him random lunches with my father and the CEO. Rex would make sure to dress nice every day on the off chance this CEO would swing by his office to escort him to my father's favorite hangouts scattered around New York.

I would take on Rex only one time and this moment of strength would mark my last day at Porsche. It was when I asked my father for his job and had proof of Rex's incompetence. An hour later Rex was fired, and he nearly tried to kill me as he was escorted out of the office. By the end of the day, my father held a meeting the CEO didn't attend and announced massive layoffs due to consolidation. For those who didn't survive this pursuit of efficiency, a decade-long paid vacation in Capri was their early retirement. My father had bought the commune of Anacapri and he turned the existing hotels into these early retirement centers for people who he claimed, "earned it early." Most of these early retirees would learn to love Capri for its views and weather and relaxation. A few did return home, only to find it had totally changed since they left. They came back to see the beginnings of true monopolization, even though my father hated that word. But it was apt, whether he liked it or not. What had happened to Porsche was just one example of thousands of consolidations. Sad thing. That was the beginning of the end for one of the most prestigious companies in the automotive industry—a raindrop in an ocean of mergers for Fep Anglish. Porsche was yet another archaic piece of business ready to be swallowed up for those growing bones of my father's visionary mega holding company.

"*Clear!*" I heard from beyond.
Rumbles off in the distance.

It wouldn't take long before my father sent me away to Capri. Before he sent me away, I had gotten into painting and felt I really had a talent for it. My expertise was in the art of watercolor. I could also do more realistic paintings and even some more contemporary hard-edge work, too. I really did it all. And I loved it and managed to gain a small following.

I sold a few for a good amount of money. And I was commissioned to do a very large one for one of my father's very rich friends. It took me a few months and I was a week late. The painting was fifteen feet by ten feet and this rich friend wanted a contemporary depiction of his wife, who had passed away a few years before. I have no idea why, but he rejected the painting for just being a week late. And it wasn't like I could even keep the painting for myself. Who wanted a painting of someone else's dead wife? And, yes, this enraged my father because it embarrassed him and showed my lack of follow-through. He had no tolerance for tardiness and had his secretary book me a room for many years at one of his properties in Capri. And I would waste away there in total comfort. Yoga in the morning. A massage at noon. And squid and shrimp and octopus and linguini at night.

The property I lived at was the best in Capri. It was at the highest elevation of Anacapri and you could see the city of Naples from the balcony winding around the edges of the island. Mount Vesuvius was right there across the water, and I wondered, stupidly, every day, when it would erupt again. Would it be when I was there? Would I see it? Would it float across the water and come up the island with magma tentacles to melt me? The imagination would run wild in paradise, with its flawless weather and constant fresh food.

I came back to New York as the man-child I am right now. My desire to paint was gone. And even if it came back, I was too scared of my father to attempt to be commissioned again by one of his fancy friends with strict, non-negotiable deadlines. I really wished that guy had told me how pressing it was to get that painting of his dead wife. I could've finished it a week earlier if I had only known. Well, guess that's how things go for artists, right? I was a failed artist like the rest of them and I would roam around this new world of my father's and dislike myself more and more and more in that passive quicksand of disappointment and jadedness. All the while my father would accumulate this unstoppable power and spread his infamy as he devoured industry around him, making Rockefeller's Standard Oil look like a local candy shop. And I couldn't believe it was all happening. Because I knew him when he was nothing—and I knew he was smart but not this smart. To see him rise above the boundaries of human ability like this was something for someone like Einstein or Mozart or Jesus or Shakespeare—not Fep Anglish, the failed Audi car salesman. It was all so odd. He used to have (like me) no real personality to think of. Not until he became what he is now.

Now he had more personality than anyone I had ever met. His enthusiasm for life was exhausting to be around. Someone so flat before was now so inflated, to the point of detonation. But when he was alone with my mother and me, he was either abusive or he was that old boring Audi dealer Fep Anglish. And when he was in the public eye, he was something else entirely. He became an idol who had more things to say about life than all the great philosophers combined, or so he thought and made others think. And sometimes, even, I thought he was something extraordinary, until I woke up and realized he was full of nonsense. Because the nonsense was just the petrol for his ego. It meant nothing. And that was the thing about it. He really was nothing. He would buy up everything and take the credit. The expertise of others he would claim as his own. He would soon become the world's leading tech pioneer and that was utter BS because my father was in no way a savvy guy with technology. He knew some but not nearly enough to be what he declared himself. Not even close. Not a chance. But he would bend reality. And people would let him do it for some reason. It was so strange how people seemed to simply clear the way for him so he could do anything he wanted. No chance that would work for me or anyone else I knew. Even the way George responded to my father. "Anything you want, Fep," he would say. Take this. Take that. Take everything if you like. When my father bought up a small computer chip company a few years after George died, he initiated what he called the stress test. That meant he gave the company forty-eight days to impress him. If they failed, he dissolved them. If they succeeded, he would rule them until they burned out. And, as it turned out, he would rule and burn out this poor little computer company. They were the best in the country and, in those forty-eight days, some genius in their forced think tank built the prototype for an identity chip. This chip housed your social security number, your passport, your credit card information, medical records, insurance—*everything*. So, when you went to the airport, you only had to walk through a *pairing screening device* instead of digging around in your bag for a passport you probably had already lost. How convenient. No more wallets. Scan your wrist and that was it. The whole chip was smaller and narrower than a fingernail and it fit right under a few layers of skin in your wrist. Sounds great, right? It did, until it became something far more sinister.

"*Clear!*" I heard from beyond.
Rumbles off in the distance.

"He's back," a voice said.
"I . . ." I attempted.
"Honey, can you hear me?" another voice asked. "Do you know where you are?"
"In . . ." I tried.
"Your mother is here."
"Dad . . . ?"
"Your mother is here," it repeated.
"My fa—"
"Your father isn't here."
"It . . .alive . . . ?"
"Honey," she cried. "Jamie baby."
I now saw that black dog running into the marshland.
"Jamie!"
I saw that black dog following a stream.
"Honey, can you hear me? See me?"
I saw that black dog disappear.
"Can you?"
The sound of gunshots in the distance.
"Yes," I murmured.
"It's Mommy."
"Mom . . ."
"I'm here. Everything is fine now. Sweetie, you're going to be fine."
A man guided her out of the hospital room, and I awoke in my asymmetrical bedroom located on the top floor of the Chrysler Building. We were back on that Fogo Island. And my mother was asleep on my Art

Deco saddle leather couch. Her silver-blond hair was hidden by that same great big yellow sunhat and that same metallic lamé dress festooned with the same glass beads and plastic sequins. And, as always, her overdressed, unfit-for-winter attire was her protest to her present condition, and by wearing those clothes she escaped from her life with my father. Even when I was like this, she still needed to escape him. That's how much he took out of her. But I'd ignore it. And the sadness of it all mixed so well with those saddle chairs arranged around her and the gold seams in the pebbled granite floor leading to a marble star in the center of the room. The angular light came in through triangular windows and large Art Deco chandeliers hung from the army green ceiling covered with hand-painted stars. Stars of all shapes and sizes. Some intricate. Some simple. Big needles painted against the wall, taking up most of the vertical depth, the tips ending right before they touched the stars.

"There he is," my mother said.

My bed was against one of the floor-to-ceiling triangular windows and the leaking sun strained the shrunken pupils of my eyes. I squinted like a drowsy puppy and my mother ran her hands through my hair to make me feel better. From the window, I could see all fourteen miles of my father's racetrack. The Empire State Building looked absurd against the edges of uneven land kissing the brink of the North Atlantic. And the Freedom Tower, farther in the distance, picked up the blue from its tremendous body and refracted stronger strips of ocean-soaked light into my eyes.

I turned away and cried, as I always would, when I could do nothing else. A thirty-seven-year-old man crying to his mother on the top floor of the Chrysler Building—what a specimen I was.

"Don't cry," she sung and rocked me. "You're home now."

"Is Dad fine?" I asked, nudging her away from me like a bratty child would.

"Honey . . ."

"Where is he?"

She made no response.

"Where is he?" I asked again.

"Honey," she belted with sudden panic. "I can't find my glasses. Where did I put my glasses? I can't find my glasses. Honey, please."

Like a dog catching a scent, she moved about the room in deep pursuit. There was no purpose to her movements, besides muscle-memory recall directing her left and then right and then left again.

"I don't know," I answered, having been through this before.

"Your father," she cried, "—he'll never buy me another pair. We have to find them, honey. We have to. Please, help me. Oh, please help me."

I couldn't move but pointed instead.

"Are they there?" I pointed.

"No," she answered.

"How about there?"

"No."

"There?"

"No. Oh, please, honey. Try to think where I left them last."

"I don't know."

"I know I had them in here."

"There . . . ?" I went on pointing again. I'd continue to play this game with her.

"No."

"Oh, under there."

She searched under the chair and then stood up in proud form.

"How did they ever get there?" she pondered.

"Always the last place you'd suspect."

"Now, honey—I'm sorry. What were you asking me . . . ?"

Losing sunglasses took precedence over everything, even my father's life.

"I was—"

"Oh, yes," she interrupted. "What was it? Oh, yes. Of course. The Miracle on Ice upset. It was wonderful, honey. So, so, so wonderful. The United States beat the Soviets. They actually did it. Greatest upset in sports history. Who would've known? Just a wonderful, wonderful thing. Really, who would've known?"

"Mom, I'm not talking about the 1980 Olympics."

"It's all over the news now, honey. Breaking news. The story is just everywhere. People can't stop talking about it. I mean, no one could've guessed such a thing was possible. I think they won four to three. Just so—"

"Mom, please!"

"What, honey? What do you need from me?"

"Mom, why are you talking about hockey?"

"I'm sorry. I know, you're right. I . . . well—you know—I just thought you would've wanted to know."

"I don't care about it. I want to know about—"

"Yes," she interrupted again, "about your father."

"Please, Mom."

"Your father," she smiled to keep the tears in, "your father is dead."

And there it was. Suicide—and attempted murder.

Her tears broke through. But she was bad at crying because she never cried out of sadness. It was always out of horror. This must have been horrible for her. I knew she knew what my father had done. It was no accident.

"I don't know," she wept.

I sank into the bed and pulled the sheets over my head.

"Honey, did you . . . well, guess what? I'm writing a memoir."

"What . . . ?" I asked through the pillow.

"I've had quite a life, you know."

"Yes, Mom," I mumbled, "I know."

"Ups and downs, of course. It's hard for me. Well, it's hard for all of us, I guess. Not much of a happy world we live in. Ahhh, you know, I'm sorry—in a lot of ways—for bringing you into it."

"Don't," I mumbled.

"I do feel bad. As a mother, I can't help but feel bad. The constant sadness in all our days. It's the end of the world every day now. The asteroids. Week after week, sometimes daily, there's another one of those rocks the size of Texas coming our way. It never hits, luckily. But, sometimes, I really wish it did. So, well, I just didn't have to worry about it anymore—worry about every day being the last day, you know?"

"Please, Mom," I mumbled. "Please."

"I begin to wonder what's real and what's not real. For you, I want to be able to ground myself in being a good mother. It's impossible in this setting. I can't be a good mother for you. I can't protect you when I don't know the outcome of things. I feel like the world is lying to both of us. It's making me a bad mother because it's making me a dangerous woman."

A dangerous woman? I asked myself. *What the hell is she getting at?*

"Honey," she sighed, "I don't even know what that means. I guess I felt like just saying it."

"You're not a bad mother," I mumbled.

"I have this strange dream. Like there's something better out there. Like this isn't for us anymore. I see it as some strange green planet. The air is fresh, untouched by people. Away from people altogether. Away from that anxiety they create. A place where I can be a good mother for you. And, honey, you know your father could've been a good father. We could all be exceptional at what we do at that wonderful green planet. It wouldn't be considered unfair to be exceptional there. I could be the best mother out there—on this wonderful green planet. We could be anything out there."

She sighed again and her voice got heavy from the tremors of panic and anger.

"Too bad, for us, it doesn't exist. I'm sorry I brought you into this world, honey. I really am."

"Please, Mom," I mumbled.

"I am very sorry. It's just so sad—every day, the end. We all want it to end badly. We want to be put down. We want that ultimate disaster because we're just so damned bored and scared. Bored and scared is the worst, honey. It makes you do horrible things. Just horrible things. You hear about the bugs, honey? The strange bugs coming for us?"

I wouldn't respond.

"These scary new bugs," she shivered. "Bugs we haven't seen for thousands of years. Big disgusting bugs. Some are poisonous, I've heard. Many people have died from them. Thousands have died."

I exhaled into the pillow.

"And why is everyone balding? Is there something in the air? In the water? People are starting to look like Mr. Clean. It's horrible. Just terrible. Just horrible!"

CHAPTER FOUR

....

Ben Woof

I t was seven months later, and little did I think of my father. There was surprise but no sadness. But the fact he tried to take me down with him. Why? So much of Fep Anglish could never be answered. His rise to unparalleled fame. His suicide. How the hell was that possible? And why in the name of God would he kill himself? He wasn't a happy person, but he had moments of happiness. Well, a different type of happiness—one brewed from defeating the other guy beyond earthly recognition. But why he finally did himself in at the end, I knew as much as anyone else. And my father meant to me as much as he meant to anyone else. For me, his death was not personal; it was historic. I could not claim Fep Anglish as my father any more than John Smith could. And all I thought about, until now, was my recovery. And it was time to leave my mother's care and return to New York for schooling.

New York had sloughed off that *Midnight Cowboy* grit and grime. It was modernized to take on the apocalyptic loneliness of Tokyo, Japan, the characterless sameness of Murmansk, Russia, and the sterilized hard-edge ready-to-assemble Nordic crispness of Copenhagen, Denmark. But crime was down, at least. And population size was also way down. And it was very clean here, too. It really was. And men and women of my generation would walk through these clean and empty streets and think, with their overeducated minds, about social injustices and other things that angered them.

It was a lonely anger because most of the people I knew left the city to rent places upstate. Off to those microbreweries. That was a trend that took way too long to end. After the Fraction Farmers turned farming into an agricultural cooperative movement, my father seized the opportunity and raided the industry despite the strict Shareholder Rights Poison Pill Plan. Fep Anglish offered up a golden parachute and managed to downsize the farming co-op into a flimsy debt-ridden heap of manure. In less than five months, the Fraction Farmers were gone, and the microbrewers took over, exploding their ignorance across the counties. The microbreweries first centralized in Sullivan County and, from there, metastasized in Orange County, and, from there, into Putnam, Ulster, and even into Clinton County. Ill-informed aspiring microbrewers dreamed of producing the best organic beer in North America.

Like the founding Fraction Farmers, these microbrewers used common ownership as the linchpin of their new agricultural theory. Microbreweries webbed their beer factories together with this common ownership ideal. It was nonsense, though. None of it worked. Too many analytical minds putting theory and political philosophies into something that was terse and tactile and demanded zero BS from the farmer or the brewer. The real farmers and the real brewers had no clue what common ownership was, and that's what made them good. But being good and productive didn't matter. The emerging elite wanted to try their hand at honest work. To feel morally fulfilled, they put these experienced generational farmers and brewers out of business. Even my father couldn't fully anticipate the power of moral fulfillment as he helplessly witnessed key members of his own company resign to join the movement of moral replenishment. Highly regarded surgeons quit their practice to seek what would widely become known as agricultural repentance. It was a misled spiritual connection with the land, which resulted in state bankruptcy. Counties that were once thriving were now open and bare and full of nothingness. Business was stagnant. A microbrewery here, a microbrewery there. But, otherwise, total bankruptcy.

The bankruptcy spread throughout the state like an infection and the people who spread it wouldn't return to the city. They'd attach themselves to anything they could find. Anything that hadn't been ruined yet. Whatever was still thriving, they'd get at. And then they'd run from it after they'd sucked the life out of it. And then they'd run, and just run, and run until they discovered Buffalo. A group known as the Brooklyn Brokers, or the BBs, founded New Manhattan there. New Manhattan was a block-for-block remake of Manhattan, spanning across 150 miles from top to bottom.

"The Big Apple you once loved," the BBs told the public, "A big apple pie spread across 153 miles. Bring it back and spread it out—that's what the BBs say."

"Bring it back and spread it out" was advertised all over New Manhattan.

The quest for a higher morality became the norm. To free yourself from big cities to help replenish your soul. A return to nature, without leaving the luxuries of technology. Keeping that hand-in-glove relationship between the man-made and the natural; electricity being the blood and blood being the electricity. Organic matter could function as hardware and hardware could function as organic matter. Although, out in nature, underneath those flowing rivers, was a deeper undercurrent of wiring and cabling that could circle the planet a hundred times over. Nature was just an affect for mankind's conscience. And it would always be an excuse to separate from each other and build more places like New Manhattan. Because one's moral authority could not be too close with another's. A thirst to remove yourself from the rest hardened into a tumorous distrust in the other individual. That individual could never surpass your morality. No surprise the moral superiority complex had blossomed into monstrous proportions.

It was a fragile thing, though. This complex was very aware of itself. It had the façade of a demon, but the inside of a bullied child. Lighter than a leaf and more breakable than a dead one. And it made you scared. You feared more than ever the impurities of others. Whether that was disease, weather change, or whatever, you were always on guard and looking to avoid that *other* creeping up behind you to corrupt you.

They created this hell, you'd say.

They are the cause of the pandemics.

They are the cause of this crazy weather.

That bad weather comes in. And that good weather comes out. And that bad weather comes back in, all within an hour.

Because of *them*—the *other*.

And you look up at that sky.

And you question everything around you.

You feel unwanted.

You feel hated.

Those *UNIVERSAL* letters circling Earth. Big block letters, each letter hundreds of miles long. That bright silver and that gleaming gold trim. Projected into space from 35,641 land locations. You could see them drifting along up there. That madness of Fep Anglish's vision. This world turned to my father's fiction. His Universal Studios. You'd see the letters one day. The next, they'd be covered by the bad weather.

That bad weather. Seasons, gone. Always random weather.

A mundane chill blanketing your 365 days.

Mundane until it became severe.

The sporadic weather representing the sporadic behaviors of these viruses in human form. That other.

All of us, infecting Mother Earth.

Nature and humans entangled in a state of hysteria.

People crying, tornadoes twisting.

People laughing, earthquakes shaking.

The end of the world, every day.

And every day sharpens your moral code so you can stab yourself with it.

Remove yourself from the corruption.

Separate.

Take away ownership. Rent. Rent. Rent! Why buy? Why have any investment in anything? Why add that to all the many things you have to do? You're just too damn busy and too wildly important. Experience. Experience. Experience! Rent an apartment. Rent a dog. Rent a cat. Rent a grandmother. Rent a mom, dad, uncle, cousin. Rent anything. But just for a little. Before it becomes a burden on you. Before you get bored and disguise that boredom with being too busy. Because there are so many more things you need to rent and then discard for someone else, to then rent again, and then discard that for something else. Rent. Discard. Rent. Discard—and on it would go.

Live on Fifth. Live on Madison. Live on Central Park West, for all anyone cared. It didn't matter. The grand life of a ten-room apartment for you—for anyone, anywhere, at any time. Experience unlimited wealth for two weeks, and not a day longer. And then go to the Catskills and rent a small one-room cabin and feel like you're the man who lives off the land. Take care of the dog that's left there for that authentic experience. His name is Ben, and he can drink beer. Everyone knows about Ben, the dog who drinks beer. Everyone's taken care of Ben at some point in time.

Make everything Disney World, even the things that once were very real to very real people. The world, one gigantic stage built to entertain you. Be poor. Be rich. Be everything all at once. Wear the fine clothes already in the closets of those Fifth Avenue apartments, once worn by people who worked for them. Eat the food in the big stainless-steel fridge, restocked like you'd refill the gas tank of a rental car before you dropped it off again. Rate how well the other temporary residents left it. Let the next people rate how you left it.

"Relocate, relocate, relocate," my father said once about New York's real estate. "You don't have to worry about location if you're always relocating."

Own nothing. Own yourself—because that's enough of a task. Be your own religion. Be your own god, with your own rules and set of ethics. Be the ultimate judge because you've experienced everything in this Disney World of yours. You know what it's like to be poor—I mean, you took care of Ben, the beer drinking dog. You know what it's like to be rich—for God's sake, you lived in the grandest duplex apartment in all of New York. You know it all. You're God. And you are the moral authority. Everyone has his or her own type of moral authority. But *your* moral authority is the most moral.

Too bad Ben died. It wasn't from old age. Rather neglect. My best friend, Beasley, told me about it one sad day. Beasley was the biggest influencer out there. Places to rent became hot because of her. If she liked something, everyone wanted to check it out. The cabin in the Catskills was a prime example of this. Find a stray dog. Find an abandoned cabin. And there's your wilderness experience. A man and his best friend, alone in the woods. With a simple fire in a simple cabin in the middle of nowhere. What a wonderful thing it was to indulge in when you knew you could leave.

But Beasley got tired of this cabin. There were newer and better things at her disposal. The cabin experience did what it had to do for that desired period. But once her followers went, they begged for more. Once she stopped promoting *Catskill Cabin Getaway (with Ben Woof)*, the cabin had no one there to maintain it. Ben sat at the entrance waiting for fresh faces, but the door never opened. His food was never restocked, and he died of starvation. Curtains drawn forever on that Catskill Cabin Getaway stage set. And Ben was discarded like a prop being put away in storage.

"I forgot about Ben," Beasley said to me, entering the freshly rented Park Avenue apartment.

"It's animal abuse," Tennyson (her almost boyfriend and my almost friend) responded with forced concern.

"Anyway," she moved on, "we finally got this apartment. Two weeks of heaven, guys—because of me."

We'd been on a waiting list for this apartment. Seven-forty Park Avenue—what an address. It was one of those understated palace apartments with their natural light drenching the walnut-paneled libraries, galleries, and many, many—I mean many—bedrooms. Totally impossible to get into unless you were Beasley. And even she had trouble. What a wait. But worth it. For a triplex apartment, in what was once the most expensive Art Deco pre-war residential building in the city; this was well worth it.

And you really felt special with Beasley. Even though this place was a little, let's say, tired and bruised. *Ravaged by rent*, it became better known as. That feeling that so many disrespectful people had been there before you. Such abuse to things only designed to be touched by the few, or not touched at all. Not even The Mop could hide the damage. They'd come in for a twenty-four- to forty-eight-hour cleanup, depending on the size of the rental, and it was their job to make the place feel fresh and new for the next round of renters. After two full weeks of *fuck you*, it was an impossible task. They still did a great job. But the disrespect was permanent.

Anyway, I wouldn't have met Beasley if it weren't for my father introducing us. He connected us on the day he announced the official name of his mega holding company: U. Beasley was one of U-Rent's most valuable influencers. Ben Woof became a mascot for this whole side of my father's business. He hated marketing gimmicks like Ben Woof, but Beasley went with it anyway. And, for that willingness to risk her job for greater profit, my father loved her and had an affair with her. I knew that because Beasley would fly right in from Fogo Island, and she wouldn't hesitate to tell me she flew right in from Fogo Island. I think she thought it was something to brag about since no one besides family went to that island. She bragged about it even if it meant she was bragging to the son of the man she was having the affair with. And my father knew I knew, and he couldn't care less because what could I do. No one cared what I knew. It meant nothing that I knew. Tell the goldfish anything; it's even therapeutic.

Anyway, my father introduced us at one of his parties and, of course, my mother wasn't there. He was holding Beasley's hand and caressing her back as he initiated an introduction. Beasley was twenty-two when they first met. And, despite her being that young, he told me I could learn a lot from her and that someone like Beasley could help me grow into an adult and become relevant to modern society. I was reluctant and embarrassed at first. But Beasley and I became close friends. It was cool knowing someone who had a paying job. There weren't many of those types of people anymore. When you signed on with U-Learn like I did (like everyone did), you found yourself knowing about the things you'd never be able to do. I was thirty-seven years old and I still taking Shakespeare, James Joyce, and Faulkner seminars. To give myself a little credit, though, I was in very advanced classes. I knew more about Faulkner than Faulkner knew about Faulkner.

But I specialized in nothing practical. My life orbited around specialized literary theory and a few other subjects I knew too much about. Obsessive amounts of insignificance weighed me down. My reference point became so narrow and so deep. I absorbed the world around me by comparing it to the tortures of my education. Objects and people had such metaphorical significance to my very esoteric, hyper-inquisitive mind. And I found myself begging my educational advisor for something new. And, surprise, surprise, he didn't help. So, I took it upon myself to take a film class. That was a big switch for me. It had been all books. Now I could sit back and just watch. It was easier and a lot more fun. A few of my friends in this film class called it a *gut course*. But I didn't think of it as that. It made me want to become a director. But I couldn't. I would never be allowed to even try. Thanks to Fep Anglish's predictive analytics.

Predictive analytics was exactly what it sounded like. U-Predict had the leading algorithm for predicting outcome. But it failed in predicting the future. Nothing could do that. Even the great Fep Anglish couldn't do that. After that reality soon poisoned his overamped ego, he scrapped predictive outcome altogether and substituted it with what he called hypothetical outcome, or more specifically, Hypothetical Algorithmic Consciousness. HAC became the single most impactful idea in human history.

The Hypothetical Algorithmic Consciousness made the past very much alive in Fep Anglish's future. HACs, in their lifelike hologram forms, ran every form of industry. The Beatles still churned out big hits. William Shakespeare still wrote sonnets and plays. Wolfgang Amadeus Mozart still composed symphonies and concertos and operas. Albert Einstein, once again, became the leading mind in the scientific community. Abraham Lincoln was reelected after his long absence following his assassination. During his inauguration, the world saw his hologram reread his Gettysburg Address. President Lincoln was now on his seventh term, and it solidified a new standard for the office. That position of power was reserved for the dead, and only for the dead. Posthumous Priority, it would become known as. And it became a real thing—a very defeating thing for those of us still living.

The dead, who had nothing to lose, were the framework of society. Anyone stuck with a beating heart was damned to a no-man's land of hopelessness and sameness, drizzled with utter confusion. A hellish confusion that sucked the life right out of you because you didn't know up from down, the truth from the fiction. To you, and what you knew of history, Darth Vader was real. Did you know that? Well, if you didn't, you should've. Check out the old footage if you think I'm lying. It's real. It happened. Watch Star Wars like you'd watch the History Channel. Watch JFK's assassination, while you're at it. Watch Neil Armstrong's landing on the Moon, too. It was all the same, right? The fact and the fiction—just data, collected information projected through some ancient LED screen. This data wasn't any different than *that* data and *that* data wasn't any different than *this* data. It was data. Data was data. You couldn't say one thing was more real than the other. To us, Darth Vader was as real as Winston Churchill. Both moving images brought to life through pixelated documentation.

For God's sake, Batman was spotted a few times walking down Lexington Avenue. Martin Luther King just made headlines leading a revivalist Civil Rights movement. Napoleon Bonaparte became Fep Anglish's personal advisor. The Emperor helped my father lead his U employees into greatness. Napoleon was his private HAC, even though it was illegal to have a hologram for personal use. But that didn't matter to the man making the rules. As his mission statement said: "A HAC must fulfill the collective needs of humanity, not the personal interests of the few."

To make the hypocrisy worse, he went as far as having an Adolf Hitler HAC. This he would deploy for idiot's delight. The dictator was imprisoned in Fogo Island, along with a few other holograms he called his holo-trainers. Hitler chanted death to the Jews, Michael Jordan gave my father private basketball lessons, and Tiger Woods helped him master the putt. In the confines of Fep House, Bob Dylan wrote him hundreds of songs better than "Like a Rolling Stone." These private HACs, slaves at my father's disposal. And no one else could benefit. Only my father. Building his hatred for everyone else by capitalizing on the dead. These hypothetical beings, his private entertainers. Ghosts producing work based on the computing power of state-of-the-art technology. The most advanced software ever built bringing back the people he adored. Algorithms of unending complexities telling him how the mind of a ghost works. Was it a lie? Was it really Bob Dylan's mind based on those trillions of detections surmising one's future body of work? If X were still alive, what would X produce determined by what X had done? Was that a real capability? Or was a computer making things up, tricking us all, including my father?

Whatever the answer was, I knew enough to know that my future was chaos wrapped in control. The fear of ever going back to what was. That dread was in all of us. Being old enough to remember what it was like. The beginning of the end. Before HAC. When Lincoln wasn't president, and the United States would swing every four years from one extreme to the other.

For hundreds of years this had gone on, the shockwaves birthed from a time before my great-grandfather. The sway from far right to far left, bending the population in the same weak spot until it would snap. With each election, the fabric further unraveling. Citizen ownership of equity becoming popularized. Holistic gain trumping individual need. Ethical socialism proving moral stature, overshadowing material wealth. Anger, self-hatred, and undying jealousy becoming the engine for social justice. A chicken-before-the-egg disaster site, where the working class demanded more payment from a condemned and battered ruling class. Fep Anglish, the last of this ruling class. He would now fulfill the demands of the people, getting taxed at 78 percent with a net worth of 793 trillion dollars and an annual salary of 550 billion a year. That means 429 billion dollars in the pockets of the working class every single year.

The individual. The individual. The individual! signs would say.

No government spending. Privatization. Free trade. Free trade. And more free trade. The end to government budget deficits. The end of a highly regulated global economy. Red-blooded testosterone fertilizing hyper-capitalist free-for-all, free-range deregulation and globalization. The private sector roaming on this laissez-faire land. That freedom to become anything. That freedom to become nothing. And, through it, the emerging dictatorship of Fep Anglish, the Emperor of Gain. The personification of the private sector using the private sector to promote the spirit of socialism. Not for government assistance, rather for Fep Anglish assistance. Showing the common man that he was the common ground. Whether it's socialism or capitalism, each arrow points to him.

He would snatch that pendulum swaying from far left to far right and take control. Fatten the private sector by smothering the government underneath it. The hyper-capitalist becoming the socialist. Bleeding his worth onto the people and awing them with generosity. Using that Napoleon Bonaparte HAC to lead the way and further invade the future. To give people everything they wanted but nothing they hoped for. To turn the federal government of the United States into the monarchy of the United Kingdom. Abraham Lincoln addressing the nation and blurring the past and the present and the future with figurehead legislation. Things not real becoming real. The public losing its grip on reality to witness a wannabe John Wilkes Booth attempt to assassinate a hologram during a speech. The sadness in the futility. The reality in the imagination. One in the same. No one jailed for what they did because there were no jails. The madness dissolving into that controlled chaos. Criminals disappearing into the futility. The fog of confusion curling up around us all. Those illuminated eyes of Fep Anglish charging at you, knifing through the fog at 243 mph. Each, and every one of us, paralyzed, deer in the headlights, unable to detach our gaze from approaching death heading right toward us. Ready to run us over. That petrifying truth that nothing could be done. The American Dream had left us, and Fep Anglish lived our dreams for us. Each and every one of us could live vicariously through Him. To witness the land of the free leaving its people behind to flee for the hills across the Atlantic.

The protected American Dream, now in Israel. This was something I found out through my mother, not my father. He would never allow me to hope the way Americans hoped in the movies. This was reality. That was fiction. Israel was fiction. There was no way Capitol Hill moved to Tel Aviv. There was no way the United States left its birthplace to claim world control via the Middle East. There was no way we were left on our own to fight off the private sector. It craved power and smelled the blood trailing from this fallen nation. My father, the first to take a bite and tear us to shreds. The real rule of law, so far away, across the Atlantic and beyond the Mediterranean. Too bad no man had clearance to go there. It was a place of gods, each of whom were even godlier than my father. Gods of Blue Planet United. The flag of that BPU, a blue globe superimposed on a white backdrop, standing tall, and flapping, and flapping, and flapping. Freedom, so far away, and flapping, and flapping, and flapping. In the distance now, like the shuttering of dragonfly wings, as Fep Anglish harvested what a dream had left behind. Buildings uprooted and moved to different locations like trees being transplanted.

CHAPTER FIVE

....

Drifter's Edge

After the political unrest lost its momentum, and the hologram of Abraham Lincoln calmed our souls with nostalgia, my father put everything under risk assessment. It was easier for him to capitalize on a sure thing than it was to take a chance on something new. That was his only way of insuring stability and control. To avoid any shift in thought, bestselling authors such as John Grisham, Dan Brown, Stephen King, James Patterson, and J.K. Rowling dominated the publishing marketplace. Each HAC churned out a bestseller every three months. The more thoughtful works of James Joyce, Ernest Hemingway, Kurt Vonnegut—and other writers of that caliber—were still published, but infrequently, every few years.

The established past was the future. And there was no room for aspirations. The industry was not taking new members. Whether it was becoming an author or a stockbroker or an entrepreneur, you'd soon find out it wasn't for you—actually, rather, it didn't want you. In fact, it didn't want to even know you existed. You were the consumer, not the producer, and success was reserved for the other guy. But there was no other guy. There was just that one guy who died a long time ago. But we all know the name. And we trust that name. So, we become the consumer and we watch opportunity slip away from us just for a good read.

"I read this in a day," Beasley said, slapping the book down on the melted-copper-and-gold-infused marble island kitchen counter of this luxurious 740 Park Avenue triplex apartment. "It's better than *Alex Cross*. He outdid himself again."

Tennyson exhaled and then draped himself on Ron Arad's famous stainless-steel sofa. The shape and reflectiveness screamed out of the African Blackwood floors and the charcoal volcanic ash, 99 percent cocoa finish was so dark the floors appeared to be purple. The deep conflict with the marble and the stainless-steel and the white-on-white created a sense of nightmare in this distilled form of opulence.

"*Along Came a Spider* is better," Tennyson murmured with high concentrations of elitism.

The curved stainless-steel sofa bent the living room in all different directions and he was unable to find a comfortable position on it.

"I'd rank *Along Came a Spider* number three," Beasley dismissed. "What about you, James? What would you rank it?"

I hadn't read one James Patterson novel and it worried me to feel ignorant in front of her. She was an influencer. A very important person.

"For sure third slot," I answered. "But I'm not going to lie because I think *Alex Cross* is a close second."

"Agreed—I'm victorious. Ha!" she declared, like a kid winning after a pouting fight.

"You always win, Beaz. And James always agrees with you because he secretly loves you. We all know this. I'm sure he's writing about you in his memoir or something like that."

"He's not writing a memoir. He hasn't done enough. I'm writing a memoir."

"Beaz, that must be a short memoir."

"Longer than yours."

"Mine's pretty long."

"Both things I'm thinking about are pretty short."

"My memoir isn't short."

"Well then—what the hell is it about? What could you possibly write about?"

"My NYPD days."

"What?"

"Yes. My NYPD days."

"What is the NYPD? Wait, wait, wait . . . you mean those stupid shirts you wear all the time?"

"Yes, in fact so."

"I didn't care enough to ask before. But now I'm intrigued."

"NYPD stands for the New York Police Department."

"Oh, wow. So, you're lying in your memoir."

"Why am I lying?"

"Well, let's see . . . to start, there isn't a police force. There hasn't been a police force since . . . well, before either of us were born."

"You can say anything you want in a memoir. What's real to me, is real to me."

"Good thing no one will be reading it."

"What did you write about in yours, my queen?"

"I wrote a lot about Fep in mine. I loved Fep, more than any other man. I'm sorry, James—but I couldn't love you, too. I loved your father. My ultimate lover."

The affair was so casual I didn't have time to react when she threw it in my face.

"Beaz, such bad taste. James, may your father RIP."

He then got up from that stainless-steel thing and dragged himself lazily to the kitchen. Beasley hopped up on the marble island and patted it for Tennyson to sit next to her. I would never sit near them. I had a bit of a mental thing left over from my father's abuse. And I couldn't help but notice a leftover strand of Lo Mein and its caramelized oyster sauce hardened like wax on the veined white marble table. It had somehow survived The Mop.

"You're looking good," Beasley said to me.

"The crash," I answered, trying to pull my eyes off the Lo Mein. "The whole thing—I don't know."

"One for words, he is," Tennyson laughed.

"Hey, that's not nice. You haven't lost a father. And you surely haven't lost a lover like I have. It's a huge loss for me. Even more than for James. To lose a lover . . ."

"Jesus—James, doesn't this make you feel uncomfortable? She called your daddy a lover. Her daddy and your daddy."

"What is wrong with you?"

"Oh, don't worry Beelzebub. Your daddy-lover will become a strapping hologram soon enough."

"That would be a conflict of interest, Tenny-bub."

"Oooh—that nickname wasn't as clever, Beelzebub. A good try. A very good try, indeed."

"I'm sure you know this," she went on, all business, "but, per contract, a hologram cannot run U."

"James, did you know that?" Tennyson asked, his face wrapped with a sick grin he only reserved for me. He knew I was oblivious. And by showing that, it gave him control over Beasley. I didn't know why exactly. But I could see that he was given a pass to treat her worse whenever he defeated me. It gave him some immunity after shoving me down.

"He didn't mention anything to me," I answered.

Tennyson laughed to himself, and Beasley was embarrassed.

"And there you have it," Tennyson announced. "The prodigal son."

"At least he had a relationship with his father," Beasley defended.

"Well, fuck you."

"No, fuck you."

"Fuck you harder, Beelzebub . . . I like this game."

They both laughed together, and I watched. I'd just watch, as always. You were subjected to a life of observation when no one had a personal investment in you. As much as Tennyson was Tennyson, he at least had someone who loved him. And I hated when people defended me out of pity like Beasley did. The pity could only go so far, to then end with a mutual laugh like this.

"Look at it," she said, changing topics and putting a stop to their laughter.

Next to her was a swan-shaped glass wine decanter. And next to that was a Riedel Boa crystal wine decanter. It snaked up into the air with curving drama and, to Beasley, it asked to be destroyed.

She picked it up and told herself how pretty it was.

"Pretty, pretty," this possessed child marveled.

"So pretty," she went on marveling.

Then—

Out of nowhere—

The decanter dematerialized into a thousand micro-fractures of glass against the oversized industrial-grade Wolf stove, seemingly taken out of some bustling restaurant kitchen.

"What the fuck, Beaz?" Tennyson screamed and lifted his feet in the air to avoid the shrapnel from the exploding glass. I wasn't quick enough and got a few pieces tangled in my leg hair. But I didn't say a thing because I never did. Brushing them off quietly, I leaned my limp body against the cold and sterile oversized Sub-Zero fridge.

"What about it, Tennyson," she laughed. "I could break everything in here and they wouldn't say shit. You know how much money they make off of me. And I ask for very little in return."

"A little of James' dad, I'd say."

Beasley searched for another thing to throw, and Tennyson caught her arm.

"Stop," he yelled.

There was always a lot of yelling with Beasley and Tennyson. They were casually dating now, and they both reacted off each other's flair for drama.

"You can't tell me to stop. James can tell me to stop. But you can't tell me to stop."

"I'll hit you with a frying pan, Beazy."

"I'll hit you with a fucking fridge, Tenny."

They started to make out and talk in between kisses. They forgot I was watching them, and I even forgot I was watching them, too.

"740 Park Avenue!" Beasley screamed, taking a breath from Tennyson's mouth. "We're here. We're actually here."

"What about 778 Park Avenue?"

"Fuck you."

"What about 1040 Fifth Avenue?"

"Shut the fuck up."

"What about 834 Fifth Avenue?"

Beasley hopped off the island and opened the silverware drawer.

She pulled out a knife and pointed it at Tennyson.

"What are you going to do, stab me?" Tennyson asked with his hands in the air.

She walked past him to Ron Arad's famous stainless-steel sofa.

"Don't even think—

"You fucking bet I will."

Even I reacted to this and ran over to stop her. But it was too late. The horrible sound of the knife scraping against the beautifully curved steel. That whole extremely rare and expensive piece, ruined. And Tennyson didn't move. He covered his mouth like a child would. There was a sick smile in the creases of his face as he did.

"That's like . . . oh my god . . ." he giggled, "like a cabillion kazillion dollars, Beaz. Not even you can get out of this one."

She threw the knife in his direction but not close enough to hit him.

"We'll be going to all of those other filthy very rich buildings soon enough. After I give 740 a shit review, they'll be begging us to go to the others for a good one. They need my blessing. 'Oh, Ms. Koch, please enjoy two free weeks at 778 or 1040 or 834—whichever you like . . . all, if you'd like . . . if that would satisfy . . .' Mark my words, I'll be the first to hit The Big Four."

The Big Four were the last late Art Deco buildings left over from the 1920s. Surviving Fep Anglish's massive city-wide demolition projects, these four Candela-designed buildings became beehives of nostalgia for old New York. The rest of the new residential buildings became homages to the obliterated 1920s and New Classical limestone façades sourced from the same quarry as the Empire State Building became the big thing. Such a Fep Anglish stamp. Massive, gigantic, and retro limestone facades mimicking something he'd chosen to demolish. It was the stuffed animal instead of the real one. But this stuffed animal had big ears and big beady eyes and a tongue that went down to the floor. And above these limestone colossuses were super tall glass needles that punctured the bulbous clouds. They were called sliver buildings because they were built on narrow lots. The sliver buildings were all the same size. The roof of the 116th floor capped off at 1,555 feet. Every block had at least five sliver buildings packed into it. From New Jersey and Long Island, the city looked like one of those old pin art games where you pressed your hand against the pins to make an impression on the other side. Small indents in the pin skyline signaled where the limestone giants lurked below.

"The first to hit The Big Four," Tennyson groaned as he took the effort to bend over to pick up the knife. "You'll be bigger than . . ."

"Than . . . ?" she asked back, wanting to know.

"Than . . ."

"You can't even think of a famous person."

"Than . . . someone I'm forgetting."

"You're pathetic."

"At least I do the right thing."

"You do the right thing?"

It got bad when you attacked Beasley's morality. Tennyson was the best at testing Beasley's very nasty self-righteous side.

"I do," Tennyson defended.

"You do nothing but follow me around. Like a fucking puppy."

"Let's not talk about dogs."

"Why in the fuck not?"

"We know what you do to animals."

Tennyson looked at me for support. I couldn't disagree with him. Ben Woof would still be alive if it weren't for her.

"My father is a racist," she deflected.

"Rick Koch is not a racist, Beaz."

"How would you know?"

"I've met him many times."

"Well, Fep Anglish was a huge racist. Ask James."

She said it like I wasn't even here.

"Beaz, Fep Anglish was Black. He couldn't be a racist. Right, James?"

"I don't know," I answered.

"See Beaz, James doesn't know much about anything."

"That's mean," she fought back in a hyperbolic sad voice. "Don't say that to James. That's really mean. Take it back. You could've really hurt him."

She hugged me and then squeezed her face against mine. The contact seemed to get Tennyson jealous.

"I can't retract facts," he said.

"You're all emotion, Tennyson. Nothing about you is fact."

"I think you're projecting yourself on me."

"James, what do you think?"

Before I could answer, Tennyson interrupted.

"Let me guess, James . . . 'I don't know.'"

"You're such a bastard."

"You're a bashful bitch."

She laughed. "Never heard that one before. What alliteration."

"Some of us go to school."

"I'm glad I don't. I can actually do something productive. Make something of myself."

It didn't even cross her mind she was also making fun of me.

"Yeah, you're so professional," he laughed, "letting dogs starve to death."

"Are you going to bring that up forever?"

"I just might have to when you bring up my education."

"You know, the one you should really be pointing your fingers at is my father. He's a racist toward animals."

"Beaz, how can you be a racist toward animals?"

"Try not to be such an ass, Tennyson. He gave our dog away when I was very young and extremely impressionable. All because it barked too much. I had to go to therapy for many years because of that. I cried for nearly a week straight."

"Did he kill the dog?"

"No."

"You really seem to forget what you did to Ben."

"I'm not a racist toward dogs like my father was—and *is*."

"This is getting boring, James. Bitch Beaz won't budge. Stubborn bitch Beaz, as always. James, oh reasonable one, are you hungry? Because I am. Let's get outta here and shut this stupid conversation down."

Tennyson and I followed Beasley to Madison Avenue's U-Eat.

"I can go for one of those tuna melts," Beasley said and skipped across the street.

"Pizza, pizza, pizza, that's what I'm digging," Tennyson said, and also skipped along, following right behind her.

I walked at my slow pace and let them play the food game among themselves. They would never wind up getting what they said.

"Ah," Tennyson yawned, "here it is in all its glory."

We turned onto 71st and Madison and walked up the avenue. Th clothing storefronts from the turn of the century were preserved, but inside there was nothing but cabling and routing for U's massive computers. The whole street-view portion of Madison Avenue came out of Paris and the classical and timeless Beaux-Arts style wrapped around the faux storefronts to express some level of integrity in a faceless city. Any floor above the first floor was torn down and replaced with a huge slab of concrete on which a super tall sliver building was constructed 1,555 feet into the atmosphere.

The Gertrude Rhinelander Waldo House was a French Renaissance revival mansion, and the first-floor façade was still intact on the southeast corner of 72nd street. A bird-shit–covered store, once called Ralph Lauren, blasted its winter collection through the panes of glass and we looked at the corduroy pants and the wool blazers and the Italian leather shoes and the Italian leather gloves and the silk scarves and those crazy-patterned ties and bowties, all handmade materials catering to the individual so long ago. So far from us now, we looked at these artifacts like one would look at a caveman rendering at the Museum of Natural History. "That's how it was?" I'd ask myself. "How extraordinary." I'd always talk to myself while Beasley and Tennyson bantered and skipped with each other off somewhere else.

"This is what people did a long, long time ago," Tennyson marveled. "The work put into every little detail is absurd. What a waste."

He slugged his sweaty hands across the pristine glass and the contact of his exuding bodily fluids made an awful rubber sound.

"No different than 740, really," Beasley dismissed, pressing her face and tongue against the glass. "I could wear men's clothes. I'd look good in men's clothes."

"Beaz," Tennyson nudged her, "get your tongue off that."

"It's not exactly clean," I interjected.

"Get your beautiful tongue off of that, Beaz."

We were all germaphobes. After fourteen pandemics over my lifetime and ten over Beasley's and Tennyson's, we learned that it was just a matter of time before disease would end us. If you wanted to die you had to wait for a pandemic, or you did it yourself. A lot of people took matters into their own hands. It was common to hear about people jumping off bridges and buildings because the quiet slitting of the wrists wasn't dramatic enough. But overdosing was much more in fashion than it used to be, I have to say. That was a new quiet, but dramatic way of doing it. Not as dramatic as jumping off the GW—but prescription pills had a sort of white-collar demise to them that we all liked very much.

Other than that, you waited for nature to eventually deliver you death. The United States government took it upon itself to weaponize pandemics to pave the way for a stratocracy. I wouldn't ask my father what a stratocracy was. That job was for my mother. My father would've hit me if I'd asked. So, my mother told me that a stratocracy was a government run by the military. Stratocracies became a power move. Since my father had depressurized the power of the executive branch to such figurehead proportions of nothingness, the government had to think up dramatic plots to overtake the hologram of Abraham Lincoln. Under Fep Anglish, the private sector was paramount, and its contradictory socialist values did anything but satiate the values of big government. The whole thing made no sense in a lot of ways. But it resulted in the call for *muscle-force*, a term coined by my father for the military. What little was left of this military could be awakened if a pandemic hit. Government control through military force was the only move the United States had left. I had lived through fourteen stratocracies, each obviously blooming out of the pandemics, and each failing once the outbreak was contained. The trick was having a virus that was lethal enough to thwart cure but safe enough not to end the world. Something that would make prolonged military dictatorship a must for survival. My father was aware of the clandestine operations in pursuit of a virus like this and black operations were undertaken across the world to foster controlled spreading of infectious diseases. My father called these black-op groups *The Breeders* since they bred viruses to execute desirable outcomes. The CDC had become a safehouse for these operations and many epidemiologists from the CDC were recruited into these black-op offshoots, once collectively called the CIA. The CIA was now an old thing out of the movies. The FBI, the NSA, and the CIA—hieroglyphics in this modern age. But they still existed in some way through the outsourcing of private companies with massive agendas. That's essentially what the government had become, factions of self-interest acting in the dark like shit-fed mushrooms. And my father would be the one to feed them. Because he also had his own inhouse operations.

It was all very sketchy. The powerful got creepier and the powerless got lazier. And as I got lazier and my father got creepier, the use of lab-rat average citizens for a coup became common practice. In our hearts, everyone knew how expendable they were, the irony of an age catering to your every need also having the ability to terminate you just as fast. I would hear about this true darkness when my father was blackout drunk. He wouldn't even remember telling me. If only he had known how much he disclosed; what his son really knew. If Rick Koch, the father of Beasley Koch and U's chairman of the board, had only known what the great Fep Anglish had told his stupid son . . . God help us all. God help Beasley. Help her for even knowing me. Because Rick would end her. He would end her just as fast as he would end me. In a lot of ways, he was far more dangerous than my father.

"You wouldn't believe what I heard," Fep Anglish would stammer through Fep House. "Fucking hysterical . . ."

When the nights got this bad, my mother acted as his little shadow throughout the house. She did this because he'd eventually drop to the floor and go on mumbling to himself.

"You like *Drifter's Edge*?" he asked, spilling the Laphroaig. The house smelled of smoky peat, as it always did. Smoky peat and lingering cigars. What a hell.

Drifter's Edge was a series produced by U-Entertainment, the first original series in the last hundred years. Nothing about it was a remake or a rehash. None of that "inspired by . . ." stuff, which was unheard of based on my father's rigorous risk assessment analysis. There's more loss than gain for new thinking, he thought. In consequence, this new was unacceptable. But, not with *Drifter's Edge*. It was a test tube idea from one of my father's think tank guys. It was the first of its kind. Something that was both new and safe. There was zero risk. Tim Argosy, the creator of *Drifter's Edge*, was the first person to write and direct an original series of the modern age. Talk about fame. Some thought he was more impactful than Fep Anglish himself. Tim Argosy—the man who created a series that truly represented our time. The characters that talked like us. The characters that felt like us. The characters that lived like us. Wow, how about that? Finally!

Tim Argosy was the god of fiction. And he proved my father's hatred of *new* wrong. And every Sunday evening, the entire country was closed for business from eight to nine-thirty. Each hour-and-a-half episode was packed with pure entertainment. And the characters became more to us than we were to ourselves. Lark McKittrick—that's who I identified with. Lark was a little unsure of himself but managed to do the right thing when he was put under pressure. The most popular character was Laurence Arlington. Laurence was, without a question, based on my father. A character like that gave a degree of hope to its viewers. They wanted to be like Laurence Arlington, and, for that, they'd watch the show just to watch him. *Drifter's Edge* was on its eleventh season, running stronger than ever. That drama. Those twists and turns. The characters. Everything, a beautiful working system of fictional wonder.

Well, until . . .

About six months ago, Tim Argosy was fired from U-Entertainment for being a clandestine agent. From what I overheard, he had accepted 250 million dollars to kill off Laurence Arlington in season twelve. Argosy hadn't written the script yet, but he agreed and took the money. The reasoning behind this was the same as the reasoning behind the pandemics. *Drifter's Edge* became so significant that fans did kill themselves when characters died. It became a huge problem and Argosy refused to change the style of his writing just because people took it too seriously. My father gave him total creative freedom and that freedom made Argosy a target.

The death of Laurence Arlington could only mean total chaos and mass suicide. But, to Tim Argosy, 250 million dollars was worth more than 250 million lives. I mean, he already had so much blood on his hands his conscience couldn't be his navigator. Money led him and powerful people knew he'd do just about anything for it. He'd even do his career in to obtain more of it. What a sad way for a creative to go. To be fattened like that by wealth. Severed from the mind that made him. Becoming a puppet for the next coup. Laurence Arlington blowing up in his favorite car. Wow, that would produce panic. Surely enough to reengage the military. This could be the very thing to end Fep Anglish. Funny how my father did die that way, though. But I have no proof of anything. I shouldn't throw things like that around. But you couldn't help but to think about the way he died . . .

Anyway, well, of course, it didn't work. My father's inside guys found out, as they always did, and he fired Argosy and replaced him with a hologram. Argosy was the first living person to be turned into a hologram. Imagine that—a hologram replacing you for the rest of your life. That's a living hell. But he could run away from himself easily. And he did. With U-Rail, you could go to the farthest place on the planet in under three hours. International travel was domestic travel and the Atlantic and Pacific Lines webbed across the globe. Those windowless human-carrying bullets shot through frictionless vacuum tunnels deep within the bedrock of the oceans. London, now fifteen minutes away. Everything so attainable and complex, all the while people remained so unattainable and simple.

CHAPTER SIX

·····································

Babe Ruth's Laws of Motion

"I've decided," Beasley garbled, her tongue still on the Ralph Lauren window. "I'm not going to be a germaphobe. We're all going to die anyway. Why not enjoy it and lick windows?"

"Uh. You'll die much faster if you lick things covered in pigeon shit."

"Pigeon shit?"

She propelled herself off the window like a frog.

"James," she asked me, "is there pigeon shit on my tongue?"

I looked in her mouth.

"No pigeon shit," I answered.

We went into the entrance of this Ralph Lauren and walked down a flight of stairs to what was once the subway. Wiring and cabling all around us. I could feel my father's influence everywhere. Flowing through those cables. His mind going at the speed of light. The pistons pumping. That smoke rising from the hood. His death, underneath this city, powering everything we relied on. He was all around us. Our Father.

"Our Father," I said, running my soft, unused hands along a cable.

"What father?" Beasley asked.

"What?" I asked back.

"You said something about a father, James."

"I'm just daydreaming."

"Dreaming James," Tennyson dismissed. "You know, I wonder what would happen if I cut one of these wires."

"You say that every time."

"I really wonder."

"Then why don't you just do it."

"Who knows what would happen if I did."

"I'm sure nothing would happen."

"Something would happen. My life would be over. I know it."

"This isn't like five hundred years ago when you went to jail for things like that."

"It involves U. That's a different sort of thing."

"U doesn't do fuck all. I would know."

The nonsense talk finally ended when we got to the bottom of the stairs.

"Smells wonderful," Beasley said. "As always, of course."

U-Eat was one of Fep Anglish's real estate visions come to life. The New York City Subway transit system hadn't seen a moving train in a while, and my father managed to buy up the space and turn it into one gigantic interworking and interlocking underground food court venue. The best was down there. Eisenberg's Sandwich Shop, Katz's Delicatessen, Roberta's, Gray's Papaya, P.J. Clarke's, Peter Luger, Russ & Daughters, Sylvia's, and on it went. Even the whole seventh floor of Bergdorf Goodman. That coffee ice cream color wicker wallpaper and those rich black moldings, purple, red, and brown in their depth. Those straight out of *Alice in Wonderland* Easter-egg blue leather chairs wrapped with an ornamented skeleton of off-white wood trim. That slightly grayer and greener light blue wallpaper with the flowers blooming from the branches and the birds perched on them. Those other asparagus-green scuffed and finger-marked *BG*-badged chairs, their smooth outer-facing hide upholstery falsely appearing as a suede due to the wear and tear. The one-off asymmetrical glassware with varying designs embedded into the whimsical and unevenly bent glass. Some had little orange dots, while others had stripes in vertical and horizontal patterns. It was all down here. The kinetic energy of the city was in the subway. Dead, above. But alive, below. What my father put out of business was laid to rest a hundred feet under, in this food court.

Roberta's wood-fired Neapolitan Bee Sting pizza lathered with mozzarella, chili, sopressata, tomato sauce, and honey. Sylvia's mound of macaroni & cheese, fried chicken, and greens. Peter Luger's butter-drenched dry-aged steaks. Katz's pastrami. Russ & Daughter's bagel and lox. Eisenberg's tuna melt. P.J. Clarke's bacon cheeseburger. Gray's Papaya's hotdogs that cracked open with an explosion of fat when your teeth went through their skin. That all appeared to be down here the way it always was. But it really wasn't. My father made it seem so. *Raising New York's Cholesterol Since 1929* ran across the Eisenberg's Sandwich Shop booth and the staff behind the booth wore black Eisenberg's shirts depicting a classic cheese, lettuce, tomato, and meat tower stacked between rye bread. Above the sandwich was *Eisenberg's Sandwich Shop* and below the sandwich was that raising New York's cholesterol quote. They sold those shirts, and I bought one the other week. It was one of the very few places in the city that sold merchandise to people instead of going through U as their retail distributor. I had no idea how they got away with it, but I liked those sandwich shop shirts. They felt one-off and original to me. With these shirts, I could feel a little different and have an object all for myself. Kind of like those old NYPD shirts. They didn't have to be traded in after a month like the rest of the shirts. I could keep it and wear it forever. This Eisenberg shirt was a prized possession of mine. The best thing I owned, simply because I owned it. And, wearing this thing of mine, I could marvel at the *RUSS & DAUGHTERS APPETIZERS* signage, with that energy-sucking green glare of the *RUSS & DAUGHTERS*, and the uninviting red of the *APPETIZERS*, and those blue and yellow bending fish on either side.

Too bad this was all fake. It was a health food center disguised as old New York. There was no mac and cheese or fried chicken on Silvia's menu. No pastrami on Katz's. Gray's Papaya had a plethora of salad options instead of grease-filled hotdogs. Russ & Daughters had a bagel made from kale somehow and there was no lox because it was said to have too much salt. Peter Luger, the steak place, didn't have steaks. It was illegal to sell meat or anything that came from a land animal, including milk. There went the mac and cheese and that fried chicken, and that juicy burger Nat King Cole called the "Cadillac of hamburgers."

There went everything except for the neon signs and the shirts, and the weird Little Italy godfather music that U played to get you oiled up and ignorant and eating. This horrible U-Eat subterranean network of deceit and aesthetic trickery. The real deal, so dead and gone and far away that no one could ever really know.

But some did. Some knew where you could get a real tuna melt from Eisenberg's and a real Cadillac burger from P.J. Clarke's. Ironically, the people who put an end to it knew where to get those things. Because they didn't want to give it up even if they wanted everyone else to. They couldn't give it up. So, they built speakeasies all over the city and made a black market out of the things people used to have. An exorbitantly expensive black market only available to the top .0001 percent. Most people had no idea there was even a black market to begin with. And the people who did know had no idea where these speakeasies were. I, the son of the richest man in the world, hadn't even been to a speakeasy. Not me. Not Tennyson. Not Beasley. Yes, not even the woman who had sex with my father.

"Your father, Jamie boy," Beasley said as she got online for Gray's Papaya, "—he really was funny, you know."

"Why is that?" I asked, getting online behind her. Tennyson went off somewhere else.

"You know," she pondered to fill the time, "my father is the reason this place looks the way it does."

While waiting in line, she would insist on educating me. My father had empowered her to do that, and this monster was already created.

"This is what Rick Koch wanted," she continued. "Not Fep Anglish."

"I don't think so," I defended weakly. "The subway project was his baby. He wouldn't shut up about it around me."

"You're misunderstanding, Jamie boy," she continued to patronize. "I don't mean to confuse you. I'm just saying the whole look of this was my father's—not *yours*. Fep was the brain. But it wouldn't have looked like this if not for my father and his aesthetic eye."

"Is that what Mr. Koch told you?" I asked, like a brat.

"What do you mean by that?"

"Nothing."

"You mean something, the way you said that . . ."

"Really, nothing. I barely knew my father. I can't defend his legitimacy. And he surely can't defend himself now. I don't know what else to say. I'm sorry for sounding that way."

"The famous James 'I don't know' line. The ultimate default."

"I'm not defaulting."

"You seem to be defaulting."

"Beasley!"

"Yes?"

"I'm not defaulting."

"I was just trying to say if it weren't for my father this really cool neon signage would not be down here. Fep wanted a very basic style that each venue followed. Neon nowhere. A simple two-dimensional red script font that carried the look and feel of U. Did you know, Jamie boy, that my father and the rest of the board had to basically strongarm him so he would give back some of his hoarded Fogo Island pleasure palace possessions to those Madison Avenue storefronts above? Did you know that? Did you know Fep wanted to tear down everything on that avenue? Have those needle-dick U buildings ground up and the beauty all gone. It was my father who wanted to keep some semblance of New York. He remembered his grandfather talking about the extravagance of the old-time retailers. The Ralph Lauren would not have existed above us if it weren't for Rick Koch. Remember that, Jamie boy."

Beasley had to take a breather from being the premier scholar on her father—and my father, too. Then she went back into it again:

"God, from what I knew, Fep hated—I mean fucking hated—what he called *the sell*. Any hacky sell. Advertising, marketing—the lowest of the low to him. I remember when I stayed over at Fep House one night, he told me that U made the world a seller's market. Renting and never owning made it a seller's market, he said. He actually put his hand in my mouth and said that if he could take the food out of our stomachs and resell it, he would. My father really is so different than him. It's scary. See, my father still believes in the sell. You still have to woo people even if you tell them what to do. You still have to sell people food. And food is the one thing you don't give back, to a certain degree . . . if you know what I mean. The Mop can't make you throw it up to package it as something else. Fep hated food for that. It had no resale value."

She went on and on and on. "My father showed me the layout for this. He had a copy of his architectural renderings and a copy of Fep's. There was a vast difference between the two."

We would always have these one-sided daddy conversations. My dad did this and your dad did that. That Superman-talk kids have before they realize their parents aren't that cool. But we never grew out of it. I grew enough to hate my father, but not enough to see any of his faults for what they really were. Seeing the humanity in the people who raised you is one of the quickest ways to shed innocence. My mother had the frailty, and my father had the faults. But there was no real humanity in either of them. Not enough to help you grow and learn life. Despite the sweetness my mother conveyed, she was a wrecking ball to a young man's courage. To be enabled, like I had, eroded the soul, and muddied the identity. I was, in the most penetrable way imaginable, no one unto myself or anyone else. Even Beasley couldn't help but patronize me. And I was older. For God's sake, I was older.

"I understand, Beasley," I gave in to her bigger and better personality.

"Not to worry, Jamie boy. Not to worry a single bit. As long as you understand, I really do like to teach you things."

She was up and she ordered some healthy dog and ordered me the same without asking. She also paid for me.

"It really is something, though," she said and gazed at the wires and cables going through the walls. "They can do all of this, but they still can't get a man on Mars."

"Well," I attempted to apply some of my great sidelined wisdom, "they got a man and they—"

"I know," she interrupted. "I mean a man living there. Permanent residence. I could be an influencer there, you know."

"The first Mars influencer."

"How about that, Jamie boy."

"You and only you."

"Fep said I was the best, you know."

Hooray for Beasley. I rolled my eyes inside.

"He did," I said, sucking my lips in.

"Jamie boy," she digressed. "I have to ask you something."

"Yeah?"

"Why isn't it—"

She stopped.

"Yes . . . ?" I prompted further.

"Why isn't it . . . like why haven't—there's been no women in your life . . . or anyone for that matter."

"I have my mother—and that's enough," I joked.

"No, seriously."

Beasley sensed I had rolled my eyes inside and this was her most passive-aggressive way to get back at me. It was her style to show false concern and to keep running with it until you gave her the most awkward answer possible.

"I don't know," I answered.

"There it is. Vintage James."

"Come on, I really don't know, Beasley."

"You have to know. You've got the looks over Tennyson—and most guys for that matter. You must know that, right? You must know that."

"I guess . . ."

"Do you even know what you look like? I really wonder sometimes, Jamie boy. You're kind of like a dog that way. I wonder if you even know it's you in the mirror."

"I know who I am."

"I'm not denying that. I'm just asking if you know what you look like."

"I'm not much into it."

"Into what?"

"The whole thing."

"People?"

"Yes."

"Why?"

"It's not you, if you're wondering."

"Do you think I'm attractive?"

She came in close to me.

"Do you think I'm attractive?" she asked again.

I couldn't even tell you what Beasley looked like. Eyes, nose, and a mouth. That's it. A talking box. They were all talking boxes. Tennyson, the worst of the talking boxes.

"You're very pretty," I answered.

She backed away. But she knew something else was going on. Her eyes zig-zagged along my face and she tried to follow my fluctuating facial expression muscle movements. There was something I knew that she didn't. And it gave me so much joy to have this power over her.

"What are you hiding?" she asked and squinted to lock down on some telling part of me.

"Nothing," I answered.

"You can be mysteriously weird sometimes, Jamie boy."

"Can I?"

"You have a smugness about you right now."

"Do I?"

"And you're digging at me."

"Am I?"

"And you keep digging. Anyway—"

The cashier handed her the food and I followed her to a communal table. To restore her control over me, she would remove herself from the dialogue we got ourselves into. But she needed time to think of a way to do it. The act of sitting down and opening the bag and serving me my food—that was perfect. She would gain her foothold by doing that for me. She would lay the napkin in front of me and then place the food on the napkin. She would even put the paper straw in my drink.

"Here you go," she said. "More napkins?"

She won. She always won. Another loss for Jamie boy.

"Yes," I answered. "Maybe just one."

Hopping up happily, she skipped over to get napkins. Compared to her other skips, this was her victory skip. When she came back, she rested her chin on her fist like that famous Rodin sculpture. Beasley was the great thinker of our time, or so she thought.

"Sorry for being so paranoid," she exhaled, with false humility. "My mind gets scattered sometimes. Too much going on, you know. Too many responsibilities. I need to compartmentalize my life. Fep always said I needed to compartmentalize. Said it was the key to success. Knowing when to press the gas and knowing when not to press the gas, you know. You can't be 100 percent, 100 percent of the time."

She really won. She really, really had.

"Did . . ." she unexpectedly began to dig at me again, "did Fep ever explain to you why Mars never worked?"

"No," I surrendered, "he didn't."

"Wouldn't have thought so. It's fascinating, really. The American Northern Lowlands and The European Southern Highlands. Utopia Planitiae, Chyrse, and Amazonis—The Three Bays of The American Northern Lowlands . . ."

She was regurgitating what my father had told her word for word. I remember him telling me, very drunk, about the different territories established on Mars. For America, he bought the American Northern Lowlands. The federal government had no money for that type of frivolous investment. But somehow Europe, Japan, France, and Australia followed my father's lead. The richest of the rich of those countries managed to acquire areas for their respective governments. Private ownership was the powerhouse, and the rule of law was a dainty cloth that wrapped loosely around it. These areas were at the disposal of their governments. But anything done there was dictated by private ownership. You really can't think of a weaker structure than that.

"The Japanese territory," Beasley went on, "known as Olympus Mons, Australia's Tempe Terra and China's Alba Mons, the European Southern Highlands, the English and French Cerberus Plains . . ."

Pausing to suck the straw, she had a searching look in her eyes. I worried she had a point here. Something that could pulverize me even more. Maybe this was information that my father had told *her*—and not *me*. Maybe this would really reveal that Daddy loved her more!

"Many generations ago, 2025 was supposed to be the big year. We'd land on Mars in 2025 and set up shop. Would've happened if the world hadn't gone to political turmoil. Then it became 2027 when we'd get there. Then it became 2029. Then it became closer to that NASA timeline, which was 2040. Then 2040 came along—and nothing happened. Then people wanted to do Venus, which Fep said was the worst decision in space history. Resulted in no man on Mars. Just machines roaming around. But now—"

The glands in her throat shifted and her tongue clicked with pooling saliva. She sucked on the straw again.

"—now that we've successfully terraformed Mars—"

Her tongue clapped around a little more. I didn't know what terraforming was. And I wouldn't ask. She couldn't know I didn't know.

"We warmed up the planet and we thickened the atmosphere. All that dry ice from the south and the north—"

She pointed down and then she pointed up. That planet was right in front of her, seen from his mind's eye, because she really did know what she was talking about.

"Carbon dioxide," she continued, "the dry ice warmed the planet. And thanks to that greenhouse—"

She had such excitement now, running away with this victory of hers, how much better she was than me.

"Radiation is no longer a worry there. Five pounds of pressure is fine for us. The water vapor now creates rain and snow. The atmosphere is totally breathable, *finally*. No need for spacesuits. And, thanks to gene manipulation, we've built people for Mars. Fep, himself, was a perfect example of successful gene manipulation. For many years, his genes had undergone extreme modification. He was worthy of Mars. There are thousands of others like him—like my father, too. My father is also worthy of Mars."

Here, she would reach her finale and claim Fep Anglish all for herself.

"My father will go to Mars. Because your father wasn't ever willing to go. You probably didn't know that. This is something Fep would only tell me. Because he trusted me like no one else. Fep confessed to me that his gene manipulation was all perception. He did it to do it—but he was never planning to act on it. Willing to spend millions on a procedure simply because he could throw the money at it. He wanted to stay here on Earth with his baby U, forever and ever. He wouldn't leave his baby. And I think, Jamie boy, I really think . . . I think he killed himself because the board threatened to vote him out if he didn't go to Mars. He signed an agreement, which my father drafted. My father led that agreement.

He would go with Fep out into space to start a new world on Mars. Fep agreed to it—by contract. A legal obligation. A seven-hundred-and-fifty-billion-dollar agreement. Did you know that . . . Jamie boy? That's seven hundred and fifty billion dollars your father was willing to throw away on a lie. A lie to himself and, worse, to my father. And, as a result, U-Space went down the drain. And now, still, my father is picking up all the pieces. He's doing Mars himself in this mess Fep left for him. Your father, *my lover*—the great Fep Anglish—was a total coward. And as my father said, "Fep never wanted to be the monkey in the rocket ship."

I had no words. To say I was surprised by her behavior would be a vast understatement. I could barely catch my thinking and even my breathing.

"I . . ." I stuttered. "I . . . I . . . had no idea," I managed to get out, stunned and angered.

Her forehead stretched back, and her nostrils expanded from the euphoria of my surprise. She needed to intake more air for this type of enjoyment.

"I'm sorry," she said.

Saying "I'm sorry" was a very popular thing for my generation. You were "sorry" for being who you were. There was regret in everything. You thought to yourself around the clock, *I really didn't deserve this because I had the upper hand.* You were trained to think this way. To feel bad for being good.

"No," I answered. "*I'm* sorry. I'm sorry my father was a coward. I'm sorry to be his son. I'm sorry. I'm sorry. I'm sorry."

Tennyson returned and I was happy to see him. The Beasley wreckage was complete, and I needed Tennyson to absorb the rest of her blows. I needed to heal, mentally.

"Doesn't James look so sad," he laughed and kissed Beasley. "Why so sad?"

"I'd say that's none of your business, Tenny Benny."

"You know what's my business, Beaaazzz?"

"What's your business, Lenny Tenny?"

"Why you have yet to donate to my Go Fund Dreams page."

"Why would I?"

"I donated money to your page."

"Because I deserve it."

"And I don't?"

"No, actually you don't. The world isn't about you right now."

"It's all about you?"

"People like me."

"But you're the one getting the money—not the people *like you*."

"Tenny Benny Lenny. Ignorant you. Helping me is helping us."

She would always have freshly made nicknames for him. And Tenny Benny or Benny Tenny—whatever it was—loved it. They would feed this stupidity into their relationship to change it up a bit. What a way of doing it, though.

"What are you two cookin' up together?" Tennyson asked us, to thwart Beasley's spewing moral superiority. "Scheming? Creating? Coming up with Babe Ruth's Laws of Motion?"

"Babe Ruth's Laws of Motion?" Beasley questioned, rolling her eyes, her soul bubbling over the brim with toxic authority.

"Yes," he answered.

"Babe Ruth didn't have any laws of motion."

"Yes, he did."

"No, he didn't."

"How would you know? You don't go to school like the rest of us do. How would you know who did what? James, back me here."

"I don't know," I responded right before I could retract it.

"Jesus Christ, James. Always with you and the 'I don't know.'"

"Calm down, Tenny," Beasley interjected.

"He goes to school. I go to school. He knows Babe Ruth is the man behind the laws of motion. And he can't say shit—because he's obsessed with you . . . and he doesn't want to hurt you—your feelings. Because he knows I'm right and you're wrong."

The fact was I would not respond because my professor taught me something entirely different. I was taught John Adams was the man behind the laws of motion. But how could I tell Tennyson that when he got like this?

"Okay, Lenny Tenny," Beasley tried to reason. "James, what do you know about the laws of motion?"

I didn't know how to react. Should I lie and agree with Tennyson, or should I stick it to him and tell the truth?

"I'm pretty sure it was John Adams," I announced after a long pause.

"No, you're wrong," Tennyson panicked. He shoved me.

"Stop!" Beasley cried.

"He's wrong, Beaz."

"Little boys, little boys, I don't go to school because of *this*. You two have no idea what you're talking about. You're learning different things. Can't you see how messed up our educational system is? Can't you see? History is a bad—*very bad* thing. And I don't learn about it, thank god. You know why? Because of this. And, also, because none of us would be welcomed in history anyway."

"Beaz, what the fuck are you talking about?"

"No, no, no. I have a point here. Let me finish. Let a woman speak, for once. Let women speak, for once. You think Babe Ruth or John Adams would be friends with us back in the day?"

"Why wouldn't they?

"Ah, Tenny, you are so naïve. They wouldn't be friends with a lesbian."

"A lesbian?"

"Yes, a lesbian."

"Who here is a lesbian?"

"Me."

"You?"

"Me."

Tennyson broke down laughing.

"You fucking arrogant jerk," Beasley cried.

"Oh, come on."

"No."

"You're not a lesbian."

"How do you know that?"

"Am I a girl?"

"What?"

"Am I a girl? Simple question."

"It isn't that simple."

"So, you're bisexual?"

"What does that mean?"

Tennyson threw his hands in the air and prayed for the dramatics.

"Oh my god," he said, his voice quivering. "You don't know what *bisexual* means?"

Beasley was now very embarrassed, and she wasn't comfortable with that emotion. It was either laughing, crying, or screaming for them. Being embarrassed was not suitable.

"Whatever, Tennyson," she said—because how could you give someone a nickname when you're on the defensive. There's no room for humor.

"You say 'whatever' and James says, 'I don't know.' I'm really with a philosophical group."

Beasley was losing this battle and I wasn't strong enough to help her fight back. Because I didn't know what bisexual meant either. I never learned that in school.

"I'm just saying," Beasley said, docile, "why learn about history when only bigots lived in the past?"

That was succinct and it won her some points over Tennyson. But would it be enough to replenish her authority over him?

"Well . . ." Tennyson stumbled.

And just like that, Beasley was on top.

"Well, what?" Beasley asked.

"I mean . . ."

"I mean, *what*?"

"It's a good point."

"Exactly."

CHAPTER SEVEN

....

Otigia Girls

To move on from this intellectual subject of history, Tennyson buried his face into a veggie burger and let the healthy juices bubble in the corners of his lips. He got bored of the burger and dangled a fried asparagus above his mouth.

"I don't like real stuff," Beasley's train of thought pivoted. She ripped the asparagus from his hand. "I like Broadway. How about we see *To Kill a Mockingbird.*"

Broadway was a miracle. It was the only industry that really stood the test of time. No matter what happened, it was always there. People went to the theater even when the pandemics made us fear and hate one another. Singing and dancing and smiling and laughing and crying, despite marriage dropping to a pathetic 2 percent. Despite less than .05 percent of the population having children. Broadway would always remain for everyone, for Beasley. She was so full of that Broadway sing and dance and smile and laugh and cry. That ability to direct her hatred and jealousy of things through the happy drama of Broadway. One second, she'd ruin someone's reputation out of spite, and the next, she'd jump about in choreographed movement with hands and legs in the air, smiles everywhere, giggles here and giggles there, skipping and jumping and hopping like an energetic, happy child.

Evil goofy people, they were. I never actually thought about it before. But Beasley, and so many others like her, were really evil goofy people.

Beasley decided for us—we were seeing the twenty-sixth remake of *To Kill a Mockingbird*.

"It really is the most telling play of our time," Beasley said, walking backward in front of us. She'd turn forward occasionally to make sure she was going in the right direction.

"Here it goes again," Tennyson sighed.

"It is, Tennyson."

"James, she's off on it again."

"Fuck you. You don't want to hear me because you're—"

"What, Beaz? What are you trying to sell now?"

"Not selling anything. It just hurts me to see you don't care."

"Care about what?"

"The struggle."

"What struggle?"

"The Black struggle."

"I'd say James' father did pretty well for himself."

"He wasn't Black."

"What do you mean he wasn't Black?"

"He wasn't Black."

"What are you talking about? He came straight from the Congo."

"Why do you say it like that?"

"Say it like what?"

"'Straight from the Congo.'"

"You know, I don't get you, Beaz."

"Why'd ya say it like that?"

"Because he was, wasn't he?"

"He was not."

"I think he was."

"You don't even know for sure. So arrogant. So ignorant."

"Beaz, what are you talking about?"

"You just assumed he's from the Congo. Because he's Black. Didn't you?"

"Someone, I think, told us," Tennyson said, like I wasn't there. "I think you did. Or James."

"Black doesn't equal Congo."

"Jesus, Beaz."

"He could've been from Asia, you know."

"The Congo isn't in Asia."

"Asians aren't allowed to be in the Congo?"

"That's not what I'm saying."

"What are you saying then?"

"The Congo is not in Asia. It's in Central Africa."

"It would be to you, wouldn't it? To young White men—*like you*—everything else is the Congo."

"You're nuts," Tennyson laughed, shaking his head. "You really are."

"As the oppressor, you see all Black people as Congo people."

"Wait—I thought you said he wasn't Black?"

"He's not the Black you see."

"What?"

"The Black you see is dark men (and women) with spears."

"That's not what I see."

"The Black I see is the founder of U."

"Why are you telling me what I think?"

"Because I know what you think."

"You don't know what goes on in my head. I only do."

"I know what you are, whether you know it or not."

"You assume too much, Beaz."

"You're just jealous."

"Jealous of who?"

"He was too successful for you."

"Fep Anglish?"

"Yes."

"When was I ever competing with Fep Anglish?"

"Your whole life. White versus Black. You oppressed him."

"No—he *oppressed* us."

"You racist bigot."

"Fuck you, Beaz."

"Not all Black people are African."

"I was saying he was from the Congo. That means he's African. Not Asian. A-F-R-I-C-A-N."

"You White man."

"What does that have to do with anything?"

"I don't want to talk anymore."

"You can't just decide to end this conversation."

"Why—because you're the decider now? Because I'm a woman and you're a man?"

"Because you know how it makes me feel."

"I don't want to talk."

"That's violent, Beaz. You'll ruin the week for me if I can't get this resolved."

"I'm not talking."

"I'm not a racist."

"I'm not talking."

"Take it back."

"Not talking."

"Beaz, please, I beg you. You're being unfair. I feel so guilty. I feel so racist."

"Not talking."

"Am I a bigot?" he begged and cried. "Really, am I?"

"I do *not* want to talk."

"I need to know. Am I a bigot?"

"No more," she sang, stomping on the ground with her fingers in her ears. "You lose. I win. You lose. I win. You lose. I win."

"Beaz, please. Tell me. I feel horrible. This guilt of mine."

"No more," she hissed in her fierce hysteria.

"Beaz, I need to know."

"No more," she screamed and drooled and laughed. "You lose," she stomped, and stomped, and stomped.

"Please, Beaz!"

"No more," she cried.

"No more," she cried.

"No more," she laughed.

"No more," she laughed

"No more," she cried.

"No more," she cried.

Tennyson began to punch himself in the head and ran around in circles confessing his sins. Beasley now sat cross-legged in the middle of the street. This was her *protest*. And she'd protest and continue to chant to herself "no more, no more, no more." And she'd keep going and keep those firm freedom-fighter fingers straight in those defiant ears of hers. For the good of her fellow people, she'd close out this world from her world. Her world. How beautiful. So equal, so fair, and so just. *That* world—Tennyson's world. How horrible. So evil, so sinful, and so racist.

"I'm sorry, Beaz," Tennyson came limping over after attacking himself. "I am a bigot," he confessed. "I am."

She then smiled.

That's all she needed to hear.

And she would forgive now.

Because she had won.

"He was a mockingbird," she admitted. "Fep was a mockingbird."

Tennyson began to cry with her.

"And then," she attempted through the sobs, "and then . . . he killed himself. Because this horrible world rejected him. Because you *all* were against him. You, the oppressors."

She cried, and then laughed, and then went back to crying.

"He was a mockingbird," she sang.

I didn't know what she meant by that. I knew very little about Harper Lee. Beasley knew everything about her. When U decided not to turn Lee into a HAC hologram, Beasley banded a group of women together to protest. Her slogan was "Rich Black People Hate Successful Women." It didn't even have a nice ring to it, but, no matter, because thousands of women got behind this slogan and my father was villainized for many years thereafter. Strange that that villainization wasn't enough to make him hate Beasley. He clearly didn't hate successful women because he loved her for her successes. It turned him on, I think. And, I guess, his dislike of Harper Lee turned Beasley on. My father told the press once, "There is no Harper Lee HAC because she's a one-trick pony. To become a HAC, historical figures must go through rigorous diagnostics. Harper Lee just didn't have enough. We couldn't see any potential growth for her since her body of work is not by any means extensive. She failed our risk assessment."

"He was a mockingbird," Beasley went on, and on, and on. "And people like you—"

She pointed at both of us now.

"—people like you—"

She stood and stretched and yawned and then collapsed into a crouched baseball catcher position.

"White men, everywhere," she sobbed and touched the ground. "No freedom in this whiteness."

She then smacked her face against the pavement.

"Too much whiteness," she growled.

She smacked her head against the pavement again.

"Too much whiteness."

"Too much whiteness."

"Too much whiteness."

"Enough," Tennyson screamed.

"Please, Beasley," I finally said.

I tried to help her up.

"Beasley," I said in heavy breaths, "you're hurting yourself."

"Too much whiteness."

"Too much whiteness."

"Too much whiteness."

"Maybe seeing a play isn't the best option," I said to Tennyson. "I think that play gets Beasley too emotional."

"Don't tell me how she feels," Tennyson barked back, pushing me aside to help her up and kiss her and then feel bad for himself again.

"James, you're right," she sniffled, flicking off her tears. "I guess it's just too damn much right now. The injustice I have to endure. And that mockingbird I loved. Oh, God—I really want this world to be as good as I can be. I want people to learn from *me*. But they just won't. They won't. They won't. They won't. And I hate *them* for it."

"Beaz, I know," Tennyson begged. "They're horrible."

"Shut up," she then cried. "You're *them*."

"Fep was such a mockingbird," Tennyson said, with such unbridled sycophancy, "but now I'm *your* mockingbird."

"Very far from it, Tenny Benny Lenny," she smiled, and then hugged him, and then kissed him. "A White man is very, very far from it. Your birth was a sin. And I pity you."

"Oh my god," she suddenly screamed, stretching each syllable into a screech as she hopped up and down in the air. These dramatics ended her quest for moral authority. There was something else that took her interest now. White oppression talk was so two seconds ago.

"Look," Beasley went on. "Look over there. Look who it is."

Tennyson followed Beasley's lead and they both went into that strange baseball catcher position of hers. The emotions were too heavy on their shoulders to stand.

"Is that really . . . ?" I whispered.

"I can't even . . ." Tennyson whispered back.

"She's just . . ." Beasley whimpered.

The HAC holograms walked right through Tennyson and this fakery didn't seem to take away from it at all. Beasley began to cry again.

"My life is made," she said. "Yoko is *so* beautiful."

"Who cares about Yoko," Tennyson said. "John Lennon just went right through me. He's part of me. His genius. His life. His work. He's part of me now."

Beasley's sobs had become so saturated in hysteria she was now unable to communicate her feelings. She was choking.

Then I heard others crying off somewhere else. Their crying got closer, and another couple turned the corner, their eyes drenched. It was just too much for them to take. John Lennon and Yoko Ono. Oh, God, what a sight to behold. And these sobers came toward us with their pampered Six Flags-lazy-adrenaline, and their cheap Disney World Mickey Mouse-ear-headband-wonder, and that cruise ship-anchored-zero-blood-flow-bobble-walk—those horrible attributes of urban decay.

"Alright, alright," Tennyson said to himself. "Enough is enough. That was a good cry. I needed that. We both needed that."

"I still need it," Beasley squeaked from the lack of oxygen. "I need this cry. I don't think these meds for my bipolar disorder are working anymore. *I need this cry.*"

"Shut up, Beaz," Tennyson broke into tears again. "Always about you. What about my cerebral palsy? Imagine living with *that.*"

"Tenny, you don't have cerebral palsy, you *fool.*"

"How do you know?"

"Because anyone would know."

"I'm taking meds for it. Look everywhere. Cerebral palsy is everywhere."

"Not like my illness."

"Fuck your illness."

"Look right there, you moron. Right over there. There's an ad for Otigia."

THINK HAPPY WITH OTIGIA

Beasley was on Otigia. She wanted to think happy. Who didn't? But I was sure of it; she didn't have bipolar disorder. I bet most people on Otigia didn't have what they said they had. But who was to say you couldn't have what you said you had? There weren't any prescriptions. You didn't have to get one. Pharma was totally democratized, and everything was over the counter. Drugs for the worst diseases imaginable were advertised like a Big Mac or a Whopper. Disease was a signifying factor for identity, a dog tag to make you something special. Beasley was an Otigia girl. What a struggle she lived with her bipolar disorder. How could she be so strong amidst something so debilitating? To be an influencer like she was. With something like that dragging her down. Power to her. Those Otigia girls were so strong. And they called themselves "Otigia Girls." If anyone else called them that, they'd protest and say they weren't *girls*—no, they were *women*. You think they would just change their name. But that would mean they gave into the demands of society. So, they created this impossible situation for the outsider. It was easier to refer to them as "Otigia People." Even then, some of the bipolar disorder crew said that *people* was sexist because it meant you were unwilling to accept the reality that bipolar disorder primarily affected women. Those stats, I knew from my father, were entirely fabricated. And there couldn't be legitimate data when there was not legitimate diagnosis. That's why my father had started to really hate the democratized pharma industry. None of it was measurable since you could pick and choose a disease based on your liking. I really did think I had OCD and some of that ADHD, though. I had real signs of it. Really.

"Depression is everywhere, you idiot," Beasley said and pointed at the Otigia advertisement.

"That's just an *in* thing," Tennyson dismissed.

"You bastard—an *in* thing?"

"Oh, come on."

"You're an ass."

"I could take Otigia right now if I wanted to. But I'm not. Because that's what everyone is doing these days. You're a follower, Beaz."

"I am *not* a follower. I *am* an influencer."

"An influencer? What a world Fep Anglish has created."

"What do you mean by that?"

"Fep Anglish was the devil," he explained, making slight eye contact with me. It was his way of acknowledging his rudeness. But he wouldn't go further than that.

"How horrid you are," she responded. "He was a saint!"

"With this monopoly world."

"He saved us from ourselves. You remember what the generation before us went through."

"I wasn't around for that. How would I know?"

"The past is alive."

"Is it?"

"Yes. We're living it. It's all around us. Like the air. We inhale it and we exhale it."

"Yeah, you're right—we suck it in and turn it to poison. Good old carbon dioxide."

"Fep Anglish saved us from ourselves. He unified us. Because we couldn't agree on anything before. Too many options. Too many opinions. No mainstream. Only boutique. The boutique ate itself up because there were too many of them all over the place. A simple nail. The one you hammer in. You couldn't even get that. Because you had to get it from some artisan who specialized in the art of nail making. You had to wait for him to make that nail in his house in the middle of nowhere. You couldn't just buy it at a store. Everything had to be handmade. You had to get it from the nail guy who had one of those stupid waiting lists of over a year—for a horrid nail. He saved us—Fep Anglish. You horrid fool."

"And that nail guy only knew about nails—and nothing else—because Fep Anglish's algorithms only blasted his limited brain with more pointless information about nails and nothing else."

"You're horrid!" she said. Then she pulled out a Fep Anglish quote that had nothing to do with their argument.

"Perfection is formless," she had memorized with thoughtless precision, "because form is found in the fingerprints of human error."

"The poster Otigia Girl who sounds like Fep Anglish himself," Tennyson announced.

"I am the poster Otigia Girl."

"The poster Fep Anglish Girl."

"That too."

"People have spotted him."

"Who?"

"Fep."

"Right. Right."

"They did. Seriously. His hologram. At Enoteca Corsi."

"His favorite lunch spot in Italy—Rome to be more exact—that's where they saw him?"

"Yes. His hologram."

"I don't believe you."

"Maybe it's just rumor—but I heard. I did."

"Anyway, true or not, I am the poster Otigia Girl."

"Alright. I get it."

"In fact, to enlighten your ignorance, I was asked to be in their next photoshoot."

"Bullshit."

"I was."

"And you just mention this now? Because you're always so modest."

"Do I have to tell you everything?"

"No, but you do tell me everything."

Out of nowhere, Beasley punched Tennyson in the face. He fell to ground with blood clots the size of teabags coming out of his nostrils. I nearly puked.

"My nose," Tennyson panicked. "You bitch—I have blood clotting problems. This will never stop. I'm going to die. I'm going to die. I'm going to die."

Empowered beyond recognition (or EBR), she towered over him and looked down at her victim like Muhammad Ali looking down at Sonny Liston.

"Silly you," she fumed from above.

"My Crohn's," he gargled.

"You don't have Crohn's."

"It's as real as your depression."

"So, Tenny, women can't be depressed, I guess?"

"That's not what—"

"They can't, right? Because they live simple lives."

"I'm not saying—"

"Only men have a right to be depressed."

"Beaz . . . please . . . I'm trying to—"

"Don't 'Beaz' me."

"I need a napkin or something."

"You need something from a woman?"

"Yes."

"From me?"

"Yes."

Before she could search her pocket for anything that could stop the bleeding, a piece of plastic stapled to her jacket began to light up and vibrate.

"Fuck," she grunted. "Time's up."

She found a flower-patterned handkerchief in her pocket and threw it at Tennyson's bloodied face. I helped up Tennyson, who had lost a surprising amount of blood. He was like rubber in my arms.

"I really loved this jacket," Beasley sighed. "Time's up already."

"Your month is up?" I asked, placing Tennyson's doll-like body on a street bench.

"Seems to be. Good old Circularity, right? Every object in this world has a lifespan now and you can't enjoy anything for too long. Just when you're starting to really like something, it goes straight back into this sustainable world of constant recycling."

"That's Circularity."

"The wallet—even the fucking wallet."

"What happened to your wallet?"

"I took it out to pay for something. Can't remember what. But someone saw my wallet and reported me."

"Why would they do that?"

Beasley needed you to bait some of her more uneventful stories with questions because it built the drama and the intrigue.

"My wallet was not a mono material," she answered.

"What's that?"

"How can you not know by now? It's an object that cannot be recycled because it's made up of different materials that have been permanently bonded together. It becomes labeled as an object lost for society—wasn't lost for me, though, recyclable or not."

"Aren't wallets usually just leather?"

"No, not this one. Fep gave it to me. Part of the wallet was wood, and it had my name engraved in it. Part of it was also carbon fiber, I think. He loved racing cars, so . . ."

The irony, I thought. The man behind Circularity handing out wallets that weren't recyclable.

"Well . . ." I said, smirking.

"And now, this jacket."

"You can get another like it."

"Now someone else gets to wear it. This jacket was a rare find. It fit me perfectly. I've never had a jacket fit me like this before. I loved this jacket."

"Try to rent it again."

She caressed my cheek with her bloodied hand.

"You're so sweet sometimes," she almost sang. "The amount of clothing in rotation—in my size—I'll never see this fine thing for the rest of my life."

My confidence shriveled up into some infinitesimal spec and my passivity held together the density of my lack of worth so it wouldn't separate and then explode into some wild, uncontained fury.

"You know so little about everything, don't you?" she said, in a sweetie piece voice. "Let me educate. Well . . . hmmm . . . I bet you don't even know . . ."

She stopped herself and continued, "Oh my god, I bet he really doesn't know this."

She stopped herself again and continued, "You know those big, great big-tall buildings your dad has on his island?"

To hold it all in, I wouldn't answer.

"Your dad was behind the Energy Efficiency Act. He ran the energy efficiency grading system throughout this city. The grading is based on water usage and other important things that have to do with saving energy. You *now* know why he has all those buildings?"

I wouldn't answer.

"He failed all the old buildings. F. And, with an F, according to the Energy Efficiency Act, that building must be removed, permanently. So, he took them . . . for himself. Now you know!"

I nodded my head.

"This is driving me nuts," she screamed and pulled on her hair.

The buzzing and blinking wouldn't stop. That's what your clothes did until you returned them to a local rental drop.

"Drop it before you get fined," I warned.

In a pretend way, I scanned for a rental drop. They were all over the city, so you had enough time when the time was up. I had never been late. Beasley was late almost every time. It was her thing to be late. Influencers had a right to be late. And she got off on her lateness most of the time. Thirteen late fees. I knew this because she bragged about it. But then something happened. She no longer wanted to be late. Another worthy influencer linked lateness to the increase of India's poverty. The connection between her clothing and India was lost on me. But that's what Beasley told me. And a lot of those types of disconnect connections were thrown around to trap people into feeling terrible about themselves. If you breathe too much, you take the oxygen away from another person in need. An influencer crop-dusted that one around. Breathe less, they said. With less oxygen going to your brain, you really felt the hatred toward the people you were protecting from yourself. That was the weird place you were put in. And—not that you cared—but you were also transient in this rent-with-guilt and give-back-with-guilt lifestyle. You really were. And most people weren't aware of those very few things you could own. The fine-print stuff. But you were guilted away from that stuff. Because anyone who was greedy enough to pay attention to the fine print was labeled as a selfish-possessor or a hoarder. Labeling and branding was very common in this puritanical culture of the modern, and the worst thing to be branded or labeled as was a selfish-possessor or a hoarder. God forbid, you owned a piece of jewelry . . . or fine china . . . or a watch— because, if you did, that meant you took the time to have it appraised when you could've been helping someone else. That jewelry you've kept all for yourself—that's six months' worth of meals for someone in need. The government understood this moral dilemma and they thwarted the need to own and hoard through high taxation and heavy-handed premiums. If you really—I mean *really*—wanted that watch, you'd wind up paying ten times its worth every month. That was the government's way of penalizing you for taking what you owned out of rent-and-release circulation. You were no longer a citizen who gave back to the community. How absurd. My father had an entire island designated for hoarding. No one seemed to care about that. But he was Fep Anglish. He was a character. A source of publicity. A person they loved to hate and hated to love. That entertainment for them. Let the clown do what the clown wants, right? But guilt the rest of us. And let the clown guilt us, too, if he wants. That'll create even more entertainment.

And this clown did guilt us. And he changed attitudes and redirected trends. Beasley's attitude was much different than it had been. Before it was so absorbed in what she could do without getting in trouble. I mean, she was so bad at keeping track of her renting schedule, one time her entire outfit went off at the same time. You had to make sure that didn't happen. I would know—God, I would know—March 5 was the day I had to return my shoes. March 16, the pants. March 24, the shirt. And March 27, the hat. Diligent people like me would return the clothing early, at varying times, so you never had to worry about having to change your whole outfit, all at once. Returning clothing early was a strongly advised tactic. But Beasley wouldn't do things this way. She was too busy influencing. But I had nothing else to do. For me, my life was mapping out my attire and going to school. I had no one to influence. I couldn't even influence myself. Beasley had bigger fish to fry and that's what led to the famous Day of Nakedness.

The Day of Nakedness—that day of the flashing and the buzzing of the shirts, the pants, the socks, the shoes, and even the underwear. I warned her about it. But she wanted this to happen. It gave her something else to do. Something else to fight for. An injustice that had to be squashed. And she pulverized the hell out of it. She could've simply returned all those clothes and the rental drop would've given her a whole fresh new set. The drops had your profile. They knew your style, and there was always drop-off accompanied with pick-up. You changed in those portable street-side changing rooms and then you gave your old clothes back. And you couldn't get away with keeping the old set, as many would come to discover, because you were always tracked and stealing clothes would only damage your credit with U. Better to be damned than to have bad credit. Better to be dead at that point. But it was all such an efficient self-sustaining system. You never dropped off to not pick up. Otherwise, you'd be naked. Like Beasley intended to be.

"Enough!" she roared that day, her body lit like a Christmas tree.

"We have rights!" she went on.

Then, the Day of Nakedness commenced, and she got fully undressed in the middle of the street. Some said it was the statement of the decade. That was the influencer in Beasley. She could bait this and serve it up as protest. And she did. An army of naked women went up and down Madison Avenue a few days after her Day of Nakedness. The protest lasted a week.

"Women have a right to wear clothes," they said.

A few men got involved, too. You'd see a naked guy in there somewhere, crying and screaming and collapsing to the ground from the weight of his own emotions. People would throw clothes from their rented apartments, and you'd see a sea of nakedness in the crowd and through the windows above and all those clothes raining down on the protestors. A freedom marcher was injured from a belt buckle. The person who did it ran away somewhere and hadn't returned since. People took care of themselves when it came to crime. It was the guilt that was punishment enough. No one could live with the guilt. Self-loathing was a jail sentence, and everyone self-loathed and, consequently, suffered day-in and day-out. But the people who committed crimes, imprisoned themselves. No jury. No sentencing. No jail time. They did it themselves.

CHAPTER EIGHT

The Society of Entropy

"My poor Tenny Lenny," Beasley said, kissing his blood-crusted face. The blood browned and flaked off as her lips detached from the beaten skin. "Make sure my love is alright. I'll drop these quick. There's a place two blocks away, I'm sure of it."

I had no idea and did another fake surveillance of the area.

"I'll keep an eye on Tennyson," I said.

"Be back in five."

She ran off with that duck run of hers. It was good she didn't make a public thing out of her running. Tennyson would laugh when she ran, and he'd even managed to smile now through the pain.

"It is a ridiculous stride," he gurgled. "I wouldn't bet on that horse."

If only Beasley were there to hear him say that. She would have done the Mike Tyson ear bite. Maybe worse. His new name could become Dickless Tenny Lenny Benny or whatever the hell it was. Maybe it would just be Dickless. I liked Dickless. Or Dick Less. Whatever.

"God," Tennyson moaned, "my nose is *sooo* fucked."

"Hurts?"

"What the fuck do you think. No, it feels wonderful. I love being bitch-hit every now and then. A good bitch-hitting is good for any guy."

"I can run and grab you bandages . . ."

"It's fine."

"You sure?"

"What are you, my fucking wife? I said I was fine. I already have one bitch to deal with. I don't need another."

For such a progressive person, he really sounded like Archie Bunker. That side of him came out when he was made a fool of. Otherwise, if he was on the other end of this, he'd tell whoever it was that they were a sexist for calling a woman a bitch. Funny how it sometimes goes when you're angry enough not to care. And when you're defeated enough to be the person you'd normally condemn. Our souls were torn in terrible ways by the things we didn't care about and the things we pretended to care about. And the world was so bitter and so clean, and the lack of war and death, and the hatred baked into the sterile social posturing of boredom, and the moral authority of self-loathing, and jealousy in the hearts of each, and every, one of us—that's what made it begin and end with *you*. To make yourself God in your own mind, meant to separate your existence from any other existence that came your way. Nothing mattered besides the things that had a direct effect on you. Because it began and ended with you. A papercut on your finger had more universal impact than another outbreak of the Ebola virus. Your world was the papercut. And that hurt like hell. Tennyson's world was his broken nose.

Funny how all it took was a broken nose to really ruin someone.

"I'm sorry," I said, to avoid being his target.

The Otigia advertisement dematerialized and re-pixelated itself into a blue-and-red Uncle Sam. He pointed at us while the words *Why do you not admire ambition in women? It's time to end the stereotypes* flashed above him.

What timing. It seemed too good to be a coincidence. Well, it wasn't a coincidence. It was listening. I was sure of it. And Uncle Sam pointed at Tennyson and called him out for what he was. Then he dematerialized and another ad re-pixelated itself, the white type appearing letter by letter against a black background. The letter would type itself and then erase itself. When it was typed again, the next letter would appear with it. This was done to build the drama and make you feel worse about yourself. It went like this:

C...
CA...
CAN...
CAN Y...
CAN YO...
CAN YOU...
CAN YOUR...
CAN YOUR R...
CAN YOUR RA...
CAN YOUR RAC...
CAN YOUR RACI...
CAN YOUR RACIS...
CAN YOUR RACISM...
CAN YOUR RACISM B...
CAN YOUR RACISM BE...
CAN YOUR RACISM BE C...
CAN YOUR RACISM BE CU...
CAN YOUR RACISM BE CUR...
CAN YOUR RACISM BE CURE...
CAN YOUR RACISM BE CURED...

CAN YOUR RACISM BE CURED?

Can your racism be cured? was an attack on both of us. America was listening and it was judging us, pointing at us, and blaming us. I felt bad for being something I couldn't control. If only my mother hadn't been so pale. The sin was in my blood. And the sin was in Tennyson's blood. We were both doomed from the start.

"I don't think anything like that can be cured," Tennyson said, paralyzed by this question. "I know I'm not a perfect person. I know that much."

I let him go on with his confession.

He needed to confess.

And I would be the one to listen.

"You can't choose your father, right," he laughed through the bubbling nostril blood. "You can't change your father. Neither can Beasley. She's about the whitest type of bread out there. She can't do a thing about that. This ad is really talking to her, you know. She's the problem. Yes, that's right, she's the problem. We're not. It's because of her we're shunned."

Tennyson stood up and paused to ground his balance.

"I'm done," he said.

"Done with what?" I asked.

"Done with her."

"With Beasley?"

"Yes."

"Why?"

"Because of that."

He pointed at the advertisement.

"Tennyson, that's unfair."

"I can't live with myself when I'm around her."

"But that's crazy. You can't be that unfair."

"Unfair? Have you heard of the Sentinelese?"

I was worried where he was going with this. It felt like he wanted to morally replenish himself by attacking me now. There was no one else around to be the victim.

"No," I responded, anticipating the worst.

"I thought so," he said, as a light blow. This was very unexpected. Maybe this was just a lecture. God, I hoped it was just a lecture.

"The Sentinelese," he went on, "are the indigenous people of the Bay of Bengal in India. They inhabit the North Sentinel Island, and they are completely removed from the world community. In fact, they are hostile to people like you and me. They are uncorrupted by racism and sexism and elitism. No civilized person has dared to infiltrate the North Sentinel Island. All who have tried have been killed, brutally. The tribe has no tolerance for racist people like you and me, or anyone remotely like us. They live amongst themselves in the purest purity and the most unmolested divinity. Centuries and centuries of this purity and divinity and that rightful hostility to the outsider. But I do know of one man, a trespasser, who went to the island and was embraced by the Sentinelese. No one knows how or why. It's a bit of a legend, I must admit. I've heard many different versions of this story. And they all lead to the same ending. That this foreigner, this trespasser, rules these indigenous people now. That he has an army. A very large army. And that India, in secret, fears this army. The Blue Planet United, I've heard from many, wants to invade this island. But I won't allow it. People like us won't allow it. The Sentinelese have a right to live by their own rules just like we do. Who gives us the right to tell them what to do? We *are* the enemy."

Tennyson began to chant.

"We are the enemy!"

"We are the enemy!"

"We are the enemy!"

"You and me—we will never let the BPU prevail against the Sentinelese."

He began to chant again.

"We are the enemy!"

"We are the enemy!"

"We are the enemy!"

Then he began to cry. This cry had no emotion. It was something closer to shock. There was an abruptness to it, like sudden cardiac arrest or a seizure.

"I love her," he said. "I really loved her—everything about her."

"And that's reason enough," I explained, confused by his convulsions.

"Not when it's like this."

"Like what?"

"Like this and that. The whole thing. The guilt."

"No one is asking you to do anything."

"I can't take this fucking boredom any longer. She's boring—and she's simple."

"She's an influencer."

"You give a fuck?"

"It's not what I think."

"I guess you don't think. You just listen. That's your thing, right?"

"Don't bring me into this."

"You brought yourself into it."

"I'm trying to help."

"No one helps anyone. Don't kid yourself, James."

"That's not true."

"Oh, it is. Very much is."

"You'll break her if you do this."

"Her fake depression?"

"We all have problems."

"Do we?"

"Yes, we do."

"Your father had problems—I know that much."

He attacked my father to unhinge me. But it wouldn't work.

"He did," I responded.

"What is it with you?"

"What do you mean?"

"The passiveness. The whole fucking thing about you. You don't care about a thing, do you?"

I wouldn't respond.

"Tell me," he cried. "Tell me if you care about a fucking thing."

I wouldn't respond.

"Maybe you just hate everyone?"

I looked away.

"Oh," he laughed, through the cries. "Is that it? James hates the world."

"You'll crush Beasley."

"She'll get beaten down just like the people she beats down."

"I'm sure she's sorry about your face."

"You think? Really?"

"I'm sure she is."

"The hell, she is."

The advertisement triggered him. It made him hate himself for being himself. Right there, it was a lose-lose battle for Tennyson. He was ridiculed for something predetermined. But that wasn't simply it. The hatred for himself pressurized underneath his conscience and the secret jealousy he always had for Beasley emasculated him and wiggled his Dickless Tenny Lenny Benny in front of his woman-beaten face. It was all a good laugh at his expense. The whole entire world was a good laugh at Tennyson's expense. Talk about being vain. This was true vanity.

"I'd ask her," I suggested. "I bet she feels awful about your face."

"Her past doesn't allow her to feel guilt."

"What?"

"The future is simply the past, unresolved."

"What?"

"White people don't feel bad about what they do. They're impervious to guilt."

And then he just walked off like John Wayne. There wasn't much of a movie sunset, though. But he turned the corner and disappeared with drama. That was the end for them forever, for just the moment. The longest relationship I'd ever seen. Approaching three months. That was done forever, until it was back on. And wow, for Beasley, that was unheard of. I don't think she ever went beyond a week. I couldn't even imagine myself doing a day. Doing the grind with another body for twenty-four hours straight, day after day after day . . . holy hell. Sounds like torture. Some other human there to breathe down your neck, always.

But Beasley. What if it'd been her? What if I was with her? How would that be? I wondered. Could I even do it? Could I be someone that another wanted to spend prolonged time with? Could I be that person? It made me sad to think that way. And I cried to myself for a moment and then got it together.

"Oh, Jamie-waaamie," Beasley singsonged from across the street. "How about this new piece of grand old clothing. Another puzzle piece to the clothing that is . . . sorta mine, ya know. You like?"

She spun on the crosswalk and giggled to herself.

"Where's poor old Tenny?" she asked, looking at the blood on the bench.

"He left," I answered.

"He left?"

"Yes, he left."

"Why did he leave?"

"I don't know."

"Don't give me that."

"I really don't know."

"You're lying."

"Ask him."

"Why can't I ask you?"

"I don't want to get involved."

"You killed him, didn't you?"

I laughed.

"You killed him."

"What?"

"You did it. I know you like me."

"What are you talking about?"

"I left. You like me. You hate him. Boom. Done. Tennyson's gone. Poof."

"You think I killed him?"

Long pause.

Beasley broke out into her spit-filled cry-laugh. It was always her laughing and crying. Together, always. So very Broadway. Like opera. The manic dramatics.

"Do you literally believe anything, Jamie boy?"

I was too embarrassed to defend myself.

"You're so cute," she went on. "Tennyson doesn't think you're cute, but I do. I assume it's because he knows you're better looking than he is."

"Wait a second," she stopped. "Wait. Wait. Wait. Wait. Do you really like me? You like me. Oh my god, you like me. Like—like me, like me. This is actually real. Your face doesn't lie. It never did. It never will."

"Alright, Beasley," I said, brushing her away. "Enough is enough."

"But you like me?"

"I don't like you that way, Beasley."

"That's a shame."

"I'm not saying you're unattractive."

"You are saying that."

"Why are you doing this?"

"Doing what?"

"What you're doing."

"I have no idea what you're talking about."

"Hitting on me—or whatever it's called."

"I am absolutely not."

"You seem to be."

"Well, you're wrong. I'm teasing you."

"Flirting."

"James, you wouldn't know flirting."

"Alright."

"Alright. Alright," she echoed me.

"You should talk to Tennyson."

Beasley began to cry.

"I'm cursed, Jamie boy."

"No."

"What a thing to say. Two letters to make me feel better."

"Beasley."

"Seven letters, not much better."

I couldn't handle the constant talk and the back and forth. Throwing up words like clay targets. Shooting each other's words down with more words. The chatter.

"I'm sorry," I told her before she could walk away. It was hard for someone to walk away when you said you're sorry. That was the big word of my generation—*sorry*. It was the ultimate white flag—*sorry*.

"Tennyson can wait," she said, full of a spunk that came from nowhere. "I won't let him ruin this day. He won't get that from me. I won't let him have a ruined day."

She rambled like me. We all rambled. There was a readiness and nervousness screwed into us by our bizarre parents. Drilled in at birth. If there could've been a human factory recall, we were the population to have it.

"Is today the day, James?"

I would let her answer her own question.

"I think it is. Oh, Jamie boy, today is supposed to be the most delightful of days. I hear The Society of Entropy is tearing down a statue. They're putting an end to the corruption of the past. That statue has offended so many people over the decades. One of my friends can't walk past it without crying. I never walk anywhere near that block. Awful tribute to a terrible past. I don't want to cry."

The Society of Entropy was a difficult thing to describe. From the little I knew they were a group of very rich people who sought to explore the universe. Once every week, spacecrafts would be launched from Central Park into the darkness of the night. The elite explorers would discover new places for two to eight months. If you had more money than God, you were out playing spaceman for eight months. If you had just enough money to do this once or twice, it was a two-month journey. People like Rick did the trip in around five months. My father only did it once. But that was for two years. The longest civilian space travel adventure in human history. Of course, my father would've done that. Two years, one month, and six days, to be exact. My mother was in a slumber most of the time. And toward the end of it she was convinced he was abducted by aliens. She told me they wanted his brain and that it was all a ploy organized by Rick. I admit, my father's omnipresence and brilliance did make people think crazy things, especially the people closest to him. You'd think being a member of his family would make him more human—well, it did the exact opposite. That wrecking of his wife, all the while he circled Saturn, Jupiter, and Pluto, to then come back and say the trip was a little boring. Though Saturn, he couldn't deny, was mesmerizing. The rest of the planets he didn't really talk about. He spoke about space travel like he was traveling to another country. Going to Pluto was like a disappointing Venice trip. Too many tourists. But he did like Saturn. Saturn he'd suggest to other people. It had great authentic alien pasta there. Five stars!

Anyway—The Society of Entropy had followers who also called themselves The Society of Entropy. They were The Society of Entropy's Bleacher Creatures. These admirers would celebrate around the launch site like some tribal group dancing after sighting a commercial jet flying in the air. The spacemen would take off and leave behind thousands of admirers below, gathering to do drugs and destroy things. For each launch date, the Bleacher Creatures tore down a historical monument. This went from being a terrorist act to a perverse celebration after enough launches had happened. And the public enjoyed it, too, because it gave their lives a good adrenaline pump. It wasn't like there were police to thwart it, anyway. The vandalism was something that would just happen and continued to happen as the launches happened. And people really got into it. And they voted, from that darkest place in their hearts, for the object of destruction. It was fun to see what innocent thing people hated most. This was about the only thing that made the city feel alive. Otherwise, it went back to being clean, empty, and barren. People came out of nowhere to congregate around this primitive ritual of chaos.

It wasn't chaos without control, I hoped. Though I would never know for sure. I yearned for the comfort of maternal and paternal control. The drunkenly divulged secrecy of private operations gave me that fulfillment. That no matter how messed up things got, there was always someone there to pat down the flames. Chaos perpetuating itself without supervision could not exist on its own. If it did exist on its own, we were more alone than we thought. That would mean Mommy and Daddy didn't always know what we were up to. And I would never want that even if I pouted about it and said I wanted them to go away forever.

CHAPTER NINE

Black Ant

"There is no *is* . . ." the voice said.

"There is no *is* . . ." voices echo her.

"Infancy—your *infancy*," the woman enunciated for sheer effect. "*That* is one stage in life where you don't look back. Too bad none of us look forward enough to remember it."

"There is no *is* . . ." she went on in rhythmic tantrum.

"There is no *is* . . ." voices echo her.

"There is no . . ." voices echo her.

"There is . . ." voices echo her.

"There . . ." voices echo her.

Echoes disappear into a slow build sparked by another voice.

"There . . ." that single voice says.

"There is . . ." another voice says.

"There is no . . ." more voices say.

"There is no *is* . . ." they all say.

"There is no *is* . . ." they all say in unison.

"The Society of Entropy," she went on, "Your story is everyone's story. And everyone's story is your story. Because there is no you. Because there is no everyone. Because there is no is."

Beasley had forced me to take drugs and her violent fingers dug into my arm fat and fish-hooked me back onto the street. I fell over and didn't have it in me to get back up. The euphoria made me want to stay on the ground forever. What a wonderful place this ground was. I could stay there for eternity and just relax. I couldn't imagine having to ever stand again.

"James," Beasley stood over me and cried, "I'm so sorry. This was my fault. You should've stayed inside and rested. You weren't ready. Please, forgive me."

"I forgive you," I said, my eyes crossed.

She snuck her arms under my weighted body and pulled me up with surprising effort.

"Leave me," I mumbled, my eyes rolling around.

And there I was—vertical. And those wonderfully and wizzfully and swishtyfully quiet electric cars. The slicing up and down Central Park West soothed me. That warm butcher knife sound going through soft butter. Ahh. Those crisp aero razorblades full of calm. Car after car after car. Impact after impact after impact, I fucking hoped. I wanted to be torn to shreds. To be taken over by this calm slicing.

"I'm fine," I said, standing on my own now. "I'm really fine."

"We need to get inside," she insisted.

"I'm fine now, really."

"You're not fine."

"I can't go back inside."

"Why?"

"I just . . ."

Like a zombie, I dragged myself away from her. She gave up easily and trailed behind me as I followed the strong woman's voice back into Central Park.

"James! Where are you going?" she cried.

"That voice. That fucking voice."

"You don't want to be a part of that."

"I'm on the drugs—why shouldn't I want to be a part of it?"

"The Society of Entropy is a ghastly thing."

"Everything is a ghastly thing!"

Her shadow echoed me, and the streetlight turned, and I hobbled across Central Park West into the park.

"You are not poor or rich," the voice said somewhere in the tree-shadowed dark. "You are *not* a man or a woman. You are not from Mexico . . . not from Algeria . . . not from Spain . . . not from the Moon . . . not from Territory A . . . or B . . . or C . . . or even from Mars . . . or Jupiter . . . or Pluto. You're not from the past . . . or the present . . . or the future. You're not even *you* or *them*. You're no one. You're everyone and no one. Fanny is Carmen and Carmen is Karma and Karma is Miss Moses and Miss Moses is Old Luke and Old Luke is Annalee and Annalee is Crazy Chester and Crazy Chester is Jack the dog."

My damaged joints began to harden, and I powered through the pain to the Great Lawn. The Great Lawn was the largest stretch of grass in the park. Before my father relocated to Fogo Island, he used to take me there every Saturday. What a memory. There wouldn't be a person in the park. It would be ours. That plot of grass left for us to enjoy, alone. What a miserably vacant society this was then and still is now. But it'd worked out for my father. He loved the park—and so did I. It was special. Different. Unique. Another piece of nostalgia poking holes in the tapestry of Fep Anglish's façade. No one understood why he didn't stamp Central Park with his U buildings. To my father, it was surely wasted space.

That chanting.

The trees parted themselves and presented to me a huge performing stage. Thousands of people chanted below it and this woman was above—like a god . . . their god.

"Because all of us," this woman said onstage.

"Because all of us," the crowd echoed.

"Because all of us," she went on, "are a *weight* that gets passed along . . . because there's no central character in this story . . . no arc . . . no twist . . . no resolution . . . no identity . . . because, in The Society of Entropy, we are all reaching the same vision. We are *all* drifting to the same fate, to that same fall—that same fog. We are *all* a collective thing that is waiting—*yearning*—to dissolve itself into something much greater."

Cheering.

Whistling.

Screaming.

Crying.

Begging.

Singing.

Barfing.

Shaking.

Running.

Dancing.

Masturbating.

Some naked.

Some with painted faces.

Some with painted bodies.

Some with both.

Some holding branches lit on fire.

Some bleeding.

Some with blood smeared on their faces.

Some fighting.

Some kissing.

Some speaking in other languages.

Some unconscious.

Some very drunk.

All on drugs.

Altogether, a permeating roar extending its range into the nonexistent night of drooping afro trees, each wooden extremity moaning in reaction to the dainty wind pushing flirtatiously through its leaves. The madness of the artificial light made you feel like you were in a doctor's examination room. Microwave silver white light refracting off the crazy eyes above the chanting mouths above the tantric torsos above the vibrating legs above the Michael Jackson–rhythmic feet. A circus set up in hell. The cursed crowd swarming the radioactive preacher's contagion. Then the holograms came in and the atom of mania split and self-imploded and a hologram entered through that classic Looney Tune vortex. Choreographed fog splintered the light cast from the vortex. The ballooned eyes and the protruded golden beak of Daffy Duck stabbed the crowd and its oil-spill-black head vanished against the night. Crisscrossing one another, the searchlights lit the hidden afro trees and their twitching movements from the slight touch of the breeze. The crowd was lost in a drift into fiction. They'd fall into that self-loathing chemical imbalance.

"Bring in the duck," they chanted.

"Bring in the duck."

"Bring in the duck."

"Bring in the duck."

Then they stopped.

"Marry death," the crowd went on

"Marry death."

"Marry death."

"Let's marry death."

"Let's marry death."

"Let's marry death."

The hologram of Daffy Duck disappeared, and the crowd swayed back and forth. The searchlights came together to focus and illuminate the woman on the stage.

"But, we can't," she said. "We *cannot* achieve greatness here. We *cannot* and *will not* do this here—not on this rock. On this rock, we live the static life of what *is*, what *was*, and what *will*. On this rock, we grow like a tumor, feeding off each other, feeding and feeding and feeding like the old ways of government wanted us to."

The crowd swayed like a rocking chair now.

"Go to war, Jack!" they said, swaying left.

"Fight the fight, Jack!" they said, swaying right.

"Be this!" they said, swaying left.

"Be that!" they said, swaying right.

"Come on, Jack!" they said, swaying left.

"Not in The Society of Entropy," she continued. "Not *here*. We— were, are, will be—*nowhere*. Here, there is no *Jack*. Here, there is no *war*. Here, there is no *fight*. Here, there is no *this*. Here, there is no *that*."

"So, *come on*, Jack . . ." they said, swaying left.

"Let's get going . . ." they said, swaying right.

"Let's unchain ourselves and experience Entropy, *finally*," they said, swaying left.

"Let's not be Jack," she continued. "Let's escape from Jack. Let's get closer to beyond . . . to that place where you (we), like milk to coffee, disperse into greatness. Jackless Jack . . . Jack of all trades (and master of none)—let's wave good-bye and slip the surly bonds of Earth to touch the face of God."

The ground rumbled and shook all around. I looked at Beasley, but she didn't seem concerned. I spread my legs apart to strengthen my center of gravity to thwart the imbalance of the drugs.

"What's happening?" I asked her.

She didn't respond and tilted her head down to pray.

Lava light burst from random spots in the park. The magnifying rumble went throughout the city like thunder. You could hear it travel through the cavernous cracks of the skyline.

"The rockets," Beasley finally answered, looking up. "It's launch time."

Magma smoke filled the air and the shuttles, pointing up like syringes, took to the stars. They fumed above Central Park.

Cheering.

Whistling.

Screaming.

Crying.

Begging.

Singing.

Barfing.

Shaking.

Running.

Dancing.

Masturbating.

"I think we better go," Beasley said.

The woman ran off the stage and the crowd went into a frenzy. They seemed to hoot until they were calmed by a procession of men and women entering the stage in a single-file line. I counted thirty-three men and thirty-three women.

"Dead Man Walkers," Beasley whispered into my ear.

The woman that'd run off the stage appeared again, trailing the sixty-six Dead Man Walkers. Four rows were formed, and she skipped to the front like a child.

"How 'bout it," the woman laughed. Her laugh echoed over the crowd. They laughed back in reaction.

"How 'bout it," the crowd replied.

"We've got a good lot of Dead Man Walkers tonight."

"How 'bout it," the crowd replied.

"We've got a lot of apologies tonight."

"How 'bout it," the crowd replied.

The woman handed the microphone to a female Dead Man Walker in the front row.

"I'm sorry," the Dead Man Walker stuttered.

The woman grabbed the microphone from her. The Dead Man Walker began to shake.

"How 'bout it?" the woman asked the crowd.

"I . . . think . . . not," the crowd answered.

"How 'bout it," she said and handed the microphone back to the shaking Dead Man Walker.

"I am very sorry," the Dead Man Walker pleaded. "Please. I'm sorry, okay. I'm so sorry."

Silence.

Beasley began to cry. It was a happy cry. She was one with the crowd now and the woman on stage tore the microphone from the Dead Man Walker's hand.

"What are you sorry for?" she squealed.

She handed the microphone back to the Dead Man Walker.

"I apologize for everything," she cried and then knelt. "I apologize for being me. I apologize for having advantages. I apologize for not offering my home. I apologize for . . ."

The woman kicked her flat to the stage floor and the microphone rolled out of her hand. It rolled offstage and the crowd swarmed it like ants on bread. One victorious person had it in his hands and he climbed up and handed it back. He then did the Richard Nixon victory sign and jumped into the crowd and people laughed maniacally.

"How 'bout it," the woman said. "Did you hear what I heard?"

"Yes," the crowd screamed.

"I knew you did. I think I heard 'my home.' I know I heard 'my home.'"

From the ground, The Dead Man Walker defended herself. But no one could hear her. The woman tossed the microphone to her like it was a handkerchief. She wasn't worth handing it to.

Still on the ground, she said into the microphone: "I'm sorry . . . I apologize for calling that home my home. I apologize for thinking it was my home. I apologize for hoarding my money. I apologize for trying to hold onto the things that have been passed down to me. I apologize for not giving away my possessions. I apologize for it all. I apologize. I am sorry."

The Dead Man Walker struggled to get up and the crowd, along with Beasley, continued laughing. The woman wouldn't help, and the Dead Man Walker rocked her body on the ground to gain enough momentum to get up. Like a turtle on its back, she managed to roll herself sharply enough to pull her weight up to its vertical stance. The woman, annoyed she got up, swatted the microphone from her again.

"You're sorry for being rich, aren't you? You're sorry for being who you are because it flies in the face of who we are. You either join, or you go away. You understand? You hear us loud and clear?"

The crowd growled like children would at a small bug or some tiny animal that wasn't threatening.

"Are you White?" the woman asked, holding the microphone to the Dead Man Walker.

The Dead Man Walker went to hold the microphone and the woman pulled it away. She wanted to hold it and have the Dead Man Walker speak into it.

"Are you White?" the woman asked again. "Are you willing to let your country die for you?"

"I am nothing," the Dead Man Walker responded. She was now tired and no longer scared.

"Do you feel the guilt?"

"I am nothing."

"Do you feel the pain?"

"I am nothing."

The Dead Man Walker then dragged herself back into formation. The woman pulled another victim out of the front row.

"How 'bout it," the woman laughed. Her laugh echoed over the crowd. They laughed back in reaction.

"How 'bout it," the crowd replied.

"We've got a good lot of Dead Man Walkers tonight."

"How 'bout it," the crowd replied.

"We've got a lot of apologies tonight."

"How 'bout it," the crowd replied.

The woman handed the microphone to the next Dead Man Walker.

"I'm sorry," he said, very rehearsed. "I'm sorry for being me. I'm sorry for being privileged. I'm sorry for being an enemy. I'm sorry for hoarding a car. I'm sorry for hoarding clothes. I'm sorry for hoarding a Rolex that's been in my family for seven generations. I'm sorry. I'm sorry. I'm sorry."

He handed the microphone back to the woman.

"That was good," she said. "Real good."

He nodded his head in total submission. The white shirt he wore was tight against his chest and you could see he was big and very fit. He looked like a marine and acted like a marine. I knew this well from the movies.

"Not great, though," she spun her logic. "Not nearly great enough. We don't accept good. I heard 'Rolex' somewhere. I swear I heard it. Rolex. Why is it always a Rolex you people try to hoard? You're not the first and you won't be the last. It's always a Rolex. Rolex. Rolex. Rolex. Rolex. I hear you say that word, and I think: 'Why wouldn't you just say *watch*?' What makes a watch a Rolex? What makes it better than any other watch? They all tell time, don't they? Why does something always have to be better than something else? Tell me, please. We would love to know."

She shoved the microphone against his chest and the thud echoed into the depths of the park.

"I don't know what a Rolex is," he answered, confused. "I call it that because it says it is."

The woman was surprised, and it seemed, for the first time tonight, she didn't know what to do. The crowd was restless and needed her to lead their frenzy.

The Dead Man Walker attempted to hand her back the microphone.

She swatted at it. And, confused, he held it to his chest. He would wait for her command. But she was thinking now.

"I . . . ," he said and stopped.

"I," he continued, "am sorry I called it a Rolex. I am sorry."

"Well, you should be," she hopped on his confession. "Brand identity is the sworn enemy. We do not believe in hierarchy. We do not believe one citizen should be entitled because their family was privileged. You should be ashamed of yourself."

"Ashamed," the crowd screamed.

Their frenzy was fueled yet again.

"Ashamed," they went on.

"Ashamed," they continued.

"Ashamed."

"Ashamed."

"Ashamed."

"Give me it," her unamplified voice barked at the Dead Man Walker. "Give it to me, you moron."

He gave her the microphone with the utmost innocence, and she looked up at him. His sheer size dwarfed her, and I could tell she didn't like the way it made her feel.

"You're a big idiot," she hissed. "Your famed granddaddy was an agent of war—an agent of violence. A hero of The Last War, some say. A villain, all of us say. A killer is more like it. An enemy of peace is more like it. Your granddaddy was a bad man."

The Dead Man Walker wouldn't say a word. Like a marine, he stood tall and confident. This annoyed her very much.

"Stop standing like an idiot," she yapped. "Stop it. Stop it now. It annoys me. It annoys all of us. It offends me. It offends all of us. You should be drooped over and sad. You should be bent by the horror of your past—that violent blood that runs through your African veins. Think about all you've done—burn in it!"

"I'm sorry," he said without the microphone. He had a stronger voice than the woman and we could hear him. He had a powerful voice.

"I'm sorry for all I've done," he clarified. "For all my family has done, including my granddaddy."

The woman wanted to overpower his natural stage presence. This was her stage, and he was nothing more than a Dead Man Walker. She was the accuser, and he was the accused. The accused were weak. The accused were small. The accused were wrong, no matter what was true. If you felt they were wrong, then they were wrong. Emotion was a garnish for fact. But everyone just ate the garnish. It was always healthier to eat just the greens.

"Sorry, sorry, sorry," she said with masculine flare, "that's all I hear. That's all we hear. I know you call yourself a patriot. A patriot, they say. I hate that word. It's an excuse. It's a weak word for weak people. It's a word used by those who want to inflict pain on others. It justifies their actions. It's a code of violence. It's an excuse for violence. I killed that person because they were the enemy. I did it for God and country. What God wants death? What country accepts violence? Not this one. Our function is peace. Capitalism always was the lubricant for war. It's the only system that rewards destruction. And you are the ant-marcher in all of it. Following the orders of capitalism . . . how disgusting. You disgust. A capitalistic ant, nothing more. A Black, capitalistic ant."

"A Black ant," the crowd chanted, "and nothing more."

"A Black ant," they went on, "and nothing more."

"A Black ant—and nothing more."

"A Black ant—and nothing more."

The woman bathed in the crowd's praise. The Dead Man Walker seemed small now. A very big, small man. But he had something she didn't have. There was elegance in his stance. The security he had in his own presence showed itself and it contrasted with her yapping. She was like a small dog taunting and circling him. When she got too close, she'd scurry away and then yap from afar. He was something out of the movies. He really was. Something out of the past. Something that wasn't her. Something unfamiliar and intriguing. Something that wasn't any of us.

"I am a patriot," he pronounced, no microphone needed as those words speared through her heart. "And I am a proud Black American."

The crowd was silent.

"Excuse me," she said. "Repeat that, please."

"I am a patriot," he said. His words were clean and true. "And I am a proud Black American."

"You have no right to be Black."

"I am a patriot."

A long silence from the crowd.

Beasley began to cry again.

"All she has to deal with," Beasley wept. "Evil men like him. And all she has to deal with."

"The evil all around us," Beasley wept on. "She's fighting that evil for us."

"Let's take a walk," the woman said to the crowd. "There's something I want to show all of you."

"Let's take a walk," the crowd chanted.

The woman glided off the stage and the proud Dead Man Walker went back into formation. The Dead Man Walkers followed her in a single-file line, and she parted the crowd like Moses parting the Red Sea.

"To Sixty-Seventh and Fifth Ave, we go," she screeched and clapped her hands in the air above her head.

The crowd clapped along and then followed behind the last Dead Man Walker.

"We must go," Beasley said to me. "A grand thing this is."

She joined the crowd and I followed her, keeping a comfortable distance.

"A grand thing," she yelled back to me.

A man overheard her and began to shake himself like a wet dog.

"A grand thing," he chanted.

A woman overheard him and began to shiver and mumble.

"A grand thing," she chanted.

"A grand thing," they all said.

"That's the power of one," they went on.

"The power of one," they chanted.

"The power of one."

"The power of one."

"The power of one."

That chanting went on until we reached Sixty-Seventh and Fifth

Avenue. The Dead Man Walkers lined up in front of the 107th Infantry Memorial.

The 107th Infantry Memorial was a bronze sculpture of those in the 107th who had fought and died in World War I. The sculpture rested on top of slabs of stone that went up like a staircase to the bronze. Beneath this staircase, three larger stones pressed together to present those etched words:

SEVENTH REGIMENT NEW YORK
ONE HUNDRED AND SEVENTH UNITED STATES INFANTRY
1917 * IN MEMORIAM * 1918

CHAPTER TEN

....

Victorian Stillness

The woman climbed the sculpture and hung from a bronze gun like a monkey. Everyone laughed and made monkey sounds. The Dead Man Walker who acted like a marine remained as still as the sculpture. The crowd formed itself up and down Fifth Avenue. I could see it stretch to Seventy-Fourth Street and down to Sixty-Second. Most of the crowd couldn't even see what was happening. I managed to squeeze my way right behind the last row of the Dead Man Walkers, where the crest of the crowd spit and hummed. Beasley, for some reason, went off with a group of wild chanters. One of these chanters was adorned with full body paint. She was very attractive, and this was her day to be a lion. Her friend, who I assumed was her boyfriend, also wore this full body paint armor. He was a wolf, and his other friend, who I assumed to be his boyfriend, was a leopard. The leopard began to cry and laugh and scream and giggle and then shake. "This year," he spat out in chaotic melodrama, "the number, another summer."

"They joke," this leopard went on, "that I'm riding through their sundown town. Their town. Not mine. Fight the power, you hear. Their power. To hell with John Wayne and Elvis—because our heroes don't appear on their stamps."

"Black is the color," the wolf howled. "None is the number."

The lion began to sing Bob Dylan's "Desolation Row."

"This is desolation row," the leopard cried. "It is. It is. Oh, it is!"

The wolf continued to howl some lyrics of another song: "The White executioner's face is always hidden."

"The White executioner's face is always hidden," the lion sang.

"The White executioner's face is always hidden," the leopard sang.

"The White executioner's face is always hidden," the wolf repeated, ceasing to sing "Desolation Row."

"Hey, hey, hey!" the woman demanded, her voice somehow cracking through the asymmetrically threaded fabric of this choreographed lunacy. "I don't have a microphone," she yelled from the sculpture. "And I don't want to lose my voice," she cried.

The woman scoped the Dead Man Walkers and cupped her hand over her eyes.

"Ah, yes—*you*," she cried. "The man this is all for. The man who is so proud. The patriot."

He detached from the rest of the Dead Man Walkers and stood next to her.

"You—you little marching soldier—you will be my mouthpiece. What I say, you say, okay? You have that big voice of yours and I want everyone to hear what I have to say."

The crowd laughed and the laughs went up and down Fifth Avenue in waves.

"The Great War," she continued, forgetting about her newly declared mouthpiece. She wanted him up there as a useless thing. She didn't really want him to speak. But he stood tall and proud and full of confidence.

"Thankfully," she went on, "most of you don't even know what that is. I'm sure you've learned your own version of it. I was taught that it was called The Great War and that it was an evil war. The whole thing was staged in Europe to make us scared. Those who fought in this war were part of the scheme. These heroic men were really cowards who went off to some place far better, leaving their wives at home to suffer. The children also suffered. They had to live without a father. The wives had no husband. They had to fend for themselves. And they did. That's why we are now the superior race. We've fought the oppression of White men who've raped our freedoms. Those White heroic men are off somewhere else breeding themselves in paradise. This statue is a misrepresentation of history—and it shall be torn down. Cowards don't deserve a place in history. The Great War was not great."

"The Great War was not great," the crowd chanted.

"The Evil War," the woman chanted.

"The Evil War," they chanted back.

"The Evil War."

"The Evil War."

"The Evil War."

She jumped from the gun and the chanting ended.

"You're useless," she said to her unused mouthpiece. "Get back into formation. At least you can act like a soldier there."

He went into formation and stood tall in the first row of the Dead Man Walkers.

"Call in the demolition," she cawed. "Call it in. Call it in. Call it in!"

"Call it in," the crowd chanted.

"Call it in."

"Call it in."

"Call it in."

"But wait," she suddenly said.

The crowd began to hoot from this misdirection.

"Why wait?" they collectively cried.

"There's someone here," she hooted back.

"Who?" they asked.

Rick Koch emerged from the mob and shook the woman's hand. He turned around and dangled his hands around, unathletically. I think it was a wave.

"The chairman of the board," the woman chanted.

"The chairman of the board," the crowd chanted.

"The chairman of the board."

"The chairman of the board."

"The chairman of the board."

Rick forced another awkward and unathletic wave. My father always said he was such a politician.

"The leader of The World Holding Company," she demanded we understand. "The leader of us *all*."

The World Holding Company? I asked myself.

She handed the mob's emotions over to Rick. This was his time to manipulate them now.

"Hello all," he said in a goofy way. Such a politician. "As chairman of the board of The World Holding Company, I am happy and humbled to say that the late Fep Anglish's prized 107th Infantry Memorial will be finally destroyed. On this day, another symbol of racism, sexism, and bigotry will be eradicated from this planet. These men in bronze who stare down at women, Blacks, Latinos, those Chinese, and any others who've got the color in them . . . these bronze men have reached their end."

Those Chinese?

"The creator of U—," this moron went on, "that Fep Anglish. He entrusted in us equality and sameness and unity. We all live by a standard and receive the same standard. None of us get more. None of us get less. We all get the same. Because we all deserve the same. We are one. The power of one."

"The power of one," the crowd chanted.

"The power of one."

"The power of one."

"The power of one."

"Fep Anglish was a weak man—I must admit to you. He let pieces of the capitalistic spirit remain to poison each and every one of us. He didn't have the strength to do the full job. Nostalgia was his weakness. Nostalgia killed him. Nostalgia made him an evil man. He was a living statue of the past."

Rick pointed up at the statue.

"This prominent statue is a bronze simile, or some sort of metaphor, or something like that, for Fep Anglish's nostalgia. He didn't have the strength to tear this down. But we do. We will. We will. We will."

"We will," the crowd chanted.

"We will."

"We will."

"We will."

The woman took over the crowd again and Rick vanished into the abyss of wild bodies.

"And we will," her voice quivered.

She shook and quivered a bit more.

"Oh, no," she cried. "We have no demolition."

The crowd moaned in sadness.

"But . . . we do have *you.*"

She paused and the crowd moaned louder.

"We do have—"

The crowd roared.

"YOU!" she shouted.

"US!" the crowd replied, unevenly.

"All of you," she went on. "We have *the power of one.*"

An explosion of sound—the crowd whistling and hooting in perfect unison.

"For our freedom. On the count of three, I want you to storm this statue like those bigots stormed the beaches of Hong Kong on D-Day. I want the patriot to come out of all of you. Take the killer out of all of you. Use the bigot on the bigot. Cast your freedom collectively on this trash. Tear down this false history. Make this history, history. And, as one, tear this trash down. We, *the power of one.*"

"We, the power of one," they chanted.

"We, the power of one."

"We, the power of one."

"We, the power of one."

"Tear the trash down," she cried.

"Tear the trash down," they chanted.

"Tear the trash down."

"Tear the trash down."

"Tear the trash down."

"1 . . . ," she counted down. "2 . . . 3!"

It took less than twenty minutes.

The bronze gun fell and punctured someone's chest.

The man lay there bleeding and the mob wouldn't help until the statue was fully destroyed.

It was too late. He was dead.

The woman didn't seem to mind, though.

She went on talking as the corpse lay there.

"We lose some," she preached. "But look what we've done. Look what a mob, with a common cause, can do. The damage that's in our hearts. The damage to make change."

"The damage that's in our hearts," I repeated softly to myself. "The damage to make change."

"The damage that's in our hearts," another person said, overhearing me saying it to myself.

"The damage that's in our hearts," another said.

"The damage that's in our hearts," more went.

"The damage that's in our hearts," the mob went.

"Yes," she replied. "We have no time for sympathy when we're in the pursuit of true morality. We must forget this death and remember that crumbling bronze."

The mob went up again in a thunderous hiss and I felt the energy tickle my spine and I caught myself chanting more and more and more.

"Down. Down. Down. That crumbling bronze."

"Down. Down. Down. That crumbling bronze."

"Down. Down. Down. That crumbling bronze."

"Down. Down. Down. That crumbling bronze."

Repetition in a bored and thoughtless mind was dangerous. And it was even more dangerous in a mob of bored and thoughtless minds. I was a part of this now, and I would be swept away in it. That numbing adrenaline would kick in and I would chant.

"Down. Down. Down. That crumbling bronze," I yelled.

"Down. Down. Down. That crumbling bronze," I yelled again.

"Down. Down. Down. That crumbling bronze."

"Down. Down. Down. That crumbling bronze."

I chanted until Rick returned.

He stood on the rubble. What a politician thing to do. How easy it was to run away and come back when the deed was done. And to stand on the rubble like that. Like you owned it and led it. What a politician. But he had to do a lot more than that to win me over. I was a member of this mob now. I was a soldier. And I chanted to myself because I was the chosen one.

I was the chosen one.

I was the chosen one.

I was the chosen one.

I was the chosen one.

"Nostalgia," Rick broke through my thoughts, "it has met its fate. Fep Anglish is a fallen figure, a forgotten idol."

The mob went still. No lingering voice still chanting somewhere. It all went still. Just like that. Ultimate stillness.

"Fep Anglish is a saint," someone screamed.

A pause.

No one followed the lead.

Stillness.

Rick would use this absence of comradery as a gesture of submission. That collective weakness was the decay off which Rick would grow like fungus. He would blossom now, fed by the odorless shit of his misplaced confidence.

"You'd think that," Rick continued. "Why not? I did—for a very long time."

He stopped and covered his face with that Broadway drama.

"I, Rick Koch, regret to say that Fep Anglish was hiding something from *all of you.*"

He waited for the mob to prod him on.

Incoherent mumbles filled the streets and he wanted to hear a chant come out of it.

"I want to know," someone demanded.

"Let us know," another said.

"Let us know," another said.

"Let us know," they all said.

"Let us know," they chanted.

"Let us know."

"Let us know."

"Let us know."

I wouldn't chant along with this. With fury, I would listen and watch

Rick tear down everything my father was. To see legacy destroyed in one swoop was the worst form of public execution. And it could happen faster than you could ever think.

"Calm," he said, holding something in the air. "Please, all. We need calm. For this is all sobering news. Sad, contemplative news. Together we have to deal with the matter at hand. I hate to say this . . ."

He paused and pushed out a fake cry.

"I was . . ." he continued.

The fake cry was pushed out further.

"Raped. Fep Anglish raped me."

"I'm sorry," they all chanted in unison.

"I'm sorry."

"I'm sorry."

"I'm sorry."

"I'm sorry," one man shouted. "I'm sorry for being privileged. I'm sorry for being a man. I'm sorry for being a woman. I'm sorry for being young. I'm sorry for being old. I'm sorry for being me. I'm sorry for it all. I'm sorry. I'm sorry. I'm sorry."

Collective crying.

"I'm sorry."

"I'm sorry."

"I'm sorry."

A drunk and sobbing man broke from the crowd and punched Rick in the face. Rick fell to the ground and struggled to get back up.

"If that's what you need right now," Rick said from the ground, "do it."

"If that's what you need right now," the sobbing man repeated, "do it."

"If that's what you need right now," the mob echoed, "do it."

"If that's what you need right now, do it."

"If that's what you need right now, do it."

"If that's what you need right now, do it."

Such repetition.

It drew you in and angered you.

This slapstick expressionism, everywhere.

Rolling eyes.

Flailing bodies.

Mucus hanging.

Salt trails of bleeding mascara.

Body odor.

Barf.

Blood.

Wrists were slit for no reason.

They lay there bleeding out on the street.

It was a part of the program.

It was just how it went with these spectacles.

And Rick got up, his nose bloody.

"I'm gonna fucking kill him," he said to the woman.

"Control yourself," she pleaded.

"No," he insisted, "I'm gonna kill him."

"If that's what you need right now," I said, "do it."

My response came out as a form of muscle memory.

"And I will," Rick answered. "All you wackos. I've had enough of this shit."

He took a gun from his pocket and pointed it at the man who punched him. The man moved toward him, sobbing. The snot hung from his nose like drool from a St. Bernard's lips.

"If that's what you need right now," the man said, "do it."

"It's what I need right now," Rick cried, "you fuck."

One shot to the chest—and two to the forehead. The man fell to the ground and twitched before he went still. The blood poured into the grooves of the sidewalk and streamed into the crowd.

"Bastard," Rick said to himself. "I'm sick of this shit—these peasants."

"Shut up," the woman said. "Keep the damn thing to yourself. You'll ruin the whole thing if you keep speaking like this."

The crowd was too busy destroying itself to listen to Rick.

"End this now," Rick said. "I just killed a man. End it now. Enough is enough!"

Rick and this woman had no other choice but to flee the scene. They retreated into the park, and I followed them, my goldfish brain forgetting about Beasley.

"Hello!" I called from behind. "Excuse me. Rick!"

Rick stopped and the woman looked angry.

"Come with us, James," he said, not surprised to see me. "A car is coming. We're going to the 21 Club."

I followed them to an empty dirt road and that electric slicing sound drew nearer. A car then pulled up fast and Rick pushed me in. He went around to the other side and the woman shoved herself in behind me. I sat between them in the back seat.

"I'm Tyler," she finally said. "I understand your name is James."

I nodded my head and was distracted by how different she looked in the car. Besides my father, and a very select few, I didn't take an interest in anyone's appearance. But I couldn't help it with Tyler. She was so different, so faded and pale but dark at the same time. Her skin was the brightest white, with a veneer of gray flaky charcoal dust. It was like the bad things she did overlayed the good in her. But how? How could a person with an aura as bland as this be that energetic woman on stage? She couldn't be. This bleached out creature with the veins in her eyelids pulsating through the thin powder skin. Her hair so black. Each eye, one big pupil. I couldn't find where that pupil ended, and where the iris began. Those crow eyes of hers. Black beads in the middle of her very round head. Her nose was so small it made her face look like a skeleton's skull.

"What a show that was," she laughed. "Saw you getting into it, too. Never really understood it. Seems a little stupid to me. You know—the chanting and the crying and whatever the rest of it is. Well, as they say, 'better to reign in Hell, than to serve in Heaven.'—right?"

Rick sank into his oversized jacket to express his displeasure.

"Silence from Rick, I guess," she remarked. "No man ever wants to talk to me. Because they're really just jealous. All men are just jealous. That whole chanting crowd of losers are all really just jealous. And, you know what, jealousy is the worst type of hate. Jealousy is your hatred toward your admiration. And it makes you an enemy of yourself. And that's why everyone's suicidal nowadays. You men!"

"Sorry," I blurted. "I—"

"I wasn't talking to you, James. You're a boy."

"Sorry," I said again.

"Oh, please," she exhaled and put her hand on my leg, "please, I beg you. None of that 'sorry' crap. It's exhausting. Just hearing you say that makes me cringe."

Rick had fallen asleep in his jacket.

"Mr. Koch . . ." I attempted.

Just snores from within his business shell.

"Mr. Koch." I said again.

Snores.

"What is it?" Tyler answered for him. "He's an old man."

"My father."

"What about him?"

"Did he . . . ? Was he . . . ?"

"Get out with it."

"A rapist."

"What?"

"Mr. Koch said my father raped him."

"He said that?"

"Yes, he did. Very clearly."

She laughed to herself. But I wasn't laughing.

"James, oh James. James. James. James."

She couldn't stop laughing.

"What's so funny?" I asked.

And just like that she stopped, and the deadness of her face frosted over my sprouting anger.

"You can't take that stuff seriously. Of course, he didn't rape Rick. Who the hell would rape Rick? He pays people to rape him. And your father didn't even like men . . . well, you know what I mean . . . in that way."

• • •

"Get up here, you little bitch," he called drunkenly from upstairs. "Unless you want me to come down there and get it over with in the kitchen?"

Eyes dry and emotions hardened into some temporary protective shell, she ran her hands through my hair to say goodbye and then went up the stairs, step by step, her oversized turquoise blue dress floating and flowing behind her.

. . .

I was very quiet now in the car.

"Something happened to you," Tyler analyzed. "I could tell. I know that look."

. . .

Step by step . . .
Step by step . . .
Step by step . . .
—the door upstairs shut.

. . .

"What's wrong?" Tyler asked.

I wouldn't answer.

"It's theatrics, James," she patronized. "It's the game we all have to play."

"What about the man who died?" I shouted back, about to cry. "Theatrics?"

"People really get into it," she sympathized. "Someone gets shot every time. It's the ritual of it. Sorry to say it, but *it is* the way *it is*. The mob loves death. It's part of the whole self-healing process. A crock of shit—but a part of the process, nonetheless."

"Destination arrival," the car announced.

Rick's head popped up and his unathletic body pushed itself out of the car. I followed him with a stuttering stride. Tyler took note of my hesitance, and she interlocked her arms with mine to speed me up.

"You're my date tonight," she told me through her forced smile.

CHAPTER ELEVEN

Boneyard of Capitalism

The 21 Club was another random monument of the past preserved by my father's nostalgia. From the outside, it looked like a funeral home. It had that surrealist and dreamy abandoned townhouse feel with the heavy overlapping wedding dress curtains against the dreamy smoked windows and that sallow light pouring onto the street from the unseen interior rooms. I could just imagine the bodies on the metal tables alone under the artificial laser-white light. Those brushes being applied to the faces to hide the tree-branched blue veins coming through the lifeless skin.

A wrought-iron gate lined the front of the townhouse, and a row of ornamental horse jockeys went up the steps to the next floor, while the rest of the jockeys looked from the balcony. A doorman led us in, and Tyler pulled me through with a giddiness contrasting to everything I'd briefly known about her. Rick went in rudely after us and then threw his blazer on the ground.

"Sir," a waiter said. "You must wear your jacket here."

"Who the hell are you?" Rick asked, in his face.

"Sir, it's the rule."

"What about him?" he punted, pointing at me.

"Sorry, sir," the waiter said, aggravated. "I didn't see he wasn't wearing a jacket."

"So, you don't pay an ounce of attention to the Black folk because they don't matter to you?"

"Sir, that is not correct. I am sorry if I have offended you."

"You're correcting me now?"

"No, I am simply—"

"You know who I am?" Rick interrupted, his pronounced words sprinkling the man's face.

"No sir, I do not."

"You should."

The manager raced in and picked up Rick's blazer.

"My apologies, Mr. Koch. We will terminate him immediately."

"Not immediately. Now!"

The manager shoved the waiter to the exit and pushed him out the door.

"He took off his jacket," the waiter pleaded from outside. "Jackets aren't allowed to be off."

"Not for the goddamn owner of the restaurant, you fool."

The waiter's face went blank.

"Never again, Mr. Koch. The 21 Club is deeply sorry."

"Why the hell are you saying it like that?"

"I'm sorry, sir. Like what, sir?"

"'The 21 Club is deeply sorry.' The 21 Club isn't deeply sorry. You know who's sorry? You're sorry. Last chance, Armando."

"Not again, sir."

Armando, helpless to the abuse, led us to a room that he called the Bar Room. The ceiling was festooned with industrial and sports memorabilia. The toys hung above the lipstick-red booths wrapped around the red-and-white-checkered tables. Tyler and I sat together, and Rick faced us. A British Airways Flying Boat hung above my head, along with a Toys "R" Us truck and a Goodyear blimp and endless JPMorgan Chase memorabilia and Apple trinkets and Bank of America stuff and Wells Fargo stuff and Exxon Mobile stuff and Microsoft stuff and Verizon stuff and Citigroup stuff and Chevron stuff and Amazon stuff and Walmart stuff and BP stuff and Johnson & Johnson stuff and Nestle stuff and Boeing stuff and IBM stuff and General Motors stuff and Facebook stuff and Walt Disney stuff and Sony stuff and PepsiCo stuff and DowDuPont stuff and American Express stuff and Oracle stuff and Airbus stuff. A PT-109 torpedo boat and a broken tennis racket and a golf club and a replica of Air Force One and a baseball bat, and more trucks, and more planes, and more helmets, and more and more and more random things, on and on and on, displaying a capitalistic world my father obliterated. The American Dream was now just a toy hanging from a ceiling—a Goodyear blimp in micro-movement sway due to the bodily activity below.

It hung there, limp, and dead. This was the boneyard of capitalism.

"Perfect, Armando," Rick praised.

"Now, Mr. Koch, the usual for you and your guests?"

Rick tried to think of something nasty to say but the creativity wasn't there at that present moment. After a pause of failure, he said thank you. I could tell Armando was surprised by his reserved behavior.

"A glass of beer," Rick demanded, even though he knew Armando was on it. "Glasses of beer, all around."

Armando nodded with that redundant "I know, I know" gesture.

"Now, run along, Armando," Rick waved and snapped. "The Spanish don't need to be involved in shop talk."

Armando absorbed the racist insult and walked away and then came back to be swatted off and then came back to take our orders with more insult. Back and forth, insult after insult, was the life Rick made for him.

"Now," Rick went on, alone with us. "James, I know there's a lot for you to take in. And I think you should free yourself from all of this and seek out the path of furthering your higher education. There's very much to learn. Very, very much to learn indeed."

Tyler looked at Rick and Rick looked at Tyler. He crossed his legs and fixed his tie before he continued his rhetoric. The tie gesture of regrouping thought.

But he didn't know what to say.

A loss for words.

Awkward silence.

"Armando!" Rick called to redirect his inferiority. "Play that song."

"Yes, Mr. Koch," Armando answered from some unseen place.

"Armando!" Rick called again. "Now, I said. Not tomorrow. Now. Do it now!"

"Sorry, Mr. Koch."

"He has time to say fucking sorry," Rick growled under his breath.

Then the music played, and the skeletal beat of the drum went on and the rest of the instrumentals carried underneath the audible. Their notes were deadened and stunted by an old speaker buried away somewhere in the cabinetry. Tyler hummed along, and Rick watched her with admiration. I wondered if they were together.

"You must go through with it," Rick sang.

"It's time," Tyler whispered—and then began to cry.

Without saying goodbye, Rick left the Bar Room and Tyler continued to cry. The song ended and Armando came sweeping in with the food.

"Where did Mr. Koch go?" he asked.

"Who the hell knows," Tyler answered, covering her face with her trembling hands.

Then, out of nowhere, it seemed—it just happened.

Just like that.

Right in front of me.

How?

How could it happen like that?

Right in front of me.

With no thought.

No questioning.

Tyler straightened herself and wiped off the tears. She opened her purse and took out a gun. This gun lay loose in her hand and Armando served the food, saying nothing.

"Bastard," she went on, her eyes following Armando's exit of this scene. "That wife of his really screwed him."

Gripping the gun firmly now, she pointed it above her head.

"I'm a lot more," she scream-cried. She pumped the trigger.

The bullet went right through the Goodyear blimp. The blimp fell from the ceiling onto the table and part of it hit my head, while the rest of it broke the plates and scattered the silverware.

"I'm sorry," she said. "I just—you know . . ."

My brain wasn't working fast enough.

My concrete mind solidified deeper in its passiveness.

I hated getting thick and passive in moments that needed my attention.

Then—

Oh my god!

A mania I had never seen before entered Tyler. It curled itself into an overflowing hysteria of astronomical proportions.

Then—

Don't!

A pause, the tension stopped midair like a freeze-frame of cigar smoke. That mania collapsed into itself and then imploded into a single definitive action.

"He always wants me to do his dirty work," she giggled. "We're victims, James," she cried. "I saw that look you had in the car," she laughed. "Something bad happened to you," she cried. "It was real," she laughed. "And I haven't felt real in decades," she cried. "I want to feel real," she laughed. "I want the pain," she cried. "I want the joy," she laughed. "I want something," she cried. "I'm done with this," she laughed. "Done with Rick," she cried. "I quit," she laughed. "I'm not going to be the one who makes the mess and also cleans it up—all so his hands are sparkling," she cried. "You should know I have no intention of killing you," she laughed. "I will not be Rick," she cried. "And I will not be your father," she laughed. "I will not give in to their demands," she cried. "I will not kill you," she laughed.

She pointed the gun at her head. "I hope you understand and can remember me for anything other than what I am—goodbye," she giggled, then squeezed the trigger again.

Mashed cauliflowers mixed in a thick and dark tomato sauce splashed against my face. Eggshell fragments cut at my eyes and my sudden shout echoed in the abrupt stillness of this horrific surprise.

Tyler's head split in two and the brain loosened itself from its chamber like a yolk slipping out of the shell onto some Teflon surface.

Armando attended to the mess and cleaned up the chunks of brain and the clots of coagulated blood.

"If that's what she needed," I heard him whisper to himself.

"If that's what she needed," he said a little louder.

"If that's what she needed," he said to me.

"If that's what she needed," he screamed.

I thought I was stuck in a David Lynch film. Something out of *Blue Velvet*. A disconnect in logic and reality. The way Armando cleaned her blood with a napkin like someone would clean spilled beer. Cupping the napkin and using his other hand to push the bits of brain off the tablecloth. The blood on his hands, no different to him than ketchup. Veggie burger ketchup must've exploded out of Tyler's head. That was the only way to explain this.

And I couldn't react because there was no reaction to prompt my reaction. A head in pieces. Like bread torn apart but it wasn't. Anyway, Armando was good at cleaning up. No matter the mess. The dirty glasses—picked up like that. The water—refilled like that. Tyler's eyeball—dropped right into his pocket.

"Why?" Armando asked himself, her eye in his pocket.

I had that look children possess when they see something different.

• • •

"Honey, honey, swim to me," she whimpered in her death. "Come on, Jamie," she called.

I treaded in the water, the dog following behind me.

"Great, see, honey, you're a swimmer."

Swimming to my mother, I asked, "Can't Daddy swim?"

"No," she answered, "but he loves watching us."

"Can't he use his arms?"

"I don't think he wants to try."

"I could still swim."

"Well, let's see. Try to swim with just your arms."

I tried to swim and sank.

My mother laughed as I rose to the surface.

"That's why Daddy doesn't like to swim. Imagine doing that all the time. It would be exhausting. And it's especially hard for Daddy after that accident of his."

"Will he get better?"

"Of course he will. It was just an accident, honey. A few broken bones is all."

She pulled herself onto the dock, helped me out, dried me off, and then went inside the house to get lemonade and coffee. I sat down on the wood planks of the dock, peering up at my father in his wheelchair.

As he stretched his stiff body downward to hand me my toy pipe, I had that look children possess when they see something different.

• • •

"A cigar?" Armando asked. He stood stiffly above me, lathered with blood. "Would you like a cigar while I finish cleaning this spill?"

I couldn't respond.

I forgot my lines.

This couldn't have been . . . this was *not* real.

No way.

I wanted the curtains drawn—for this to be all over.

I'm done, I'm bored . . . time to move on to something else.

Let's put an end to this.

I'm done.

Mommy, please?

Daddy, please?

I'm too tired and lazy to think about this anymore.

But why . . . ?

What?

—right in front of me!

—and, just like that.

God, this fucking world.

A mystery.

Such evil things done in the dark.

Every day—*the end*.

But never *truly* the end.

Those paternal and maternal forces protecting me.

And *only me*.

Because there was a master plan for *me*.

I knew that much.

That paternal and maternal force—stronger than anyone had ever known.

Protecting me . . . and guiding me.

Mommy!

And Daddy—my father!

Watching over me.

Dictating my reality.

Something I hated them for.

Something I loved them for.

The comfort they brought me.

That comfort I could kick and scream at.

"Go away," I'd say. "Leave me alone!"

But I knew it wouldn't go away.

And I knew I never wanted it to go away.

I yearned for it more than I yearned for anything in this world.

I never wanted to be alone.

I wanted to pretend I wanted to be alone.

But secretly, I needed comfort.

I am too delicate, you know.

Too delicate to be stressed.

Too delicate to have guilt.

And too delicate to deal with fear.

But Tyler . . .

Fucking Tyler.

She brought all that negative energy to me.

How was I supposed to cope now?

I guess I'd just have to.

Well, you know, all I could do now was forget.

It was easier that way.

That goldfish memory of mine.

"Stop asking questions, James," I'd say to myself. "*They* have a plan for you."

So, just like that, I'd forget.

Such a lazy mind of such an unreliable narrator.

Correction!

Not lazy—busy!

I'm so busy, I don't have time to worry.

Because I'm so important.

I'm doing things—so much to *not* do.

It's really just too damn tough to think on the things you'll never get the answer for.

"A cigar, Mr. Anglish?" Armando asked again.

"Just the check, please," I answered—the words coming out like leaking air.

"Mr. Koch has it covered."

"That's very nice of him," I said.

"A cigar?" he asked yet again.

"Yes," I answered. "Thank you."

It wasn't lit and I let it hang out of my mouth.

"Mr. Anglish, would you mind if I light it for you?"

I looked up at him.

"It needs to be lit," he insisted. "I can light it for you."

"Yes. Thank you."

"My pleasure."

Armando twisted the cigar against his moist lips and ballooned his mouth to ignite the tobacco. The puffs rose in slow motion against my thudded reaction, and I thought of Jaclyn. My sweet sister, Jaclyn. The one I kept from *you*. The girl who makes me an unreliable narrator. I'm sorry I kept her from *you*, dear reader. I hope you can still trust me. Because I'm a bad storyteller. And the deceit continues to grow as I continue to write without Jaclyn. I don't want to hide her from you anymore. I've kept her away from you for too long now. It was really the only way I could keep her away from me. She was locked away, blocked by the firewall of my conscience.

"Jaclyn," I said.

She would never flood my memory all at once.

It would take time, a small tear in my subconscious.

But it would dribble, drip by drip, into my recall.

Drip.

Drip.

Drip.

Soon enough.

It would be.

It sure as hell would be.

This poison would make its way down the layers and levels of protection. And my OCD would embolden and strengthen this hammerhead past, that aftertaste of Jaclyn never undone. The lingering burnt toast smell and the dry and fizzling ginger ale taste of her, readying to hemorrhage in my brain. It would be the end of me. I would become a passenger for this OCD—its prisoner, its slave. Paralyzed by its venom.

CHAPTER TWELVE

....

Alpina B12 6.0 E38

"**D**emocracy walks into a hospital room," Fep Anglish said. "It sees America in bed watching *SpongeBob SquarePants*.

"'Dear friend,' Democracy says, 'why are you doing this to yourself?'

"'Because, Democracy,' America answers. 'I am Atticus Finch. And I feel like Holden Caulfield.'

"'My dear friend,' Democracy pities, 'you must judge history as it *was*, not as it *is*. Your life depends on that.'

"'Then I must die,' America answers.

"'Then I must go,' Democracy responds.

"'Then you must go,' America accepts.

"Defeated, Democracy walks to the door.

"'Democracy,' America calls.

"'Yes,' Democracy answers.

"'Your pick—a hell that's fair or a heaven that's unfair?'

"Democracy sighs and exits without an answer.

"'I guess I won't be seeing you in hell,' America laughs to itself, as SpongeBob continues to chase jellyfish."

This bizarre little story, a joke told at Club Paris in Anchorage, Alaska. I didn't get the joke, though. The Atticus Finch and Holden Caulfield reference, no one seemed to get it.

(Drip.)

But my father would tell these weird stories. This time it happened to be in a room filled with his praise-seeking subordinates, in North America's last legal steakhouse.

Club Paris was Fep Anglish's hangout. It was the place where he told that strange anecdotal SpongeBob joke from one of the many licorice-black leather bar chairs. They were finished in a clouded sugar-coated gloss following the curve of the head cheese–pattern marble bar. Behind this bar, an overdressed man wearing a red tux and a black bowtie had both hands planted against the cold and glowing marble, the refracted glare from its surface forming slits of light against the wet lenses of his cat-like eyes. The old show *Mad About You* played on the retro TVs and the theme music spun around my ears with its distinctive, once-happy 1990s piano bar sound.

Pixelated mist from the *Seinfeld* logo glazed its light pollution onto my sterilized state of existence, as that egg yolk–colored oval with those red superimposed letters and the little dawn-blue upside-down triangle sitting there on top of the *I*, all shown top secret against my blinking awe, the whole cheesy wedding cake look of it, the horrific design of it, this logo seemingly manipulated by a pastry chef who combined dried egg albumen, modified starch, cream of tartar, and wheat starch composite for their edible art. And despite this edible art, and the music, and that man behind the bar, and the leather, and the marble, everywhere else had sun-bleached candy cane 1960s depressed-looking upholstery. Altogether, Club Paris, a meat lover's haven, slipped straight out of hell, satanic in its Edward Hopper isolation against the quiet mountains and the dead cold air and the monotonous sad faces bringing life to the joint like blood to the heart. Pumping at midnight and hemorrhaging at dawn. The cycle of Club Paris never changed. It just got tired.

Mount McKinley got tired, too. Sprinkled with that powdered-sugar snow and those gingerbread buildings scattered on hills burnt with little sallow lights, the whole void seemingly crafted out of birthday cake icing in a plain bakery I'd imagine was called Greenburg's. This Club Paris, as sad as it was, buried into that gingerbread village feeding the wealthy, red-blood-craving lunatics drenching their soaked tongues that wiggled against the bubbled and liquified oil fat of a New York strip and the vintage alcoholic grape of some very rare 1999 Saint-Emilion Bordeaux. These big-brained bugs fluttering in for a dead meat meal. The kitchen door swinging open for the feed, the cold cast iron bleeding out John Lennon's "Happy Xmas (War is Over)," the waiter kicking the door open to hand out the chunks of forbidden cow, venison, and lamb. Colorful Christmas lights festooning the interior, the lights metastasized on plastic miniature spruces, their green-dyed needle arms supporting the dangling Bergdorf Goodman *Thank You Enjoy* Chinese takeout box ornaments. These lights trailing from the little trees and, from there, snaking off between the TVs and the leftover artificial bliss of Grey Goose and Laphroaig 10 and High West Campfire and Oban 14 and those Absoluts and that top-shelf Blue Label. Slithering on from there to underneath the furniture and, from there, into the bathroom layered with caramelized beer and frothed urine, the low-quality Bose speakers hidden around the urinals playing the light hum of Phil Spector's "A Christmas Gift from Phil Spector." Then "White Christmas" came on. Then "Frosty the Snowman." Then "The Bells of St. Mary's". Then "Santa Claus Is Coming to Town." Then "Sleigh Ride." Then "Marshmallow World"—and on and on, forever on loop. These Christmas songs, only bathroom songs to me, since I had no idea what Christmas was.

It was a holiday that didn't exist anymore. That's what I knew. But they—those bar-goers—saw something else in it. It brought them somewhere hopeful. But, to me, it was nothing more than hell's elevator music. Those Christmas lights, a strand of happiness leading me through this Christmas Chernobyl like Henry leading Karen through the Copacabana in *Goodfellas*.

To then end dead in one quiet and colorless room—

(Drip.)

—this quiet and colorless post–atomic age bunker was packed with hundreds of copies of George Orwell's *Nineteen Eighty-Four,* along with good-old-boy Beretta magazine–style husks, antlers, and animal heads, and contrasting Eames chairs and Knoll couches. A figure stood in the middle of this in salty sweat-stained gray sweatpants and a loosely fitting white t-shirt with *1984* stitched into it. The Band's "The Night They

Drove Old Dixie Down" played at the brink of audibility. When you listened to the music, you noticed more of the room's dressings. Scattered everywhere, the German expressionist *Superman* movie posters hung, Superman standing tall in each like a skyscraper. A woman who felt just like Jaclyn standing tall by this washed-up good-old-boy's side. This Jaclyn figure wearing little clothing. This sweatpants-man-beast squeezing Jaclyn because he owned her for the night. They both stood by each other's side like the couple in Grant Wood's *American Gothic*. My sister had the look. And, forever, her eyes would be somewhere else.

"Help me, James" I imagined her cry through her soundless stoic stance. "Get him away from me," she pleaded more in this silence. "He makes me sick," she begged and begged and begged.

(Drip.)

His name was Frederick Moonch. He was the creator of this newly revamped and demonized Napoleonic Superman. Moonch made it possible to attack the integrity of people who didn't exist. He had proof Lois Lane was a racist and Clark Kent was a pedophile. And it wasn't so farfetched. A year before these allegations came out, Moonch had Spider-Man erased from Marvel. Spider-Man was proven to be a serial killer. The day he was convicted, a mob gathered around the last standing comic bookstore in the world.

Zee's Comics used to be down on Fulton Street. Zee refused to let the crowd burn his Spider-Man merchandise and was labeled a sexist for protecting that "web-making demon." One of the members of the mob told Zee to hand over Spider-Man. Without success, Zee tried to explain that Spider-Man was a fictionalized character. They wouldn't have any of it and, with the help of Frederick Moonch, the store was shut down that very day.

My father called Moonch both the Comic Book Killer and Nineteen Eighty-Four. Nineteen Eighty-Four stuck better because Moonch was the grandfather of revisionist history. He managed to convince a vast portion of my generation that even Batman was not the superhero everyone assumed he was. He went as far as suggesting Batman was the leader of the Nazi Party. The idea of this didn't completely take, but the questioning allowed Moonch to attack Batman's family and, essentially, ruin the legacy of this comic book hero. For kids to question the integrity of their superheroes was a dangerous way to grow up. Idols were gone. They were objects subjected to unending scrutiny. They were examined for flaws and, flawed or not, they were always torn down. No individual was allowed to be a mentor to another. There was only *you* and *your* ethics, and the ultra-powerful hidden away somewhere, instilling their rule in deeper, more sinister trenches of power and corruption. The by-products: people like Beasley and Tennyson. Those who filtered what they saw through ignorance brought on by shallow morality.

Manipulation was Frederick Moonch's trade. And, just like *Nineteen Eighty-Four*, he bent and warped history so much that the line between the real and the fictional was gone. Allegations were stronger than reality, and he could get people wrapped up in conviction even if there was no one to convict. He attacked ideas as facts and, because of that, he could attack facts as ideas. This revisionist history led to a mass confusion. The ignorance went out of control, and people lost their reference point in history. Captain Jack Sparrow was the dictator of North Korea before the United States invaded North Korea. President Hannibal Lecter, the forty-eighth president of the free world, led the invasion and liberated the North Koreans. That became fact when Moonch gave it his approval of authenticity.

Nineteen Eighty-Four was skilled. But he wasn't skilled when it came to his ego. Fep Anglish was the man to follow into the modern and Nineteen Eighty-Four refused to believe that. If he could control the past, he could control the future, he thought. My father was a nobody. He was a young cowboy getting ahead of himself. Nineteen Eighty-Four even told the public once: "I won't follow a mass murderer and a serial rapist into our future."

Bad move. Very bad move. Because that was that for my father. Nineteen Eighty-Four then met a higher power who would finally put an end to his reign of manipulation and rewritten history. My father removed Nineteen Eighty-Four from the public eye entirely and built him his own *Legacy Suite* crypt in the back of Club Paris. This was Fep Anglish's passive aggressive way of putting his insubordinate subordinates out to pasture. There were two other Legacy Suites in

Club Paris, occupied by the hall of famers no one cared about anymore.

"Sending the bitch off to corporate," he said very drunk to someone in front of me once.

But Nineteen Eighty-Four learned not to mind it. Living in this little palace wasn't such a bad thing. In that room, everything began and ended with Frederick Moonch. My father made sure to satiate the ego in a very controlled and closed-off environment. He gave the old man his taste in interior décor and, of course, those ego-pump Superman posters. Nineteen Eighty-Four could come and go as he pleased. But he wouldn't. Because the world outside this room had already forgotten about him. Inside here, he was the emperor of his Legacy Suite. My father knew what he was doing. The legendary Frederick Moonch learned to like his crate and played with the toys my father threw in for him to exploit. What a good, well-trained dog he was. But what hell for my poor sister.

(Drip.)

Moonch the Mooch. That's all he'd come to be at Club Paris. That's all my father would allow him to be, as he weaponized his lifework for his own vision. Nineteen Eighty-Four's history had been revised. And I hated him. I really hated him. But I can't deny he was more than Moonch the mooch. I mean that to say he did more than rewrite history—a lot more. Without Frederick Moonch, there would be no Fep Anglish. But no one cared about that. No one cared that Nineteen Eighty-Four was the first person to weaponize the pharmaceutical industry by selling the disease instead of the cure. Sounds crazy. But it's true. People wanted to feel alive again through death . . . or the process of dying, rather.

The leading cause of death became suicide. As you know, if you didn't kill yourself, modern medicine made sure you'd go on forever in boredom. Suicide was a quick way of feeling alive again. But just for a few seconds, which really was worth it. I'd know. I'd know very well about that. I tried to overdose four times. But I won't go into that any further. I'll continue to lie to you and be an unreliable narrator.

Okay. Fine. All I'll say is . . . well, I wanted to buy cancer after the overdoses failed. I had stage four lung cancer on my mind. And I would've bought it if it weren't for my father. Rightfully so, he put an end to the production of disease. The thrill of dying was no longer legal. You had to go about trying to kill yourself once again. Old school—what a thing. I never overdosed a fifth time. I'm not lying about that.

Anyway, my father learned a lot from Nineteen Eighty-Four. The cultivation of big pharma. Something Nineteen Eighty-Four would get no credit for. And I wouldn't get an ounce of credit for revealing it. You'll see that I even forget about Nineteen Eighty-Four as I begin to attribute all great findings solely to the wonderfully innovative Fep Anglish. I was conditioned that way. We all were.

Heil Father!

Heil Father!

Heil Father!

How wonderful. Man's most prolific pioneer. And man's most prolific crook. A total fraud in most ways. But we won't talk about that. Just like we won't talk about my suicide attempts. And just like you won't hear very much about Frederic Moonch's abolishment of *pastime pleasures.*

A pastime pleasure was something like the Super Bowl or the World Cup or the Oscars or Christmas or the Fourth of July—anything celebratory and unifying. Nineteen Eighty-Four demonized football for being too masculine, soccer for being too foreign, the Oscars for being too superficial, Christmas for being too materialistic, Fourth of July for being too nationalistic, and on, and on, and on. And the public followed his hatred. They wouldn't trust anything anymore. Tradition became a terribly racist thing. Nothing was to be enjoyed unless it had a 100 percent chance of thwarting the label of racism, or any *ism* for that matter. And most things had an *ism.* So, consequently, most things were not allowed to be enjoyed.

(Drip.)

That was a good and effective way of numbing the mind. Increase life expectancy. Increase the boredom. And allow technology to control humans. Because, out of laziness, we relied on this technology for everything. We could be anything we wanted with it. I became a licensed doctor after I adopted a robot. For way too much money, you could buy a robot and name it after yourself. The one I picked happened to be a surgeon. It didn't look like a surgeon. It was just a small claw thing at one of the hospitals. But it had my name, and it did amazing things.

"James" did amazing things. And it earned me a license as a certified doctor. It was all so fake, you know. But I had already achieved one of the most complex brain surgeries in history. What a thing for someone who knew nothing. Nineteen Eighty-Four's world, what a thing it was.

But—that, too, went away. Fep Anglish put an end to it, so I won't talk about it anymore.

RIP, Nineteen Eighty-Four.

(Drip.)

I'm trying to keep this story going but Jaclyn is tearing through me. I'm sorry.

(Drip.)

"James," she murmured. "I'm so sad all the time."

(Drip.)

"James," she cried. "I can't do this anymore."

(Drip.)

"James," she screamed. "I want to die."

(Drip.)

Tyler's other eyeball hung from the light smothered by corporate toys. Armando balanced himself on the table and stretched up to pinch the eyeball from the light. Without disturbing the toys, God forbid, he put her eyeball into the other pocket like it was a soiled martini olive that'd fallen from an overly ornamental glass. He then disappeared into the kitchen and came out again with another tablecloth. Flapping and fluttering it in the air, he so genuinely hoped to get the wrinkles out for Rick's approval. Flapping and fluttering in the air, I could feel the memory of Jaclyn coming in again, sweeping by my eardrum with dragonfly-wing lightness and briskness.

(Drip.)

Sweeping by my eardrum with dragonfly-wing lightness and briskness, the tent cover over the car in the barn flapped and fluttered in the air.

Flutter. Flutter. Flutter.

Flap. Flap. Flap.

Overlapping layers of smoke, acrobatic in their movements, looping, and looping, and looping, unraveling, and unraveling, and unraveling.

The air damp and dry and the dawn blue and tired and very pale and dying. Everything lit as a weak lantern in the muted dawn. An unknowing in the birth of morning and the mixture of heavy egg white bleaching the blue in the rising sky, leaking into the house in a granulated haze and dreamy beginning to this day of death.

That horn blaring on and on and on in the distance, somewhere. The Christmas music, relentless in its disappearance. My father running out of the house in his robe. Me, following behind him, now watching from the screen door—because, as a kid, you always stopped at the door during the odd hours. At daytime it was different. But at dawn you followed the etiquette of youth.

And that cold came in from the air holes of the screen to preach of the death I would soon experience. And it would taunt me straight into a hellish beginning and, thereafter, a strange life. Death at youth is a little off, with an almost breezy sea-salted and copper-oxidized lime lightness normally subjugated to a happy summer-lit beach bathroom sink or doorknob—but now instead, for me, something of a coming night-fogged funeral. That salted-over tired blue light of dawn painted over white and illuminated with the life of coming day makes the severe understanding of death Victorian in its emotionless reflexive reaction to the horrific. It makes you weird—a child when you should be an adult and an adult when you should be a child. In consequence, I frown with sadness, and I smile with happiness. There's no between.

And there never would be a between after my father opened the doors of the barn and saw my sister in the car, a rare BMW Alpina B12 6.0 E38, swallowed by fumes, her head pressed against the steering wheel, our lives thereafter forever changed. Now, and forever after, I'd be the boy looking from the screen door buried in myself. I'd have that look children possess when they see something different. And I'd always have that stillness. That Victorian stillness. That passiveness.

"Rosebud," I heard my father cry from inside the barn.

He called my sister Rosebud when he wanted to.

"Rosebud," he repeated.

His voice died away in despair as he said this over, and over, again.

"All because of me," he went on with a pathetic shriek like a fawn being attacked by coyotes. "Because of me. You're dead because of me. I'm a bastard. I'm a bastard. A fucking bastard."

He came out with her body that drooped over his shoulder like a dummy or a sack of dirty clothes. My sister, a sack of stagnant blood ready for burial. What a thing. What a thing for a brother to see. A father figure melted down to his pleading youth and a sister stripped down to corporeal bone-and-tissue worm food. What a thing.

Then he fell and the body bounced against the ground and then lay limp. The bag of laundry was too heavy, and my father looked at it . . . and looked at it . . . and looked at it . . .

"James," he called through the sobs. "Please go. Please. You shouldn't have to see this. Please go. For me. Please. Get your mother. Where's your mother? Get your mother. Those pills of hers—and look what she's done to my little girl. A mother up there like that. Look what she's done to my little girl."

"James," he blared. The sobs took over and swallowed up his audible words.

"James," he attempted again. It sounded like he was drowning.

"Jesus, James," he finally got out. "Get away."

My father dragged the body to the front door, and I had that look children possess when they see something different. I followed him like a dog would after his master brought in groceries and my father buried his face in his hands and then dragged them along his cheeks, so his eye sockets seemed freakishly stretched. Sitting down in the chair, he sobbed with a whimper mixed with anger and an anger mixed with regret. A deep remorse propelled something I'd never seen before.

Then he stood up tall.

"Help me, James," he demanded. "Grab her legs."

I went into shock and lost consciousness.

Waking up in the living room, I smelled that metallic scent of blood.

"Where is she?" I screamed, still in a haze.

No answer.

"Where is she?" I screamed again.

No answer.

I made my way to the garage and my father was there tidying up.

He took his rough paint-stained sponge from an empty Quaker Oats container and cleaned his wooden worktable.

"Where is she?"

Pointing to the six black plastic bags, he smiled and laughed to himself.

"What's in those bags?"

"Domestic abuse is a terrible thing," he said, washing his hands in the sink that looked like a wheelbarrow. "I'm going to start a women's rights group. Their bodies are sacred. And men can't treat them like meat."

This was the very beginning of an ill-defined man, sunken so deep in image he didn't have to be anything. That was ultimate power. He was so big in his own mind. He didn't have to be one person. He didn't have to possess a single set of values. He could have them *all*—and justify it. I am Fep Anglish, he'd say. Reasoning ended at the edge of morality for Fep Anglish.

"So much violence," he fake-cried and slashed my cheek with a small screwdriver. It took a while for the blood to respond to the quickness of the slice. I felt the split skin and I waited for the blood to pour out. And then it did.

"What are you doing?" I asked, more confused than ever.

He threw me a rag and I held it to my cheek.

"And we need to condemn the fathers who hurt their sons," he announced. "We need to fight for the children who can't fight for themselves. We need to end sexism. We need to end ageism. We need to end racism."

The rag was drenched with blood, and my father handed me another one. He held the bloodied rag under the faucet and then squeezed the blood water out of it.

"Dad," I begged, "how can you say that and then do this?"

"Good. Good. You get it," he answered, scrubbing his hands under the faucet in a slow, neurotic, and ritualistic way. "I am the watchmaker. The watch. Time. God. All things. And *you*—*you* better quickly get that, or I'll let death happen to you. I won't stop it. Your choice, boy."

"You're not God, Dad, you're the devil," I screamed and threw my rag at him.

"You bitch-brat!" he barked.

I ran out of the garage toward the barn.

"My father is the devil," I yelled, running with that awkward long-limbed youthful stride.

"My father is the devil," I repeated.

Inside the barn, I went into my sister's gravesite—that Alpina B12 6.0 E38. It reeked of gasoline. The seat was stained with her death sweat and urine.

"My father is the devil," I called from the driver's seat.

"My father is the devil," this memory echoed on.

"My father is the devil," it echoed.

"My father is . . ."

"My father . . ."

"My father . . ."

"My Father . . ."

CHAPTER THIRTEEN

Dracula's Coffin

"r. Anglish," Armando said, herding me out of 21, "I hope to see you again very soon."

"Armando, it is?" I asked.

"Si."

He corrected himself before I could talk. "Yes, sir, Mr. Anglish."

"Armando," I went on, sweating and panicking from the bombardment of memory. "Can I ask . . . ?"

"Si?"

"What just happened here?"

"I'm sorry, sir?"

"Don't give me that, please."

I acted like a cop from the movies now. I imagined myself having some New York accent in a low-budget seventies film.

"I'm sorry, sir. I'm not trying to offend. I mean no offense—but I have to say I do not know what you're referring to."

"Come on, Armando. Stop. Just stop. Tyler!"

"Si. I'm sorry about my English. Rick has been very generous with me. My English tutors are working on me . . . to make me better—how you say . . . ahhh, around the corner . . . or ahhh—"

"Armando, please. For my sanity, what just happened in there?"

A bomb went off in Armando's mind.

"I can't," he sobbed. "Rick wouldn't . . . I can't . . ."

"What can't? What can't you do? Armando, what are you talking about? Tell me. Fucking get it out. Tell me. What is going on here?"

I grabbed him by his collar like a good cop would. The information would come out one way or the other.

. . .

"James," Jaclyn called from one of the streams in the marshland. "Look what Daddy and Mommy bought me."

I waded through the water and made my way through the grassy mud toward the dock. Drudging through the mud, my feet suction-cupped into what my child-mind always thought was quicksand.

"Hurry up, James. You have to see this."

"Coming," I said.

My feet were like sponges against the long boardwalk, and I ran down to the dock like a wobbling wet duck. When I got to the end, Jaclyn was swimming next to a little Sunfish sailboat.

"Is that for you, Jaclyn?" I asked, mesmerized.

"Yeah, isn't it the coolest thing you've seen?"

"Yeah," I said, caressing the side of it with my muddy hands.

"Don't get her dirty," she warned like kids warn. "I want to keep her perfect."

"She is perfect, Jaclyn."

This was our first sailboat, even though it was hers.

"I know there's only one seat, James. But you can fit—and you can use it whenever you want. As long as you don't get her too dirty. Because I know you like to play in the mud like all boys do."

"I promise I won't play in the mud when I use her."

"You know what I call her?"

"What do you call her?"

"I call her Miss Jamie."

I giggled to myself.

"Why would you call her that?" I asked, talking through my shirt, embarrassed and proud.

"I wish you were more of a big sister. But you're a boy. You can't help it. So, this is my big sister all the time. My little Miss Jamie."

We both giggled together.

"That's funny," I said.

"It's not replacing you. It couldn't replace you."

"I know."

"I think Mommy and Daddy gave it to me because I'm sad."

"I think Mommy is sad."

"Maybe I have that same sadness then."

"You aren't as sad as Mommy."

"How do you know that?"

"You don't sleep all the time."

"I actually wake up pretty early."

"See," I confirmed, "you're not as sad as you think you are."

"I still want to be a princess."

"You can pretend. Be a princess when you go out on Miss Jamie."

She giggled to herself when I said the name.

"No," she sobered up from the laughter. "I want to be a real princess."

"That wouldn't be possible, Jaclyn."

"I know," she sighed. "Well, I think I wanna go out now."

"Need help?"

"No, I got this."

She pulled herself up onto the dock and untangled the rope from the wooden pole. With careful precision, she dipped one foot into the boat while keeping the other on the dock. Jaclyn was incredibly flexible and full splits were a common practice for her.

"Are you sure . . . ?" I asked one more time.

"I'm sure."

The other foot on the dock followed the lead of the rest of her body. And there she was, in the boat, setting the sail and bound for the larger body of water beyond the marshy horizon.

"I'm off, James. Wish me luck."

I waved goodbye like she was going on a transatlantic voyage.

. . .

"Mr. Anglish, are you alright?" Armando asked.

In this deep thought, I let go of his collar. I wondered if this is what it felt like when my father got swept up in his own dark thoughts. Like father, like son.

"I'm . . ." I answered. "I'm fine."

Jaclyn laughed from somewhere in the walls, and I could hear her calling me.

. . .

"Look at the wind carry this, James," she said. "I'm sailing. I'm really sailing."

. . .

"I'm sorry for an unsatisfactory evening, Mr. Anglish."

That poisonous voice vanished again, and I knew I wouldn't get anything out of Armando.

"It's fine," I said, far away from him. "It's all fine."

"I really am sorry."

"I'm sure you are."

"I am, very much am—you don't have no idea."

He opened the doors and I walked out questioning everything I knew.

Was this reality even real in the first place?

I really—God, I really wondered.

And it scared me so much to wonder.

Was I going insane?

Was that it?

Insanity.

"Hey man," someone said to me from across the street. "Hey. You there."

"Yes?" I asked, unable to clearly see him.

"Come over here."

With caution, I crossed the street, assuming it was one of Tennyson's pranks.

"Hey man," this random guy said, holding out his hand for me to shake it.

"Come on, man," he said, still holding his hand out to be shaken.

"What's wrong with you, man?" he whined. "It's only peace, man. I'm offering peace in this crazy world, man."

I couldn't see his eyes through his tinted aviator sunglasses, and he wore chocolate brown corduroy pants with bright red peace signs stitched into them. His white T-shirt was clearly battered from mob protest activity. And he had a blood stain by his collar bone. And those big aviators of his partially hid a bruise that had now turned green, with an outline of yellow. He pointed at his filthy shirt, and I reluctantly read what it said:

NO WAR BUT CLASS WAR

"The truest words I know, man," he assured me.

I wouldn't respond.

"You're a quiet man, man," he laughed and lit a cigarette. "What's your deal?"

I still wouldn't respond and was thinking up my polite exit.

"My name is Regis," he insisted, the tip of his fingers now jabbing into my chest, his whole hand still waiting to be shaken.

"James," I answered, making my final refusal to shake this hand. It was covered in blood.

"That's good enough for me," he said, finally at ease, his hand slowly making its way back to his hip. "What are you coming out of that high class place for? You high class?"

"A friend of mine."

"So, your friend is high class?"

"Guess so."

"What's your friend's name?"

"Rick."

"Rick who?"

"Rick Koch."

Regis stumbled back and caught himself.

"Rick Koch?" he asked, laughing.

"Yes."

"*The* Rick Koch?"

"Yes."

"The big number two for the richest man in the world?"

"Yes."

"Hey man, wait a second. I know you. I've seen you, man. You're something. I've seen you, man."

I attempted to walk away, and he grabbed my shoulder and turned me around.

"Bad manners to just bolt like that, man," he insisted and pulled down his aviators to reveal his bright blue eyes. "Who the hell are you, man?"

"No one you would know," I said and kept direct eye contact with him.

"Exactly. No one I would know. But someone I've seen somewhere. Holy fuck. No way, man. You're Fep Anglish's son. No way, man. Holy cow, man. I'm talking to James Anglish. Far out, man. Really far out, man. Holy cow, man."

"You got me. I am. It was nice meeting you. But I have to—

"Wait. Wait. I'm sorry, man. Hey. Hey. Would you come with me, man?"

"Come with you? Where?"

"Paris, man. I got two U-Rail tickets—the Atlantic line, man."

"I'm good. Thank you, though."

I firmly walked away now. Regis followed behind me with uncontrolled excitement.

"Hey man, please. Come on, man. Two tickets. Train leaves in twenty minutes and we're there in seventeen, man. Come on. I got round trip tickets, too, man. Come on, man. Hang in Paris with me. For like a few hours—and we'll come right back, man. Round trip, man."

I kept walking but still talked to him. Maybe I would go to Paris. I had nothing to lose. Nothing to do. Nowhere to be.

"Why do you have two tickets?" I asked.

He scurried in front of me and walked backward, matching my speed.

"Oh, man. Hey, man. There was another. A friend. Really a girlfriend, man. She went off somewhere. In the protest, man. She joined another crowd somewhere, man."

"You don't want to find her?"

"No, man. She's off doing her thing, man. You don't want to crowd the GF, you know. Never want to crowd them, man. Like clipping their wings, man, if you crowd them. She's a keeper for me, man. So, I don't want to crowd her, you know."

I believed him, and Regis could tell I was warming up.

"Good thing, man," he went on, "I got two U-Rail. Great thing, man. Paris is where it's at, man. Got friends in Paris that can show you around. Like the cool places, man. The wartime places."

"Wartime places?"

"Yeah, man. There's a war going on, man. A world war—all of us wrapped up, man. Where you livin' at that you don't know this?"

"What world war?"

"World War II, man. With Germany and Italy and Japan, man. You don't know this? What classes are you taking, man? Thought they would teach you good, being an Anglish and all."

"Guess they haven't."

"They really haven't, man. You should take a current affairs class or something like that, man. I got some good professors, man. I believe what they say—really man, I really do."

"It's good to trust someone."

"You trust me, man?"

He asked that with such genuine intent, and it disarmed me.

"Yeah, I actually do," I responded, truthfully.

"Well, great, man. That means I got someone for this extra ticket of mine. This is great, man. The station is right here, man. Like meant to be, man. U-Rail like two blocks away. How about that? Just two blocks away. Riding along with James Anglish. This is one for the books, man. Rosey won't believe this one."

"Rosey your girlfriend?"

"Yeah, man. She's the one who fills the glass half empty end of my heart. It's always been Rosey. You got another half?"

"No, not yet."

Regis stopped walking backward and grabbed me, his face now right up to mine. He pulled up his sunglasses again.

"You'll get your other half, man. I promise. We all do."

His sunglasses dropped against the bridge of his nose, and he went on walking beside me. He could only talk with the assistance of dramatic body language, and I became one of his playful punching bags due to it. More of a punching bag for slight nudges and elbowings of friendly reassurance. He seemed to me to be the type with an extremely annoying father. Because he got these bad habits from somewhere and it was always the father who gave it to the son. I thought about these possible tendencies of his annoying father until we arrived at the station.

The U-Rail stations were about as sterile and bland and modern as you could get. White on white. The walls were white. The floors were white. The color temperature of the LED bulbs above were set at the most severe level, devoid of any natural flair of blues or greens—rather this death-like examination room, knife-edge white, on white, on white, on white, on white. It pained your eyes, but you could at least know also killed the germs. Unlike a normal train station, U-Rail was completely sanitized by this colorless LED bacteria-killer. And the white seats intensified any blemishes, which only made the job for the U-Rail employees constant, around the clock. There was no room for error when it came to a blemish-free train station, especially when the whole place was a stark white. My father made sure of that. And that's why he wanted it this way. You couldn't hide dirt here. The U-Rail employees really had the hardest job and I felt bad for them, knowing how many of them my father fired over the years. If you had any respect for these employees, you wouldn't sit anywhere. You'd just stand stiff and avoid touching anything. The lightest brush against a seat could result in the end of someone's career. No scuff was allowed to be left unattended for more than ninety seconds and the hidden cameras made sure of that. The U-Rail employees would come out of nowhere wearing hazmat suits. They would spray and scrub and spray and scrub and then disappear into this bleached-out white nothingness. I always wondered where their offices were. Probably somewhere depressing with lots and lots of camera monitors.

"Five minutes to spare, man," he said and jumped onto the white bench with his filthy shoes. "Got us good tickets, man. The best of the best. All the way in the front, man."

For a man who looked and sounded like him, he seemed to have a lot of money to throw around. But that's how it went with a lot of the protestors. They had money and they spent their lives trying to hide the fact they had the money.

"Those are expensive tickets," I commented.

"Yeah, man. What can you do, right?"

I laughed because the response was so stupid.

"What, man?"

Embarrassed by my unintentional transparency, I answered: "Oh, sorry. I suddenly thought about something funny."

"Oh, yeah. I do that all the time. Funny thoughts always pop into my head, man."

The sound of a U-Rail highspeed train entering a station is something you just need to experience for yourself. But to give you an idea, it sounded like wind going through an elevator shaft. That eerie sound would occur about two minutes before arrival because the air pressure in the tunnel was shifting. Then you would see way down, at ultimate vantage point, the tip of the locomotive. This tip was three-hundred and nine feet long and it was all engine, and it had a light, jet-black, form-fitting body. For three-hundred and nine feet, it sloped down to a bright yellow needle-prick point and this slope would curve around the stretched oval super high-beam Mars Lights headlamps. The whole train was skinned with a flexible glass nearly as thin as a strand of hair but stronger than any metal out there. When the train entered the "hundred-mile radius of entry," this glass skin would untint itself from its dark façade to show its full translucency. You could see the interior of the train like you could see a person through the frosted glass of a shower door. Undefinable shapes would move around inside, and you would always guess who they were before the thin glass doors slid open and bled out the passengers. All ten-thousand feet of this mechanical centipede would bleed out people until this centipede was suddenly replenished with fresh blood like us. Before you entered, you would look down the single piece of perfectly curved flexible glass and see it bend with the track, the insides of this centipede one continuous forever hallway that contorted and flexed without a groan from its material properties. There were no railroad cars segmenting this train and, when it reached top speed and the air was completely sucked out of the tunnel to create a vacuum, the glass body would tint to black, so the passengers didn't get sick from the relative motion. Even though it was enclosed in a tunnel, the sheer sight of lights and different wall textures passing by caused instant nausea. You could only imagine how fast we were going if we could get to Paris in seventeen minutes.

"Hey, man," he said as the train pulled up. "James Anglish, man. I'm gettin' on a train with James Anglish. How about that, man."

After the train fully evacuated its passengers, Regis raced inside to grab his egg-shaped seat by the glass body. I had the other egg-shaped seat next to him, which aligned with the middle row. The train had three rows and the one I liked least was the middle row. It was a control thing. I felt like I had more control over the machinery if I could touch the sides of it. I know it sounds strange, but it was just one of the weird things you had when you travelled. I assumed everyone had at least one. It really comes down to how many anxieties your parents had planted in you since birth, I guess.

Then the lights inside transitioned from a warm red to a light blue to a lime green when the automated U-Rail voice came through the speakers under the seats.

"Welcome to U-Rail," it said, "We are pleased to have you aboard our XP237 Highspeed Atlantic U-Line. Your estimated journey time is seventeen minutes and thirty-three seconds. We kindly urge you to remain seated until we have reached maximum speed and the vessel is in full-tint mode. Your *fasten seatbelt* indicator will turn off when it's appropriate to move about the cabin. Thank you—and have a wonderful journey with the XP237 Highspeed Atlantic U-Line."

The doors slipped closed, and the buzz of the electric motor pulsed through the skin, and we inched out of the station until we reached the Atlantic. Most of the travel time was spent above ground exiting New

York City and Long Island and then we would finally see, after eight full minutes, the entrance to the Atlantic Line tunnel. The entrance started a few miles from the coastline, and it went over nine-hundred feet beneath Long Island City so the train could accelerate without causing a building to collapse above. It would reach top speed fifty miles off the coast of Long Island and cut cleanly through an airless tunnel buried in the ocean's bedrock. Then, like that, you found yourself climbing out of the bedrock on the other side of the Atlantic and, soon enough, there it was—Paris.

Regis and I headed to 112 Rue du Faubourg Saint-Honoré. To the left of its orange and red stained-glass front doors was a gold plaque with etched black letters reading, *ERNIE'S RESTAURANT*. A man wearing a white dinner jacket opened these stained-glass doors and his eyes were distorted by the thick, low index lenses of his spectacles. The street behind us was bent and warped in the strange lenses of his and they fogged from the warmth of his own steamy breath. He seemed nervous and gave us a good stare before asking for our names.

"Names?" he asked.

"Regis Lobosco."

The tone of Regis' voice changed when he said his full name. He sounded normal and rather sophisticated. That was probably the way he spoke to his parents behind closed doors. But outside—no, outside he was the "hey, man" freedom fighter who had somehow dragged me to Paris.

"And . . ." the man looked rudely over to me.

"Oh, this is James Anglish."

He gave me a second look because he recognized the last name. But only a second look. *Must be a coincidence,* I assumed he thought.

"Alright," he said, only looking at Regis. "Please enter."

The interior was richly red, and the walls were draped with velvet wallpaper transitioning in tone from raspberry to burgundy to maroon. This velvet could've only come out of the inside of Dracula's coffin. And this death red was further abbreviated by the dark wood accents in the framework of the doorways and the ceiling, and the further magnification brought on by those gold leaf frames and those bubblegum pink and lipstick red flowers. The velvet almost turned the air red around it and a woman emerged from this haze wearing a green dress and her pale candle wax skin and her green stained-glass church window eyes approached me and she stopped right there and then turned and her perfect features came into complete focus and that burgundy, and that raspberry, and that maroon thickened and darkened around her, forming the richest saturation of red I had ever seen. Never had I seen someone become what they really were purely through surface observation. Her whole life was written on her complexion, in those magnificent contours and outlines of her body. It was all there, for me to read in a glance. Not until now had a human awakened me from the hatred of my terminal passiveness. I wanted to know more about her. The newness of it all—of caring and loving. Had Jaclyn been reborn in her? Had she?

A waiter in a matching red velvet jacket showed us to our table and Regis maintained his sophisticated persona.

"Thank you," he said as the waiter sat us down. "I cross the Atlantic only for Ernie's."

The waiter bowed and nodded awkwardly because the comment was so pointless. How does anyone respond to something like that—really? But Regis managed to turn into a corny old man out of nowhere it seemed. That's a record for personality shift. It must be a record.

"Good food," he said to me. "Great food," he corrected himself. I'm sure he did that because his father said it was great food, not good food. Big difference in high dining for people who have a subtle and distinguished palate.

"Excuse me," I heard a very light voice say from the bar. It was that woman in the green dress. She had forgotten her bag and it was sitting on the chair of the table right next to us.

In my mind I would grab it for her. But I didn't. Rather I watched the waiter grab the bag for her and watched her smile at him with that perfectly symmetrical thin upper lip of hers. I watched her leave and saw myself do nothing about it.

"Regis," I suddenly said.

"What's up?" he asked.

"Gotta run quick," I said. "Be right back."

"Run where?"

"Bathroom."

"Past the bar to the left."

"Thanks."

I pushed my way through the thick red syrupy air and the man with the strange spectacles opened the door for me. I could see the woman in green far down the block and I made my way toward her with that fast-walk, slow-run of mine. But it was never for something like this. I usually moved that way to get away from people and avoid awkward conversation. It was never to see into someone else's world like this. There was never that interest in people. I wasn't built like that. Because I was taught people were the problem. So why ever focus on the problem, right?

Now I found myself getting too close, so I slowed down to keep a good enough distance. If she turned around, it was far enough for her not to think anything of it, even if she recognized me from the restaurant, which I'm sure she wouldn't.

Then she stopped.

Shit!

So, I stopped.

What do I do?

Turn the other way?

Keep walking?

Then she did a 180.

Now she was coming back toward me.

Shit!

What the hell do I do?

I was frozen.

Shit!

Shit!

Shit!

"Keep moving, James," I said out loud to myself.

I had to say something.

We would intersect.

I had to.

Right?

Or could I keep walking and pretend like none of this ever happened?

Go back to normal.

And not care.

About anyone.

Or anything.

I could do that.

Right?

She stopped again.

Turned around.

Was she lost?

Then she went into a flower shop.

I walked over to it.

I looked at some flowers in the front.

And there she was—the woman in green—asking the man at the counter about something.

He answered her and she gave him that perfect smile, and before she walked out, she admired some flowers. These colors, everywhere.

Bright yellow flowers.

Purple.

Pink.

Blue.

Orange.

Green.

White.

Brown.

Cream.

Crimson.

Electric indigo.

Violet.

Scarlet.

"See you again, Scarlett," the man at the counter said and waved goodbye to her.

"Scarlett," I whispered to myself.

"See you soon," she called back, letting go of her admiration for the flowers to exit.

She walked right by me, and I stood still and watched her turn the corner. And that was it. I would never see Scarlett again. And I would never see Regis again. Because I went on walking and got the next train out of Paris to New York.

I'd had enough of people.

Especially Regis.

And I'd had enough of those beautiful colors.

Because I had seen these types of colors before.

Off and on.

Now coming altogether to form her.

This woman in green in Paris.

Was she even real?

Or was she just a combination of colorful emotion?

Insanity.

CHAPTER FOURTEEN

Cut Plug

Back in New York, I wandered up Park Avenue to 740 and I stood outside the building, thinking. The gorgeous marble-and-granite entrance framing the gray awning, cold at the touch. It didn't want me. The curling flowers etched in and my fingers running along the grooves to feel no pulse of the past. The inhaling and exhaling ribcage of 740, motionless, ceasing to expand and contract, dead due to my deeper longing for something. I was a foreigner now—a cheat. Someone that shouldn't have been at 740. It felt like I was touching a dead body when I touched that building. Jaclyn's death—that woman in green—was in it. She was buried in it. Was it granite or marble? That was a way to stop thinking of her. It worked before. But it wouldn't work now. I knew that. Tyler's death had broken me. My power to keep Jaclyn away was gone. She would sail on in my mind, forever. And ever. And ever. Her death would be my life. That woman in green.

"Is it marble?" I asked myself in an audible stutter. "Or is it granite?" I inspected the underlining layers of brown in this unknown material. "Is that mud? Is that rust?"

My self-obsession grew on itself, and I was concerned for my wellbeing. God, that building was so cold to me now. It was just a building. Something expensive and rare—but that's what it was. I now saw it the same way Beasley and Tennyson did. I was one of them now. There was no longer any use for appreciation—the one good thing I'd learned from my father. And Jaclyn took it away. It was really the only thing I had. Now I was Beasley and Tennyson. And I'd go upstairs as Beasley and Tennyson. I'd no longer smile at the doorman, like I'd done the first time, and muster up the courage to ask if the side entrance door to 740 was made from solid brass. I'd no longer worry about having to ask questions like that because this art deco masterpiece was a nineteen-story limestone tombstone. A big fat makeup-lathered gas-pumped body ballooning off the sides of a metal slab. The pulse was gone. This passion was gone. James Anglish was gone.

But was this passion to begin with? Had the living details of things become the smokescreen of the truth? In my mind before, objects took on more character than people did. They had to. Because people were the problem. They did not build. They did not maintain. Or preserve. Or mentor. Rather they used. Beat down. Tarnished. And bruised the jewelry of the past. Building 740 was a diamond on Park Avenue. And I saw it as that. I felt I had a duty to protect it and understand it, while everyone else wanted to rent it to suck it dry. Suck out the experience it offered and say you went there. Suck it out until it becomes worthless. Fuck it silly, why don't you. Permanently damage that nostalgia running in its pipes. Make this thing, which never wanted you, your little bitch-brat. Rent it. Say "I did it. And it wasn't that great." And then move on to screw up the next. Because that's what you did. Slap it around for two weeks until you felt better about yourself. That's what people did. Users and destroyers—*renters*.

I couldn't even tell you what most people looked like. Beasley and Tennyson were blobs with annoying voices. They were blobbed silhouettes that wanted everything to be blobs just like they were. Blobs, everywhere, full of opinions, skewed reasoning, and misplaced morality. Blobs that occupied 740 like a virus in a living organism. The building was sick with them. They were its two-week cold. And it was a nasty cold.

What a nasty thing for 740 to have. To have them inside watching U-Today, instead of reading one of those great leftover table books. That table book they didn't bother to read, which now had a big wine-ring stain on it. They both knew it, but they both wouldn't clean it up. They'd just blob around the apartment and give U-Today 10 percent of their attention, which was fine for them and the program itself. Because Beasley and Tennyson were the type of people who'd travel from some faraway place to wait outside U-Studios and wave at the cameras. They'd smile in the cold and eventually say "hi" to someone who knew either a little less or a little more than they did. That giddiness in their eyes. The love they have for the earrings the host wears each day. Those earrings that are just so wonderfully unique and different, every single morning.

· · ·

The Sunfish sailboat shrank away into nothingness within that definitive vantage point of the horizon line. Her faraway voice sounded like a distressed seagull, and I cupped my hands over my eyes to block the beating sun from my tunnel vision of her.

It was always about Jaclyn. The one person I loved and trusted. A big sister that gave life to the lifeless. My protector from the abuse of my father and the neglect of my mother. My parent, my sister, my best friend. The reason behind everything. My purpose to live.

"Jaclyn," I said softly to myself. "Please come back. Don't ever leave me. Don't ever grow up."

I removed my hands from my face and turned around to look at that Victorian house.

It was watching me.

· · ·

"Hello," the doorman greeted me. "Hope you've been enjoying 740 Park Avenue."

I walked through without answering.

"Quite a party upstairs, Mr. Anglish," he called from the door as I entered the elevator.

I didn't look back.

The elevator opened and I walked into the apartment.

"Uh, oh," Tennyson's words went up and down. "Look at who it is. Jamie boy of Jamestown."

He hung his arm around my neck and pulled me further into the mess of these wild animals. His breath smelled like my father's. I knew that smell all too well.

"What the hell have you done?" I asked.

Half the apartment had been spray-painted. That light-refracting sofa had been keyed beyond recognition. And the kitchen had plastic cups scattered all over it. The vandalism was a "navigational tool," I was told. Chris, the spray-paint artist, labeled the rooms so the partygoers knew where they were. The living room had big bleeding letters that read, *LIVING ROOM*. And, so on, the labeling went. Chris was proud of himself for doing this. He introduced himself to me as "Chris the Spray." Whatever the hell that meant.

"If someone back in the day wanted an apartment this big," he said after the introduction and through the smug puffs of smoke leaking from his nose, "then they should let their guests know where they are. Common people aren't used to having a bedroom for their dog."

He spray-paint-labeled the kitchen as *THE DOG'S ROOM*. The paint trickled down the marble from its thick application.

Beasley was in her drunk slumber upstairs and Tennyson began to lecture his guests.

"Welcome to 740," he stammered after a few failed attempts at climbing onto the marble kitchen countertop.

He clinked his lead crystal glass and stood proudly above us all.

"The height of American elitism, at my disposal," he pronounced.

"At our disposal," the crowd chanted and laughed.

You could hear a few glasses breaking through this chanting and laughing.

"I'm speaking for my piss-drunk girlfriend, too," he wobbled and then righted himself as if he awoke from a dream. "The other host who I get to . . . well, you know," he leered.

The crowd laughed again, and more glasses broke.

"But there's also another host—who I shall never . . . you know . . . fuck over—well, maybe."

His eyelids were losing their strength. He was talking from the deck of a small boat in the middle of a hurricane. Left to right, right to left. Swaying. Swaying. Swaying. Would he fall? I bet these partygoers placed bets. But you really didn't know what they were thinking through this collective smugness. They hid behind the hoodies and the tattoos and the chain smoking and the prolific drinking. To then wake up the next morning like a child with a very bad stomachache and either forget or regret what they'd done the night before.

"Jamie boy," he finally got out through his drooping and melting drunken affect. "Get over here, Jamie boy, and say hello to these fine people."

I was reluctant at first until a smug silhouette slapped my ass.

"Make 'em proud," a dehydrated frat voice said.

That was enough to get me moving and I stood with restless posture by this Frankenstein monster of Tennyson.

"Good boy," he breathed on me.

His alcohol breath cut at my face and the zombie crowd clapped and clapped and clapped.

"The guy who almost got her," he announced and smirked. "The guy who wanted *it*—but never got *it*. 'Cause I got *it*. I got it *good*." He sat on the last word an extra beat.

"What are you talking about," I leaned over and whispered in his ear.

He answered me by braying to the crowd. Tennyson was on stage now.

"You know what I'm talking about, you little slippery fuck."

The crowd was too drunk and high to understand what was brewing. And then Tennyson swayed too far to the left and fell off the countertop onto a woman who was pouring her red wine from that beautiful wine decanter, which was surely hundreds of years old. The decanter shattered and the women's palms dug into the glass upon their impact with the floor. She bellowed like a goat being slaughtered and Tennyson was faceplanted in the mess, the glass embedded in his cheeks.

"Are you alright?" a partygoer asked with fake concern. She had that glazed look in her eyes like she was trying to fight through her highness to act appropriately for the situation at hand. "Can I get anything?" this partygoer continued to ask.

The woman sat on the ground crying. And Tennyson didn't answer because he was passed out.

"This fucking party," she sobbed. "And my fucking hands. Look at them."

She shoved her bloody palms in my face.

"It's your fault" she growled at me.

This was the puritanical blame I knew too well. Someone always had to be blamed. It was exfoliating for people to sentence someone else for something they didn't do. I mean, why take ownership if you always rented, right? Repercussions could work the same way. Rent them!

Her two friends came over and picked her up.

"It's your apartment," they both said in unison to me, the woman hanging on both of their shoulders. "And you have nothing to say for yourself?"

"I . . ." I tried.

"Well," they dragged her off. "I guess we're leaving."

"I'm sorry," I got out.

They slammed the door behind them, and a picture frame fell off the wall. Chris huddled by me as if there were a small fire we were congregating around. He even breathed into his hands like it was cold.

"Bitches always be bitches," he confessed.

I smiled because I didn't know what else to do.

"That's a song of mine," he went on. "You should listen to it. Got. Like. Four thousand fans already. Good shit. My father fucking hates it. But he doesn't understand good shit. I feel like you feel me—like you get good shit. You'd get the lyrics—I know you would. You seem like you know your shit—like your shit don't stannnk. You feel me?"

His skin was so white it was red. He reminded me of a cooked lobster.

"I feel you," I said, to slough his BS off me.

"Bro, I knew it. I knew you'd feel me."

I smiled and exhaled out of my scrunched lips.

"Yeah," I said.

"Yeah," he said back.

"Yeah," I said.

"Your father doesn't feel me, though."

"What do you mean?" I asked.

"Ah," he laughed. "Now you really feel me."

"I do. What do you mean?"

"Brother to brother, I didn't like your daddy. And my daddy didn't like your daddy. See, my daddy used to be the director of the CDC. That is, he used to be."

"Why are you telling me this?"

He enjoyed that he was spinning me up in this. Now I would really listen to him. He had me. He had the attention he lusted after.

"Calm, calm," he said, softly. "You don't want to hurt yourself. Brother to brother—because you are my heart-to-heart bro—*your* daddy took over the CDC. He ended the CDC. And he told the little perching and chirping cameras around him that my daddy had some loose screws. My daddy was just a hardworking American just as all of us are. Hardworking and hard partying. What's that they say? 'Work hard, play hard.' I must admit, I like the latter a whole lot more, my brotha. A whole lot more."

He opened his arms to show me how much and a small screen underneath the skin of his wrist lit up. It never lit up. None of ours did.

"Oh my," he said with a Southern accent. "What is this?"

The screen in my wrist lit up too and then the entire crowd quieted. Indulgent chattering seized, and heads were down. I flipped my arm around to watch the report.

"Breaking news," the headline read.

"Off to you, Douglas," the anchorman said. It was a strange quick cut to Douglas.

"Mark, this just in," a simulated onsite reporter said. "A potential pandemic coming America's way. I'm here in Territory H-(B) or, as some call it, Gonda—a district of Uttar Pradesh, India—where a new, more vicious strand of the Marburg virus has unleashed itself on 513 citizens, killing 496 of them. Experts say this is by far the deadliest virus in world history. According to Dr. Barnstormer, India's leading epidemiologist, there is no current cure for this *quote* Marburg virus on steroids *unquote*. Back to you, Mark."

"Thank you, Douglas. We hope that we'll learn more about this in the coming days."

Douglas' speaking box, which housed his head, went offscreen and Mark took full screen.

"Let your heart not be troubled," he said. "U-News has successfully gotten ahold of Dr. Barnstormer, coming to us from Territory H-(B). Dr. Barnstormer—"

A pixelated box of Dr. Barnstormer's head opened and split the screen down the middle.

"Beashock Barnstormer here," he answered, surrounded by pixelation, his face seemingly riddled with scar tissue. "The state of India is in a panic. Gonda, alone, has lost close to 500 of its residents—and I'm sad to say—this is only the beginning."

"As a responsible reporter, I want to try to avoid total panic. Is there any bright side to this, Dr. Barnstormer? Any at all?"

"I feel that I must report the truth, if that's what you intend for me to do?"

Mark touched his earpiece, a Journalism 101 tactic, or nervous tic, every reporter used to buy themselves enough time for a professional response. It had to be fed to them by U management.

"Can you hear me?" Dr. Barnstormer asked.

"Yes, I can. Please, let us know what's exactly at stake here."

"The virus, from what we know so far, constantly adapts. It is the fastest-evolving entity I've been lucky enough to see in my career. Its reproduction is messy and, as it copies its genetic material, the mutations compound exponentially. The virus creates trillions of copies of itself in a single day and I do believe, I regret to say, that modern medicine is not up to the challenge. We simply do not have the tools at our disposal to catch up with its swiftness and intelligence. What we can do only is protect ourselves and stay inside, avoiding any interaction. We've dealt with viruses like this—but not *this*. The last pandemic outbreak was infant in comparison. I don't think we will ever see a virus of this magnitude again. Nor will we ever fully get out of this one."

"Dr. Barnstormer, is there a contingency plan for your location?"

"As of yet, no. It's happened too quickly to have effective response without total panic. We are looking at 500 dead now, and we expect those numbers to rise into the thousands by tomorrow. There are rumors about an outbreak in Territory E (3-3-C)."

"That's over two thousand miles from where you are."

"Yes. We have no other information other than that possible outbreak. We cannot confirm this is the same virus though."

"Symptoms," Mark declared, running out of time. "Can you enlighten us?"

"It's similar to Ebola, in that it can cause hemorrhagic fever."

"Dr. Barnstormer, do you mind elaborating."

"Certainly. A hemorrhagic fever is a fever accompanied by bleeding throughout the body. This will result in organ failure—"

"Then death?"

"It's unfortunate—but yes."

"Have all the cases seen hemorrhagic fever?"

"Yes."

"And then organ failure?"

"Yes—for those who did not survive, yes."

"Is there any ETA for us?"

"We do not know. If the other outbreak is in fact the result of the same virus, then the timeline is very different for the world."

"Would you say a week, a month . . . ?"

"Prepare now. I cannot advise any further than that. It's up to Rick Koch. I'm afraid Mr. Koch will have to pick up the pieces left by the late Fep Anglish. The collapse of the CDC was Mr. Anglish's single greatest misstep. His partnership with America's federal government was subpar, to say the least. The death toll of the last pandemic did not have to be anywhere near where it was—80 percent—if he had put in place an effective disease control agency. But I'm sure this is not why you have me on. I'm not here to talk about Fep Anglish's failures. The CDC was not 'a factory for the dramatics,' as Mr. Anglish once infamously said to those who were dying."

The smugness on Mark's face grew.

"For another time," he blurted and straightened his face. "Dr. Barnstormer, thank you for your time on such short notice. And stay safe. We'll talk soon."

"Thank you, Mark. Stay safe."

Dr. Barnstormer's box dematerialized.

"No need to be embarrassed," Chris sympathized and patted my back. "We all have dicks as dads."

I nodded my head.

"Yo—look at this? Check this. You've seen this before."

He put his wrist over mine to show me one of his digital tattoos. It was a woman being penetrated by a snake.

"Pretty chill, right?"

"Yeah, that's something."

"It's chill as hell. Came out of your daddy's shop. He did do cool things, bro."

This was Chris' way of making me feel better.

"Digital Tat. That's what it's called. My blood has some sort of plasma in it. I'm Plasma-Man. Shooting out plasma n' shit. No web out of this hand, bro. No web."

I turned off the screen on my wrist and was outwardly annoyed by him.

"Did I offend?" he asked, noticing.

"No," I lied. "A lot of things on my mind."

"A lot of things on all of our minds."

"Yeah."

"Check it."

He pointed his wrist at the wall and the tattoo jumped onto the wall.

"Cool wallpaper, man. Check it."

The woman being penetrated by a snake turned back into *Star Wars*. The preview had just ended, and the movie had started.

"Chris always has the gadgets," one guy said.

"He's got the money," another woman added, jealous.

"Alright, alright," Chris defended. "Cut the side comments and watch the documentary."

"It's not a documentary," someone else said.

"You're all fools," Chris insisted. "This shit is history. Space travel in the old days."

"This is called fiction," a guy patronized, dressed like a Greek philosopher. His long shirt went down to his kneecaps, and he wore Nike shoes with huge transparent bubbles under the sole. His hair was greased and pushed back, revealing his widow's peak.

"Yeah, fiction n' shit."

"This is a movie," he philosophized. "Darth Vader is not portrayed correctly here."

"Bro, you mad."

"Darth Vader started World War II in Ancient Egypt right before the Revolutionary War. This film is inspired by the real rise and fall of Darth Vader. This film is fiction, and it is a metaphorical exploration of the life of Darth Vader via a separate diegetic medium, which happens to be space travel in this case. Can't you see that, Chris?"

"Diegetic fiction n' shit," Chris laughed. "What you mean? Fiction what? What's diegetic about this fiction?"

"By fiction, I mean not real. Never happened. A movie. A story."

Chris looked at me for assurance and I'd give him none. Not out of dislike, but out of *whatever*.

"Alright, alright," Chris said, now very uncomfortable. He turned *Star Wars* off to pretend this conversation never happened.

• • •

"Where's your sister?" my father asked and then slapped me across the face. I tasted the peat from the Laphroaig evaporating from his breath. He was lit. Very lit.

Twitching from the impact, I held back the tears and searched the horizon line running alongside that body of water beyond the marshland. No sail swept by the wind and no happy girl called me to help her set up anchor. Just a gray that becomes grayer in absence and those gathering clouds above, their flat and silver-bottomed puffy bellies congregating as one ceiling above us.

"I don't see her," I answered.

"Why did you let her go out?" he snarled.

"I didn't."

"What do you mean you didn't?"

"She just went out."

"You weren't with her?"

"I was. But—"

"You want her dead?"

"What?"

"You heard what I asked, boy."

"I love Jaclyn."

"She won't make it through this storm if she went out into the Atlantic."

"Mommy!" I cried.

He slapped me across the face harder.

"Shut your crying."

"Mommy!" I cried again.

.   .   .

The crowd went back into their collective vapid word-dribble.

"Peeps are crazed," Chris said to me, relieved and forcing his affect to a limit beyond the absurd. "I'm not fightin' them no more."

"Check it," the affect went on. He was very much into saying that.

"Feel my lip," it went on, and on, and on, and on.

"Your lip?" I asked.

I thought it was slang for something else. It was characteristic of the very rich to downplay what they had through slang talk. Chris was a common occurrence. Slang was his defense mechanism. A way for him to roll over and play dead for the very jealous and the very nasty, which was just about everyone at this party.

"Yeah," he insisted, "feel my lip."

"I'm fine," I insisted.

"No, really," he insisted back. "Feel it. Promise, no weird."

I gave in and touched his lip.

"The upper lip," he corrected.

I touched his upper lip.

"Feel it?" he asked, with a goofy searching look in his eyes.

"Yeah."

I felt a bump.

"What is that?" I asked.

"That's cut plug."

"Cut plug?"

"You know—like tobacco."

"Yeah, I know."

"I'm not just showing you tobacco, duh."

"What are you showing me?"

"Bruh. Something a little different."

He was starting to really annoy me now.

"Yes . . . ?" I asked back.

"It's the answer to that crazy Marburg virus older baddaa brothaa shiiit."

He took what appeared to be chewing gum out of his mouth.

"I got this from Beashock," he went on. "He was real tight with my dad. He used to work for him. Everyone used to work for my dad before yours jacked them all up off their feet. Then he . . . well, then he—he killed himself."

His inability to be clear stabbed at my patience. And his breath smelled awful from whatever this cut plug thing was.

"Your dad killed himself?" I stated in the form of a question.

"They hatin' each other in heaven."

"Who?"

"Your dad and my dad. They both got tired of livin'. Kinda makes us brothers of anotha father."

When he said "father" he went out of character. I wondered if he would be able to continue faking it after that slip up.

"He jumped off the GW," he said like the rich guy he was. "I guess that's what they all do."

"At least he didn't try to kill you," I commiserated.

Chris laughed and then cried. He had no idea what I was talking about. But he still laughed and cried.

"Man," he said in broken words, "it's tough being us. Directionless offspring with nothing much to show for. Growing off the image of our dads, knowing we'll never make an impact ourselves. One rich brat to another," Chris continued, understanding the purpose of my silence.

"This cut plug is an extended-release cure for the virus. It isn't approved, but Beashock sent it to me and gave me directions to chew two a day. He sent me packs of them—a supply for twenty-four months."

"How do you know him that well?" I asked.

"I told you. He'd worked for my father. They were very close. I called him Uncle Beashock. He's my godfather."

I imagined Vito Corleone.

"After my dad killed himself, Beashock sent me a lot of things from India. He let me know about the outbreak before anyone else found out. I think it's been going on a lot longer than he's leading everyone to believe."

"Why are you telling me all of this?"

"I . . . I feel we connect. I just . . . you know, I don't know."

"I won't tell anyone, if you're now worrying."

"I wouldn't have told you if I had any doubts."

It was nice having someone trust me like this. My father trusted me only when he was blackout drunk. Who knows, Chris could've been blackout, too. If he was, he composed himself a hell of a lot better than my father ever did.

"That's nice," I said. "Thank you—I appreciate it."

"Yeah, brotha of anotha fatha. And enough of a brotha to give you some cut plug, if you want?"

"What is it exactly?"

"Beashock didn't go into it. I'm supposed to take it at least three days before initial exposure. And I've been on it for two weeks already."

"You've known about this for two weeks?"

"Yeah, Beashock called and told me all about it. He said this cut plug would stabilize my fluids and electrolytes and maintain my oxygen and blood pressure status before and during exposure. It replenishes lost blood, fights infections, and helps my blood clot. All through my gums. Amazing, right?"

I was getting inpatient again.

"Is it here already?" I asked.

"The cut plug is here."

"No, the virus?"

"I have no idea. I have more cut plug in my pocket if you want to get started now. You can come over to my apartment to get more of it, if you want . . . my Uncle Beashock is a great guy—he'll always send me more. But I can't ever tell him I'm handing this stuff out. Especially not to the son of the guy who disenfranchised him."

"I'm sorry."

"He dissolved the whole CDC."

"I'm sorry."

"I'm sorry, man. It's just that my uncle wouldn't be in India if it hadn't been for your father. Your dad not only got rid of him, he ruined his reputation. Epidemiology is now a dirty word in this country because of your dad. And India was the one place left that greeted disease control with open arms. And it happens to be the place where this shit storm is brewing. How about that? What are the odds of that?"

"I'm sorry."

"Beashock wanted him to move to India."

He took a beer from the fridge like this was his apartment. It wasn't mine, either—but it was more mine than his.

"How retro," he commented, as the beer cap flung somewhere on the ground. He wouldn't pick it up. "Where did you get these?"

"Already stocked in the apartment," I answered.

"Good to know. I don't know if you know, but Beaz got me on the list for this place. I'm renting it in a little over two months."

"I didn't know."

Pleased by my answer, he took the cut plug out of his mouth, wrapped it in a handkerchief, and put the handkerchief in his pocket.

"Lucky number seven," he said and then chugged the beer.

I took a beer from the fridge and chugged it. Chris was better at chugging than I was.

"You want some cut plug?" he asked.

The beer dripped from the copper-wire hairs of his mustache.

"Sure," I answered.

He pulled the cut plug out of his pocket and his keys fell out with it. A woman talking next to us picked them up for him and then gave him a flirtatious look.

"Your keys," she said in a sexy voice.

"Thank you."

"What's that?" she asked.

"What's what?"

"That."

She pointed at the cut plug.

"This? Gum."

"That's not gum."

"It is. I assure you it's gum."

"Can I have a piece?"

"This is for my friend."

"Can I have another piece then?"

"I don't have any."

"How could you only have one piece of gum? Who has one piece of gum?"

"I had multiple pieces of gum—and this is the last one now."

"So, he's more important than me?"

"No, that's not—"

"He deserves the gum, and I don't."

"That's not exactly—"

"He's a man. And I'm a woman."

"No . . . I—"

"I get it. You're a pig. A man-pig."

She stormed off five feet and spoke to another person about how horrible Chris was. I knew this because she was still close enough for us to hear her say how horrible he was.

"These Society of Endoscopy people are bizarre," Chris commented, his eyes still on her.

"I think you mean Society of Entropy," I corrected.

"Whatever."

"Should I put this under my lip now?" I asked.

"It's best if you start it in the morning. Remember, twice a day, twelve hours at a time. Then just spit it out in the trash. Try not to eat or drink with it. Take it out like I just did and keep it in something that's clean. You do not want to contaminate it."

"Thank you."

"If anyone asks you what you're packing in there, simply say it's cut plug. Don't say gum because they'll then be like that one over there. Amazing, isn't it? She's still talking about me. Look at the other one she's with looking at me. They hate me!"

"They sure do."

Chris was a good guy. I could tell. But he was too transparent, and I feared that he'd been taken advantage of a lot in his life. Left with fortune, unfortunately.

"You ever think about being more . . . ?" he asked, looking up at the lights of the ceiling.

"I don't know," I said, as a surrender.

"Really. Seriously. You're a guy in a similar position. Do you feel like we're, I don't know, kind of a waste of time?"

I wouldn't answer.

"I do," he went on. "My father never tried to make me feel worthless—but he did it by not trying. It made me feel more pathetic because he tiptoed around it. I think of things," he continued. "I think of new ideas all the time. But I can't do a thing about them. I'm not given the opportunity to make them real. Our parents can make anything real, but we can't. I bet I have more great ideas than most people. I've thought of a solution for almost every major world issue. I've tried to pitch my ideas. No one cares. Even for people in our position, no one cares. They don't want us. No one wants us to succeed on our own terms. We're stuck. Just stuck. With nowhere to go. To just live in the shadow of our fathers."

I grabbed another beer.

"I'll get one," Chris demanded, snapping his fingers at me.

I threw him the beer.

"Tim Argosy," he said between big gulps of the beer. "Fucking legend. First guy to do his own shit. Breaking boundaries. Tearing down that mold we're all stuck in. How the hell did he do it? To work under your father and do what he did—all on his own. How the hell . . . ?"

He burped. "Tim Argosy is my idol. If only I knew him well enough to be my mentor. I would kill to learn from him. To see how he did it. What he did. The impossible, really. The only reason why I built up my music career was because of him—Tim fucking Argosy. The legend. The man who defied all odds. The world working against him . . . and he still wins."

He stopped. And something sparked in that quaint mind of his. The spark was like a pilot light not catching.

"Hatin' n' heaven," he echoed his internal dialogue. "Hatin' n' heaven. Hatin' n' heaven. Hatin' n' heaven."

I would let him tease out whatever this was.

"See, man. These are the ideas that flow in, second after second. Like this one. A new song of mine. I know we're friends, but our dads weren't very fond of each other; let's be honest. But they're in heaven together, I believe that. I truly do. They're onto the next life, hatin' each other in heaven."

He took on a Southern accent again, like some country singer. I don't know why.

"I'm gonna write a song about fathers. Hatin' n' heaven. The song I'm remembered for. I'll be the Tim Argosy of music. Because if any of us have to hear another big hit Eminem song, I think we're all gonna fucking blow our heads off. People need something fresh. Not another piece of music from a hologram. They need real heart and art. Not for everyone to blow their fucking heads off."

• • •

Mashed cauliflower mixed in a thick and dark tomato sauce splashed against my face. Eggshell fragments due to bad cooking cut at my face and my sudden shout echoed in the abrupt stillness of this horrific surprise.

Tyler's head split in two and the brain loosened itself from its chamber like a yolk slipping out of the shell onto some Teflon surface.

• • •

I cleared my throat and scratched my leg to nudge the thought off the edge of my conscience.

"You alright?" Chris asked.

"I think I have to—"

"You allergic to something?"

"Headache, you know."

"You're clearing your throat and scratching yourself—that seems like an allergic reaction."

"I'm fine," I answered, needing him to just shut up.

"Got the old PTSD," he smirked and smugly reflected on some very big-small event in his past.

"It's written all over you," he went on, "unless you're about to go into anaphylactic shock. Why don't you sit."

Then he had me follow him into the living room like he was my bodyguard. Parting the crowd, the severity of my situation gave him a level of importance in this ensuing drama. He craved possible disaster and he hoped to be lead actor in this scene where James Anglish, the son of Fep Anglish, finally meets his end.

I sprawled out on some other couch covered with half-eaten hors d'oeuvres and mopped red with wine stains.

"Jaclyn" I said, in a daze.

"Everyone," he announced to the party. "Back the fuck up."

"What's happening?" they all asked.

"My friend has a fever."

"Oh gosh," the crowd responded. "How bad?" they asked.

He felt my forehead.

"Jesus Christ," he announced. "He's burning up."

"Oh no!" the crowd panicked. "He has the virus."

"No," he announced. "It's not the virus."

"How the fuck do you know, Dr. Chris?" a guy screamed, separating himself from the crowd.

"Carl, it isn't," Chris insisted and felt my forehead again.

"Let me ask again—how the fuck do you know?"

"Well, I don't. I mean . . . I think he's having a panic attack. He has PTSD. I know because I have PTSD."

"The fuck you have PTSD."

"I do. You know what, fuck you, Carl."

Carl pushed his chest up to Chris like some animal. A knife was in Carl's hand.

"You want to fuck with me, Chris?"

Chris stood like Russell Crowe in *Gladiator*. He would be the hero, Carl the villain.

"I'm not fucking with you," Carl warned.

"What are you going to do, Carl?"

"I'm warning you."

"This man is sick."

The knife went into Chris' lower stomach and blood flowed out in its warm and calm way. It was such a clean puncture through the clothing and then the skin. Went right in, very deep. The blade came out in a swift motion, and he wiped off the blood from the knife with his shirt.

"I warned him," he told the crowd.

"He didn't say sorry," they said together.

"I'm sorry," they chanted.

"I'm sorry."

"I'm sorry."

"I'm sorry."

The hysteria built on itself and reached a fever pitch like it'd done in the park. People began to cry and laugh and dance and shake, all within the confines of this extravagant apartment. For the first time ever, I really needed Beasley and Tennyson. What a thing this would be to tell them after they woke from their drunken denial in the morning.

Chris lay dying on the floor and I lay still from those memories of horror crashing through my skull. The pain of bad memories. The blood bubbling out of Chris' organs and some severed artery. Watching it spread across the floor, the coagulation gripping into the grooves and the blood still liquified enough to move on its own. Streams of blood marching through grooves, through the indifferent crowd, through the furniture, splitting at the walls, and running along those edges.

CHAPTER FIFTEEN

Remember, The Mop

"Honey, honey, swim to me," my mother called, standing in one of the streams running through the marshland. "Come on, Jamie."

I treaded in the water, the dog following behind me.

"Great, see, honey, you're a swimmer."

Swimming to her, I asked, "Can't Daddy swim?"

"No," she answered, "but he loves watching us."

"Can't he use his arms?"

"I don't think he wants to try."

"I would still swim."

"Well, let's see. Try to swim with just your arms."

I tried to swim and sank.

My mother laughed as I rose to the surface.

"That's why Daddy doesn't like to swim. Imagine doing that all the time. It would be exhausting."

She pulled herself onto the dock, helped me out, dried me off, and then went inside the house to get lemonade and coffee. I sat down on the wood planks of the dock, peering up at my father in his wheelchair.

As he stretched his stiff body downwards to hand me my toy pipe, I had that look children possess when they see something different.

"Daddy," I asked, fingering the pipe in that distracted way kids play with toys, "Mommy won't ever tell me. Why are you in that wheelchair? Did you have an accident, Daddy?"

"Did Mommy say anything?" he asked.

"I wanted her to—but she wouldn't."

"That's good. That's good."

"Daddy, why is that good?"

"Because you wouldn't want to know."

"I do want to."

"I don't think you would."

"Please. Oh, please. I promise I won't tell Mommy I know."

He inhaled in that severe way of his to suck in as much oxygen as possible.

"You want to know, boy?" he asked again, now to tease.

"Yes, please. I won't tell anyone."

"It's not much of a thing. You'll be very disappointed in this story. But I'll tell it because my son wants me to tell it. I was in an accident, James. I broke both of my legs. They're shattered in about a hundred places—each leg."

"How did you do that?"

"Well, I was driving—and I didn't stop. I wouldn't stop."

"Was there something wrong with the car?"

"No, boy, there's something wrong with me."

I had that look children possess when they see something different.

"It's an adult thing," he continued. "Why don't you ask your sister about it."

"Why would she know?"

I put the pipe into my mouth and my teeth clanked against the polished wood.

"She's your big sister. She knows everything."

He called Jaclyn and I saw the sail reverse direction.

"She's gotten pretty good at it," he said, proud. "Very good at it. That's my rosebud."

"Dad," she called. "Give me a second."

"Take your time, Rosebud. Take all the time you need."

"Want a real pipe?" he asked me.

He was bored of waiting for my sister and wanted to entertain himself with my ignorance and youth.

"Mommy said I can't have a real pipe."

"But what about Daddy? What if he says it's fine to have a real pipe?"

I was unable to give him an answer.

"What if I was to say you could take a puff of my pipe right now?"

"Daddy, where is your pipe?"

"It's in my pocket right now, ready to be lit."

"Mommy said—"

"No need to worry about what Mommy says. It's what I say, you hear?"

"Yes, Daddy."

"Call me *Father*. Because I am The Father."

I had that look children possess when they see something different.

"Who brought you into this world?" he went on.

"I came out of Mommy."

"But who went into her to get to you?"

I was unable to give him an answer.

"I guess you're not big enough for my pipe. Your sister is, though."

"Jaclyn has a pipe?"

"Oh, she likes pipes. My pipe, especially. She's my rosebud, you hear."

Jaclyn docked her Sunfish and had a beaten obedience in her stride as she answered to my father.

• • •

"Take it," Chris said.

The cut plug was soaked in blood and his hands shook. His body was shutting down.

"That's mine," a woman said, puncturing the crowd to tear the cut plug from Chris' weak and shaking grip.

"The asshole who wouldn't give me his gum," she went on and put the cut plug in her pocket.

"Grab . . ." Chris attempted.

"Grab tha . . ." he attempted again.

"Grab the cut plug," he got out through the blood bubbles forming from his lips.

"I know this is something else," her voice said as she disappeared into the crowd. "This has something to do with that virus. Don't think I didn't hear you two. I know when guys are up to something. Both of you."

She didn't know me. It was more about me as a man than it was about me as an individual.

And then the crowd went silent.

Chris was dead.

The woman entered through the crowd again and took firm centerstage.

"Tell us what this really is," she demanded from me.

Eyes all around.

"Tell us," the hysterics began.

"Tell us," the crowd chanted.

"Tell us."

"Tell us."

"Tell us."

"It's a cure," I confessed.

"A cure?" she asked.

"Yes. A cure."

"What—you chew it?"

She inspected the cut plug.

"You put it under your lip."

"And then you're protected?"

"From what I was told, yes."

"How many do you have?"

"I don't have any."

"Liar!"

"Liar!" the crowd went.

"Liar!"

"Liar!"

"Liar!"

"I'm not lying. I promise, I'm not lying."

"Check his fucking pockets," she said.

Two guys came over and picked me up from my armpits and a third guy searched my pockets.

"Seems clean," the guy said.

The three went back into the crowd.

"Where can we get more?" she asked, tapping her foot, and crossing her arms.

"He said he had some at his apartment."

"A lot more?"

"From what he told me, a lot."

"You know where he's renting?"

"No."

"Don't lie to *me*."

"I don't know where he lives."

"Anyone," she belted, "anyone got this dead man's address?"

Many raised their hands.

"*You*," she barked, picking one from the crowd, "the overly eager one over there."

"One Eighty-Five West Seventy-Fourth Street," the woman said. "I've been there a few times."

"Have you seen this cut plug thing?"

"No, not when I was there."

"Well, let's find out, shall we."

She was a good leader and the drama she built really did grab people. This crowd was hers until—

"Who put you in charge?" some frat king said from the crowd. He appeared from the layers of bodies and stood in front of her, chest out and towering.

"Get your White pretentious creepiness away from me," she said and turned around.

"Excuse me," he said and walked around her.

"You heard what I said."

"I know what you said."

"I can say whatever the fuck I want. I wrote a book about *you people*."

He laughed. "You wrote a book?" he breathed into her face. "That makes it okay, right? Because you wrote a book."

"In fact, it does. You see, I'm a bit of an authority on White supremacy and White elitism. I've self-published two books on it already."

"Did you write anything in those books about me?"

"Those like you. That's enough for a trilogy."

"What about my white ass? You write about that?"

He bent over to show her his butt.

"Certainly not," she retreated into some proper Jane Austen character. "How dare you say and show such things."

"I dare say anything I want," he moaned and grabbed at her.

"Get off of me," she went on, still British.

"Is God Black?" he asked and then knelt, now eye level with her.

"God is most certainly *not*."

"What is he then?"

"I wouldn't know. I have not written about God yet."

"So, you will?"

"I haven't thought about it."

"But you said 'yet.'"

"I guess there's always a chance."

"Do me a favor."

"Yes . . ."

"Tell me what He looks like."

The frat guy pulled out a gun and laughed and cried and moaned. He sucked on the gun and then rubbed it along her face.

"I can't," she cried.

"Here's your chance," he screamed and then giggled like a child.

He fired the shot right to her temple. Vaporized blood shot out the other side of her head like steam spewing out the neck of a teakettle. The bullet wouldn't stay in her brain and made a new home in someone else's head. Without intention, this man killed two people. Dominos!

"If that's what you need right now," the crowd said.

"If that's what you need right now," they said again.

"If that's what you need right now," they chanted.

"If that's what you need right now."

"If that's what you need right now."

"If that's what you need right now."

The chanting wouldn't stop, and the floor was painted in blood.

"That's fucking right what I goddamn need right now," I heard him declare through the chanting.

"One Eighty-Five West Seventy-Fourth Street," someone called, redirecting the chant.

"One Eighty-Five West Seventy-Fourth Street," they said.

"One Eighty-Five West Seventy-Fourth Street."

"One Eighty-Five West Seventy-Fourth Street."

"One Eighty-Five West Seventy-Fourth Street."

The Society of Entropy could not be contained by 740 Park. Emotions were pressure-cooking themselves to collective suicide. Seven people from the chanting crowd opened the windows and jumped out to their deaths. Living bodies fell like dead leaves. Three more followed, still chanting as they were falling. And another two went after that. Death was the escape from having a nervous breakdown. And this crowd was one big nervous breakdown.

The frat king began chanting the street address and he punched a woman in the face due to his firing testosterone. A few guys from the crowd got into a brawl and a broken wine decanter was used as a weapon. It worked like a knife right into another guy's throat. He fell to the ground, breathing through the blood-bubbling hole in his neck. He scratched at something in the air as he tried to grab another breath. The other guys kept fighting around him and one of them stepped on the dying man's face.

A few more brawls broke out and women undressed and danced around the fights singing and crying and shaking. They wiggled their breasts around and curled their faces and made disturbing gestures. Spitting on the ground, they then hopped up into the air and then fell to the ground. They then got up and hopped up in the air and then fell to the ground once again. On the ground, they rolled around, pretending to foam from the mouth. Fake convulsions. It was horrible, but it looked like they were making fun of that guy, now dead, with the cut-open throat.

It was wicked. Not just the death. But the lack of control. And the ability to do very bad things in such a casual manner. And I was wicked for watching and doing nothing about it. I was a horrible person.

Then—more guns went off.

A wacko with a small machine gun sprayed the crowd with bullets. Bullet after bullet after bullet. It seemed to never end. I took cover in the bathroom. It was a safe place because no one knew where it was. Beasley and Tennyson peed on the floor, so they never looked for it. They peed in front of each other, too, throughout the rest of the apartment. And, like a coward, I remained in this bathroom until the machine gunfire stopped. And then I heard a knock on the front door. I could hear the wacko walk to the door and answer it like he had a pizza delivery.

"Yes?" he asked and opened the door.

I was unable to hear the other voice.

"Sorry," he answered. "There'll be no more noise coming from here."

The door shut and the wacko walked past the bathroom door and talked to himself.

"Chatter, chatter, chatter," he said. "And I shut them *all* up."

ALERT, the speaker in my wrist said. My wrist then vibrated.

ALERT, the speaker in my wrist said. My wrist then vibrated.

ALERT, the speaker in my wrist said. My wrist then vibrated.

"Shut the fuck up," I yelled through a whisper.

"Who's there?" the wacko said.

I covered my mouth like all those characters did in the horror movies.

"Who's there?" he repeated. "I know someone's there," he went on. "Ten seconds to come out!"

A pause.

What do I do?

What do I do?

What do I do?

"Come out, come out, wherever you are!"

"Ten," he counted down.

"Nine."

"Eight."

"Seven."

"Six."

"Five."

"Four."

"Three."

"Okay!" I gave in.

I opened the bathroom door and walked over to this wacko.

"Look!" he laughed, his face covered in everyone else's blood. He looked like Carrie from that Stephen King story. "The man of the house!"

I stopped about three feet from him. I was on trial for my life.

"I had to stop the chatter," he told me, kicking someone's hand away from his shoes. "Too much of it all around, you know."

"Yes," was all I could say.

"You're here with Beaz and Tenny?"

"Yes."

"They're niiice."

"Yes."

"I'm glad they invited me to this party. I'm not part of this Society of Entropy, you know."

"I didn't know."

"You assumed I was?"

"No, I just didn't know. I didn't think to even assume."

"I know what you're thinking."

"What am I thinking?"

"That this is the most horrible thing you've ever witnessed."

I didn't say a thing and held my breath and tried to move as little as possible. I wanted nothing to be mistaken as aggression. To an unstable mind like this, a twitch could mean a lunge.

"They were going to kill themselves whether I did this or not. They're a suicidal bunch."

No movement on my part.

"I'm glad Beaz and Tenny didn't have to see this. I'm sorry you had to."

"I'm sorry," he repeated.

"I'm sorry," he chanted.

"I'm sorry."

"I'm sorry."

"I'm sorry."

"It's fine," I finally said to put an end to this chanting. I would risk my life to get him to shut up.

"I'm kidding," he giggled.

No movement on my part.

"You know," he stuttered. "I'm not a brutal man. I just do brutal things."

"It's fine," I repeated.

"It's so much easier to hate than to love. Loving takes work."

He moved so gradually toward me I hadn't noticed how close he really got.

"Loving takes so much damn exhausting work," he said, his lips now inches away from mine. "If I could only tell you how much work it really takes."

The sticky wetness of his lips now slugged along mine and then that filthy, wormy tongue entered.

"If only you knew," he moaned between kisses.

I was like kissing a statue. And I could tell he was getting impatient.

"I know," I said, gradually kissing him back so he got the attention he craved.

"We're very alike," he moaned. "I know you have real disease. I have real disease."

"I know," I repeated.

"You know how I know?" he asked.

"How?"

He searched the dark cherry red floor with his feet, smearing the blood around while smiling. Then he found what he was looking for. He leaned down in a girlish way and pulled at an arm from the pile of bodies. It looked like he caught a fish and he yanked away at this arm and the body finally released itself from the mound of death.

"I can't believe it," he said, crying and laughing. "Someone here is wearing a purple dress."

I didn't know how to respond.

"What if I put on this purple dress?"

I really didn't know how to respond.

He tore the dress off the body and released her back into the sea of blood.

"I wonder . . ." he pondered, putting the tip of his finger on his lip as he held the dress up to himself.

"It . . . could . . . just . . . work!"

He clapped his hands and spun with the dress tight to his chest.

"I love it. I love it. I love it," he chanted to himself.

He put the dress on, over his blood-soaked clothes.

"Do I look divine?" he asked me.

"Yes," I answered.

It was the brightest and purest purple I had seen—an electric purple.

"You don't approve?" he sighed, as his face went from a wickedly extreme smile to a clownish frown.

"I . . ."

"And you're nervous."

"I'm not."

"Shhh. I'm not the one to be nervous about. It's *them*—"

He pointed out the window and checked the sky for aliens, I assumed.

"You know what they do out there?"

"What do they do out there?" With someone like this, it was best to repeat their own words.

"What don't they do?" he giggled. "They put stuff in the air to make us all nuts. They want us to kill each other so the world can be run by holograms. They want humanity gone. We'll be in those computer chips soon enough. Downloaded consciousness. Ghosts moving about. You understand? This is choreographed. You, me—we're in an apocalyptic musical. 'Apocalypse, A Musical.' A very, very, very dark play."

"And, and, and, and . . ." he continued before I could cushion the conversation with my filler talk. "Your mother. I met her in the loony bin, you know. Real disease there. Not like these dead creatures all around us who spent their days begging for attention. I have this. I have that. Help me. Help me. Help me!"

He was speaking into my throat as he talked between kisses. And I hated myself for it. You always knew you were faking it well when you hated yourself for it.

"They don't have the problems we have. Like social anxiety is a fucking problem. Maybe because people like Dr. Barnstormer create panic and tell everyone they're going to bleed out of their eyes and die. And it's funny—hysterical— because all the people in this little party were worried to death about death . . . and look at them now. I am the virus. We are the virus. Your father was a virus to your mother. Did you know that? Well, I do. Your mother told me that in the loony bin. And for all your indifference, you're pretty fucked up, too. I can see it. You want to eat the eyeballs right out of my head, don't ya? Pop them with your teeth. Let the eye juices explode from the pressure of your teeth. Suck out the juices, right? Suck them all out. You don't love me. You hate me."

He pulled away and I kept my composure.

"Look at you," he laughed. "All the squeaky wheels around you have gotten greased and you're still waiting for it—and you're the rustiest fucking one. No one cares about you. No one cares about me. You influence or you're influenced. And, if you're not either, you're not in existence. You're a nothing. A ghost. We're ghosts, you see. Floating about and killing things. I knew your mother well in that loony bin. Wowie, I knew her *in* and *out*. But . . . we won't go there. I have manners. I was raised well. Raised proper. Proper breeding. Prized, I am. Very prized. A thing to behold. Fine, fine, fine—*very fine*—breeding."

I kept my composure. Not a sound.

"We're buried in other people's problems. Our daddies and mommies can't get to us until they get to the rest. Those fakers. Sympathy sluts."

He pushed his hair back and the coagulated blood acted as mousse for the strands.

"But we do like the melodrama, *you and me*. I mean, I don't know what to make of all of this."

He broke into uncontrollable laughter, which then turned into a song, which then turned into bursts of sobbing.

"There are just so many dead bodies. And, I have to say, it's kinda funny. Alive one minute, dead the next. Boom. Done. Outta tha pahk."

He now had a Boston accent.

"Should I cry? Should I laugh? Should I kill more? Should I kill myself? Should I just scream for the rest of my life until my head explodes? A self-induced stroke, possibly."

The Boston accent fell into a very odd Australian-American one now.

"I can see your eyes rolling around in your head—just like mine. We don't know what to feel. And we do horrible things to try and get a grip on the correct emotions. But not even murder can do that. I don't even feel remorse. I feel everything all at the same time. I could laugh through the crying and cry through the laughing. You feel the same. I could tell. Your indifference tells of it. You have it even worse than I do, though. The emotions have cancelled each other out in that head of yours. There's so much coming in all at once, they've managed to cancel each other out. You can't feel a thing—and I *love you* for that. You're still alive right now because I love you so. Because you may pretend to yourself you fear me. But you don't. Not a bit. I can see it in you. A threat on your life means absolutely nothing. Why, I wonder . . . ? It's not that you don't care about yourself. Because *you do*. We're all vain as holy hell. It's that you don't know what to believe anymore. The emotions are so untrue, and the facts are so bendy. Really, what can anyone make of anything anymore? Are these bodies around you really even dead? Was this one big act? This is all in your head. And, even if it's not, did I do a bad thing? I'm the judge of my own moral code. And I think this shootout was very well deserved. It's not like I'm going to jail for it. See, I'm the one to decide my sentencing. But I don't care. So, I'll move on from this like I move on from everything else. Isn't it horrible . . . no one cares when bad things happen to others. They'll cry about injustice and inequality but they don't care about each other. They wouldn't fight for each other. They, instead, fight to prove something to themselves; the contradictions, the lies—I've been lied to enough, and I'm sure you've also been lied to enough. You *really, really* seem like someone who doesn't know what to believe anymore. A*m I even real*? The world plays games with you, as it does with all of us. We've been lied to."

He pushed his hair back again and the hardened chocolate-fudge blood flaked off as his creepy long fingers wormed through his sticky hair strands.

"Guess you'll have to call up The Mop for this one."

He threw his gun out the window and I heard it crash against the concrete.

"I guess," I replied, so weakly I could hardly feel myself say it.

"You will," he laughed and rested his hand on my shoulder. He was so close to me, and I could feel his jealousy and anger and hate for humanity through the proximity. I knew it very well from Beasley and, sometimes, even more from Tennyson.

"I will." I corrected myself.

"Because—" he whispered, "I'm going to take Chris' slot and rent this. You can hold like four-hundred people in here. What an amazing space to entertain in. A party apartment. And such a luxurious zip. Beaz gets what she wants, you know. I'll call her up tomorrow when she wakes up and let her know I'm taking Chris' spot."

He took on another accent and threw his jacket over his shoulder. He would leave with the dress still on.

"Remember, The Mop," he called from the door, opening it slow enough for it to shriek.

"Remember, The Mop," he said again, closing the door behind him just as slow.

"Remember, The Mop," he said once more, his voice now muffled behind this closed door.

Then—

Silence.

Those dead bodies . . .

All around me.

Oh my god!

CHAPTER SIXTEEN

....

The Sentinelese

The Mop came the next morning. They didn't ask questions and tacked on a huge fee to the rent. I expected that. But Beasley and Tennyson had a bit more of a surprise.

"Thirty-three thousand dollars!" Beasley cried. "How in the hell . . ."

"Thirty-three thousand," Tennyson chimed in, unable to fully open his eyes. "What happened last night?"

It was amazing. The cost of cleanup was more of a concern than the Blue Alerts we were getting all morning.

The Blue Alert was an alert of maximum urgency. It was only issued by Blue Planet United and, when it came from Israel, you might as well be prepared for the end of times. But the sensationalism of the lethally addicting world-ending news coverage numbed us to any alert really, whether it was blue or orange or green.

A charge of $33,000 would take priority over this Blue Alert, for now. Even when that high-priority alert allowed government officials from Israel to hijack your Body Tech (aka the phones in our wrists) and transmit messages that traveled through the nerves up into the spinal cord and, from your spinal cord, into the cells of the brain, all in an organized effort to peddle this torturous inner monologue of paranoia. In short, Blue Alerts hijacked your thoughts with Breaking News updates. It took a lot of sensationalist-numbing to be able to ignore that Breaking News voice in your head. And, recently, through certain human rights initiatives, this hijacking of human thought was banned for most circumstances. Alerts were very rare now, but we still had them under certain political and security loopholes.

"What happened?" Tennyson asked again, like a father would ask after a long night of work.

"I have to go to school," I answered, too tired to get into it.

"Before you go off to school," Tennyson insisted, "why don't you tell me what in the world's hell happened here?"

I had anger in my calm. And Tennyson felt it.

"Well," I began, "when I came in, you guys had the whole Society of Entropy here. They made a mess—a huge mess. So, I had to call The Mop to clean it up. You guys know the premiums of off-schedule cleanups."

"Exactly," Beasley said, "so why didn't you wait for us to clean it up? We could've done it ourselves."

"I don't think you would've wanted to."

"Why not?" they both asked. How cute—in unison. Angry parents, they were.

"Well, for one thing, there was a fucking massacre."

"A massacre?" they both asked. How cute again. Two for two!

"Yes, a fucking massacre. You guys invited a loony to our apartment, and he shot up the whole place, killing everyone."

"Who was this?" Beasley asked.

"I have no idea. I'm just glad he spared my life. But he knew you guys. He said you invited him. Other than that, I have no other information."

"He killed all of them?" Tennyson asked, pretending to care about the casualties.

"Not all. A few jumped out of the windows. But I'm assuming they're dead, too."

Tennyson went upstairs to think, regroup, and go back to sleep.

"This is horrible," Beasley panicked. "I think I know who he is. I shouldn't have brought any of them here. I was just . . . ahhh, so messed up, you know. The drugs. And the drinking. The heroin. The crack. The nicotine. The methadone. The crystal meth. The barbiturates. The alcohol. The cocaine. The amphetamines. The benzodiazepines. All of it. That's what they do, the Society of Entropy. I don't know how they do it . . . why they do it. And they got me into it. What it does to you, how it makes you think. I shouldn't have brought them here. It was a mistake."

"It was a mistake," I said, out of character.

"I'm sorry?"

How dare I question Beasley's authority, especially when she's strong enough to admit her own faults. That's real power, admitting your own faults.

"The Mop had to clean up a lot of bodies," I continued to move on from her combative response.

"I'm sorry," she gave in. "I really am. I don't know what else to say."

"There's not much else to say."

I searched for my backpack and found the L.L. Bean bag my father had given me years back. It was over a century old, and it had the silver nylon reflective diagonal strip that went along the front zipper and below the stitched initials that read "FA." This was the bag my father had worn when he went to school. It was the one thing of his I owned. The backpack of his youth. The object that would keep me a child forever because it represented my condition, a student for life. This L.L. Bean backpack was his lasting gift to me and I paid (well, my trust paid) the government close to $17,000 a month for it. For a hundred-year-old L.L. Bean backpack. And, unfortunately, it didn't take my classmates long to discover it was a "hoarded possession." A few months of wearing the same thing flagged me as a hoarder. And they hated me for it. It was the scarlet letter on my back. Until, of course, I became the good old storyteller I was and revealed the truth to these students of grand opinions and unmatched moral authority. This wasn't just any backpack. This had once been worn by Fep Anglish himself. Right then and there, I had them. Their insatiable anger converted into hungered intrigue—unending wonder. This put an end to the shaming. And it also blossomed my popularity. And I took care of this bag like a bear takes care of its cub. It was important to my reputation, and I made sure it was in perfect shape. And I'd worry about it all the time. And I'd worry about it now. Was there some unseen blood stain on this precious item? Was there?

Let me check. Let me check. Let me check. Jesus, a massacre had just occurred the night before and I was worried about bloodstains on my bag. And I scanned it like a bloodhound searching for a body in the woods. And Beasley watched me from some faraway place, the lenses of her eyes clouded by a stress she had never experienced before. Those eyes of hers resembling dead cataract fisheyes peering out of a mucus-lathered carcass chilled on ice. She wasn't there. Fried by the guilt, she was off somewhere else. I had never seen her wear that type of emotion before. And it made her realer than ever. Her hair, a mess. Her face, white and gray and cadaver-like. But, as authentic as this was, it was still such stunted emotion. So stunted, she put toast in the toaster. So stunted, Tennyson was upstairs asleep. So stunted, I went off to school.

The professors treated me like Harry Potter at U-University. After I survived my father's suicide and returned to class with those scars on my face, I was really like Harry Potter to them. The boy who survived the accident. I must've had special powers. The force was with me. I think that's from *Star Wars*, but whatever. Both are fantasy stories.

Anyway, Rick had organized my schedule. Well, Rick's minions had organized my schedule. I had two classes in the morning, a one-hour lunchbreak, and then three more classes in the afternoon. My morning class was a creative writing course. We would read a book and then write a short-story version of that book. The class was designed to make you think as concisely as possible. *The Great Gatsby* was our first book. It wasn't long, which I liked. And the story wasn't that hard to paraphrase. But when I used the word "paraphrase" in class, the professor took personal offense to it.

"How dare you," Professor Nelson said. "It isn't paraphrasing. I'm not here teaching you to paraphrase."

"I'm sorry, Professor Nelson," I apologized.

• • •

My father punched me in the nose, and I fell backward into the stream running through the marshland. When I came to the surface covered in my own blood, I could see that sick and twisted and gnarled smirk he had on his face. Like the Grinch from Dr. Seuss' *How the Grinch Stole Christmas!* I had watched so many times. That type of extreme contortion of the face muscles to convey sudden gratification. He was a very sick man, my father.

"Don't be a bitch," he laughed. "Pull up your own weight. Get on the dock, boy."

I was tired and floundered in the water.

"Come on," he yelled.

I floundered more.

"Pull that dead weight you are."

I still floundered.

"Enough of the drama," he snapped and lunged his wheelchair toward me.

"Alright," I said, catching my breath.

"It's always breaktime with you. Catching your breath. Feeling your emotions. Cry here, cry there, cry over there. Cry boy. Cry boy. Cry boy."

My soaked clothes added weight and I made sure I had enough forward momentum the first time to pull myself up. If I'd failed and had to pull myself up a second time, my father would've surely slapped me for that. I was young and had no excuse to be out of shape. I had to be able to pull my own weight. And I did. Success! And, shivering with self-reward, I took a moment to survey the horizon line and caught sight of a sailboat entering the marshland.

"I think that's her," I said, jumping up and down. "That's her!"

"Are you sure?"

"Yes. It's Jaclyn."

"You better be sure, boy."

"Jaclyn!" I called.

It echoed down the wet moss and thick mud.

"James!" she called back.

"Quick, Jaclyn, quick. A storm is coming."

"I know. I know. Coming in."

I paced the dock and chewed my nails. My father rolled himself back to the house and watched us from the back porch. My mother was surely asleep upstairs.

I could see Jaclyn's face now. She was close enough.

"Amazing," she said. "So amazing out there."

Unable to stop my pacing from the excitement, I decided to jump into the stream to put an end to this jittering.

"What was that for?" Jaclyn asked. She had great balance and stood on the sailboat and tied it up to the dock.

"I don't know," I answered, spitting out water.

"Are you bleeding?"

"I slipped."

"Oh."

I pulled myself up from the stream and Jaclyn effortlessly hopped off the sailboat onto the dock.

"Did you go to the ocean?" I asked.

She saw I was cold and wrapped a towel around me.

"How did you slip?" she asked, ignoring my question.

"On the dock. I had a running start for the stream, and I slipped on the wood."

"Oh."

"Did you go to the ocean?" I asked again.

"Amazing. Don't tell Mom and Dad. I went really far out."

"How far?"

"Farther than I've ever been."

"How far is that?"

"I'd say . . . ten miles. Actually more. The whole coastline was so far away, and the wind grabbed me a couple of times. I really had to fight it."

I began to cry.

"Jamie James."

She tucked me under her armpit, and I walked with her down the dock to the house. Our father was watching us.

"Come on, Jamie James. I'll always come back. Trust me, there's—"

Our father's Grinch face cut Jaclyn off, mid-thought.

"Hi Daddy," she said and put her hair in a bun. My father demanded her hair be in a bun when she was around him. My sister always let her hair out when she was alone with me.

"Where the hell have you been?" he burped the words.

"Sailing."

"Don't be a *bitch* with me."

"I was sailing, Daddy."

"Yes, I know—but *where* were you sailing?"

"Right beyond the streams. Under the bridge."

"We didn't see you."

"I was about fifty meters beyond the bridge. You can't see that from here."

"Does a *bitch* like you take notice of the weather?"

"I did, Daddy. I came right back. I saw the clouds and turned right around. The wind made me a little slower."

"You were out too long," he burped once more and then turned his wheelchair around to go inside. My sister could fight him off and I loved her for that. What a big sister. More of a mother, really.

"We're sorry," I said for her, knowing she had already won.

"Rosebud!" my father called.

Her face turned white, and her tiredness manifested itself through her sunken eye sockets. She was too young to have that. My mother had that.

"Yes, Daddy," she answered.

"Come inside with your brother. Leave him downstairs and come up to me. I think you know what happens on stormy days. I want my rosebud."

. . .

"I'm sorry," the class echoed in unison.

"I'm sorry," we all went on.

"I'm sorry."

"I'm sorry."

"I'm sorry."

If one student did something wrong, the entire class had to apologize for their actions. It was the professor's way of promoting the collective, never the individual. None of us were individuals. We could take this class to learn how to write, but none of us would really be writers. Tim Argosy was an anomaly, and those anomalies happened once every two hundred years. I'm saying two hundred years because Professor Nelson said things like that happened only once every two hundred years. He also bragged about knowing Tim Argosy. I doubted if he really did. But I believed he met him. I just didn't believe they were friends. Professor Nelson and Tim Argosy didn't seem like similar people to me. And I knew they didn't know each other very well because a real friend would know about the present condition of Tim Argosy. What my father had done to his career.

"Mr. Argosy and I have been friends for years," he said.

Even though the average age of this classroom was thirty-five years old, Professor Nelson still referred to people as Mr. this and Mrs. that.

"Really, Professor," an idiot behind me marveled. "Oh, what is he like, Professor?"

"More normal than you may assume. He's been in this classroom before. He came to visit many years back. I had him as a visiting student for two weeks. It was an honor."

The shock and awe pervaded the classroom. It smelled of sweat and wet wood. Too many adult children packed into one lecture hall.

"Mr. Argosy can turn any one of these books into one-page masterpieces. He could turn *The Great Gatsby* into a paragraph. My objective is to find the Tim Argosy in *you*. To see if it's there. For you to write with firm precision and excel by learning from the greats. I've been a professor now for, what is it, a little over forty years, and I've yet to publish something of any worth. If professors can't get published, the likelihood of any of you getting published is a very, let's say, *daunting* proposition. Is there a Kuzmanovich amongst us? How about a Dickens? Maybe a Hemingway? Could there be a James Joyce?"

To become a professor wasn't an easy thing. It took decades of being a student and maintaining an average GPA of 4.0 and above. That was nearly impossible. The grade deflation at my school was so intense that getting a B- felt like getting an A. Professor Nelson refused to give out an A, not even an A-. Eric Bonofaci, the most brilliant student of this class, had the benchmark GPA of 3.3, which really wasn't much of a benchmark. And I knew something the professor didn't know. This little B+ model student of his wasn't that brilliant. His deceit was brilliant. By that I mean, he plagiarized in a very skilled way from the school's highly regulated archive. Professor Nelson, like all the other professors, had such focused fields they knew everything there was to know about three things and three things only. If it wasn't about those three things, they knew absolutely nothing. For example, Professor Nelson's expertise was in creative writing. The books he chose for this creative writing course were the only books he ever read. F. Scott Fitzgerald's *The Great Gatsby*. Ernest Hemingway's *The Sun Also Rises*. And James Joyce's *Ulysses*. He talked about other writers, but he knew nothing about them. That was the only way you could maintain an average GPA of 4.0 and above. You had to limit your exposure and master minutiae. These educators had all mastered their very specific minutiae to become professors. I could've begun my story with "To be or not to be" and he wouldn't have known the difference. He'd probably give that a C+. If he saw the name "James Anglish" above the type, it was a C+. And, yes, my average was 78 percent. I was a C student, like the rest of them. A class of fifty-eight students. One with a B+, four with a B, two with a B-, and the rest were Cs. At least I didn't have a D. There were about five of those and it was shameful to even look at them. You didn't want their bad grades to rub off on you. Luckily no students were failing. It was almost impossible for you to fail because that reflected on the professor.

Anyway, about seven years ago, I heard there was one student who received an A for the semester. She was in Professor Nelson's creative writing class. I think her name is Heather Davitt. I know for sure her first name is Heather because Professor Nelson used her short stories as inspiration for us. He did this so there was something attainable we could strive for. To be honest, I didn't think her short stories were that good. Derivative, at best. They did what they had to do. I really didn't see how it was any better than the stories I wrote. But, if you became derivative, and maintained that GPA of 4.0 for ten years straight, you were invited by the university to become a professor. It was a strange club to be a part of and I remember my father telling Rick it was a weird club. It was odd if Fep Anglish said it was odd. Because he had a hell of a threshold for strangeness, and it took a lot to break that threshold. And as much as my father supported the educational system, its behaviors made his interactions with these universities very limited. Rick became my father's point of contact, and Frederick Moonch became Rick's point of contact.

Frederick Moonch, or Nineteen Eighty-Four, was a god amongst these professors. Moonch proposed a furthering of educational elitism through his Master of Study program. To be a Master of Study, a professor had to have taught for at least twenty years and, for those twenty-plus years, had to have obtained an average fellow faculty approval rating of 100 percent. With a faculty of eighty-eight judgmental eggheads, a 100 percent approval rating was just about impossible. But if you worked twenty years and everyone unanimously loved you for all those twenty years, you earned the right to buy the rights of your study. That meant a Master of Study who specialized in the plays of William Shakespeare could rewrite *Hamlet* if they so desired. They could erase *Macbeth*. They could change William Shakespeare's name. They could pass off Shakespeare's work as their own. A Master of Study owned their study and could rethread the fabric of history if they desired. They could have their class read *Romeo and Juliet*—a play now written by MS Professor Oscar Kuzmanovich.

There was only one MS Professor at my U-University and thirteen nationwide. The majority of the fifty U-Universities didn't have an MS Professor walking about their campus carried in that throne in their own mind. Oscar Kuzmanovich had a throne on this campus, and he was beloved by the faculty and, in consequence, became a tyrant unto himself. He took everything away from William Shakespeare, the centerpiece of his studies. The only play he left in Shakespeare's name was *Othello*. No one knew why, but he never taught it and the faculty loved him too much to question it. Even Frederick Moonch approved of him, and Frederick Moonch didn't approve of anyone. I mean, how could you not admire a man who wrote *Hamlet, Macbeth, Julius Caesar, King Lear, A Midsummer Night's Dream, The Tempest, The Merchant of Venice, As You Like It,* and on and on his resume went. Oscar Kuzmanovich was the greatest playwright in history, maybe even the greatest writer, ever. That was up for debate. But arguably, he was. And Frederick Moonch pushed that narrative and sent Oscar Kuzmanovich one of those GOAT shirts, with the stupid grazing goat on it. Kuzmanovich would wear this shirt to his class every Friday. He laughed about it, but he loved it more than anything.

"Professor," one of the oldest students asked, "are you friendly with

MS Professor Kuzmanovich?"

Matt Lawrence was almost sixty years old, and he spent much of his life being patronized by Professor Nelson. If anyone was called out in the middle of class, it was Matt. He was an easy target for this professor, and he would take it because he wanted more than anything to publish a book. His class average was a lot worse than mine, and his nickname was "Sock Drawer." Professor Nelson implanted that name, knowing it would stick. A Sock Drawer writer was a term used to describe writers that would never make it. The desire was there but the talent would never meet that desire halfway. I was a Sock Drawer, too. Well, we *all* were. But at least we weren't called it to our face like he was. It was a bad thing to be approaching sixty and finding yourself still bullied. It was a sad thing to watch. And every one of us wondered if Matt Lawrence would become another suicide statistic. I would've if I were him. I already felt like a loser. I can't imagine what it was like to be Matt Lawrence.

"Matt," Professor Nelson spoke from his chest, "why are you interrupting class again?"

"I'm . . ." he attempted.

"I'm . . ." he went on stuttering.

"What, Matt? What are you trying to get out?"

"I'm sorry," he gasped, pushing the words out.

"This is a class about making you a writer. It's not a class about Professor Kuzmanovich."

He was very jealous of Oscar Kuzmanovich and refused to refer to him as MS. Matt had a way of asking him all the wrong questions at all the wrong times. This question of his wasn't designed to push any buttons, rather it had the makings of absent thought presented by an absent mind. And this absent mind of Matt Lawrence was the easiest thing for a man of education to make fun of. I really felt bad for Matt. I hoped he didn't choose suicide. It was too easy to get dramatic and hurt yourself when things didn't go your way.

"The MS thing," the Professor pronounced, "is a bit of a fad. It doesn't say much about one's ability. It's more about popularity. A popularity contest, really. And very, very political. Games and politics. It's not what it seems."

BLUE ALERT.

Wrists vibrating.

Wrists illuminating.

BLUE ALERT.

Wrists vibrating.

Wrists illuminating.

Professor Nelson paused the class to check his update. Even though everyone got updates, too, this was his update—just for him because he was that important. Most of the class watched him check his update instead of checking their own.

BLUE ALERT.

Wrists vibrating.

Wrists illuminating.

Then the voice I ignored so well came into my head.

"BREAKING NEWS," it said.

"Draft notice," it went.

The class held their breath and Professor Nelson was sweating through his shirt.

"A draft?" he questioned.

A few students began to cry, and one had a convulsion on the ground. Professor Nelson didn't help and continued to listen to the update. The convulsing student was flopping on the ground like a hooked fish out of water. Then, he stopped and the foam oozed out and his eyes clouded over.

"You are hereby notified that you are, on the seventh day of June, legally drafted in the service of Blue Planet United for the period of (TBD), in accordance with all provisions for enrolling and calling out the national forces, and for other purposes. You will accordingly report, on or before the seventh of June, at the place of rendezvous, or be deemed a deserter, and be subject to the penalty therefore by the Rules and Articles of War."

Professor Nelson sat down on his little stage set and the students were stunned because he never sat.

"They can't do this," he said. "I'm too old. This isn't fair. It's racist. It's sexist. It's . . . I'm not going. I'm not. I'm not. I'm not. They can't make me."

He began to cry and went into a tantrum. Then he rolled around on his stage with his round body and begged someone we couldn't see for forgiveness.

"Take my students," he begged, "but don't take me."

"Take me," one student said.

"No, take me," another said.

"See," this Professor went on begging, "take them. Not me. I'm too weak to fight."

More Blue Alert information came in, but the class was so distracted by Professor Nelson's prayers. This was too entertaining to ignore. And with the influx of this relentless apocalyptic headline frenzy, it was hard to believe anything anyway. You had to use 5 percent of your brain for breaking news, otherwise you'd lose your mind. You'd go into a state of mania if you gave it your full attention. Like looking at the sun too long, it would blind you. It would sweep you up and make you convulse and die like that guy had. He had a convulsing problem to begin with, but you get what I mean. But I have to say, it was unusual for a Blue Alert to come through like this. That unusualness would raise my attention span to about 10 percent, maybe 15 percent.

Now the professor went into the fetal position and continued to cry.

"I don't want to go," he said in his deepening hysteria. "I don't want to. You can't make me. I have rights. You can't make me. I don't want to die. I don't want to die. I don't want to die. Please, I don't want to die. Take the students. Please, take the students. I don't want to die."

The class cried along with him, and I would try to listen to more of the Blue Alert.

"Oh, god," he went and then the class went.

This was surely interrupting my focus.

"Oh, god," they chanted, following the professor's prayers.

"We can't go to war," they went, shadowing his words.

"We can't," they said.

"We can't."

"We can't."

"We can't."

"Not me," they chanted.

"Take them."

"Not me."

Matt ran to the lecture stage to console Professor Nelson, and he pushed Matt away and continued to bathe in self-pity. Matt cried along with him and, also, rolled around on the floor. A woman behind me started to spit for no apparent reason and a man next to her took out his gun and shot himself. Death was the only option now. You either killed yourself or you cried. Or did what I did, and you just watched the professor and Matt roll around and urinate on themselves. Yes, Professor Nelson began to pee, and Matt followed along.

"Not me," he cried, still peeing.

"Not me," Matt echoed.

"Not me," the class echoed.

"Not me," they all said together.

"Not me," they went.

"Take them."

"Not me."

"Not me."

"Not me."

"The Sentinelese," the Blue Alert punctured through the gale force of this distracting hysteria. I tried to listen. I peeled my eyes off the addicting drama. It was so hard to, but I tried.

"The Sentinelese," the alert continued, "have declared war on Blue Planet United. With an army of less than fifty men and women and a navy with less than a hundred men and women, the BPU will have to defer to the citizens of the satellite states. These citizens will be deployed to Israel to fight on the behalf of the government of the BPU. The Sentinelese, inhabitants of North Sentinel Island in the Bay of Bengal, are a hostile people who readily reject Western values and beliefs. The Nicobarese, the Jarawas, the Great Andamanese, and the Onge have joined forces with the Sentinelese army of three thousand, each obtaining an organized armed force of thirty-five hundred. The Sentinelese, along with their allies, intend to invade Israel with their collective armed forces of 17,500 men. Reports indicate Beashock Barnstormer, former CDC epidemiologist, infiltrated North Sentinel Island and put in place an authoritarian government built to be the powerhouse of biological warfare. With the sole purpose of weaponizing a doomsday virus, Dr. Barnstormer intends to spread this infectious disease throughout Israel and Israel's satellite states, unless the BPU's initiated civilian deployment ceases. Yesterday, Dr. Barnstormer, via satellite state news and other international media outlets, documented the lethality and infectiousness of his virus. Reports from the inside indicate viral culture samples disappeared from thousands of test labs throughout India. Expatriates from the decommissioned CDC are reportedly at the forefront of this weaponization, led by their newly instated leader, Beashock Barnstormer. The hierarchy of leadership and the size of this leadership are unknown. The naval fleet guarding North Sentinel Island makes it impossible for BPU's special forces to gather intelligence. The BPU's military council, as of now, refuses to cease deployment of their citizens and, in reaction, issued a first-wave special forces initiative, aimed at penetrating the island's supposed biological warfare plant. By attacking the source, the BPU's military council believes they can bypass civilian deployment. Until further notice, a draft is still in effect."

"There may not be a draft," I yelled across the lecture hall. I couldn't help myself. It just came out. I was thrilled. I didn't want to fight. There was really no country to fight for anyway. Why would I fight for a country that bestowed upon me this boring life?

Professor Nelson and Matt stopped rolling around on the ground.

"How do you know?" Professor Nelson asked.

"Yeah, how do you know?" Matt asked.

"The report," I answered. "The Blue Alert. It said."

"It said what?" Tweedledee asked and then Tweedledum asked.

Neither of them knew what they were asking. Not a person in this classroom listened to the alert. They reacted and panicked and cried and died and rolled around and spit for some reason. But they had no idea what was going on. A draft, that's what they heard. They only had to hear that. Not why there was a draft and the chances of that draft even happening. There wasn't a need to go further into anything. There was just a simple animalistic impulse to react and flail their arms about until someone else did something about it. I was that someone else because I took the time to listen. I listened to the information that was at hand. I really took the time to listen. A classmate of mine had just died because he was worrying about dying. Our professor was willing to make a fool of himself to get out of something he didn't want to do. He had no duty to anyone else besides himself, and his teaching, and this little learning-world classroom of his.

"There might not be a draft," I repeated as my answer.

Professor Nelson wiped his cheeks and stood up with bad balance. I thought he'd fall over again but he didn't. His massive frame wobbled, and his beaten parrot stood and cupped his body with his wide arms and open hands to catch the professor if he happened to fall. The confidence came back when the tears dried, and he was prepared to continue lecturing.

"There will be no draft," he announced to his class, ignoring the fact I'd given him the information.

"James is a liar," one student said and threw his classroom tablet at me.

"Liar," the class said, throwing theirs.

"Liar."

"Liar."

"Liar."

CHAPTER SEVENTEEN

....

Zeus

"Where's Mommy?" my sister asked, her eyes retaining the building water. Her hands were shaking but she would try to hide it from me.

We walked in together and I stood next to her as she called up to my father from the stairwell banister. She would never go upstairs unless she had to. Her conversations with my father would always begin from the bottom of the stairwell.

"She's asleep," he answered. "Had a long day."

His wheelchair was right at the edge of the first step. It was part of the torture he'd put himself through. My father would drag his broken body up the stairs like a slug. He would do that to prove to himself he had a will to live. He would go back down the stairs the same way and struggle with the wheelchair before he would yelp one last time from the pain and pass out, his body resting in the most awkward of positions. My sister, as kind as she was, would reposition his contorted body and he would wake in his wheelchair and roll over to the Laphroaig.

"What if she wakes up?" my sister asked, no longer in control of her tears. They now showered down her face and she tried to keep this shame away from me.

"She won't, you whore. She never does. Now, I'm losing my patience.

I want you to station your little loser brother down there. Throw him some snacks and let him chew on them like the cow he is so you can come upstairs to Daddy. Let him chew away with that cow chew of his. Chew. Chew. Chew. Moo. Moo. Moo!"

"Come on, James," she sobbed. "What do you want to eat? I have to go upstairs."

"I'm not very hungry," I answered and sat at the kitchen table.

"You know where it all is if you get hungry?"

I was so used to people doing things for me. This house didn't feel like my house when I was alone in it. It was a daunting thing to be in when I had to wait on myself. I needed my sister so much for that.

"Yes," I answered, resting my head against the table. "Go upstairs."

"I'll be back."

"Okay."

"Try not to come up."

"Okay."

"Please, Jamie James."

"I won't."

"I just need to put Daddy to sleep."

"Fine. I get it. I won't go up."

"He needs us now."

"I know."

She ran up and I covered my ears as I was trained to do. My hands hollow against my earlobes, I could hear the ocean in them. That ocean. Forever it went somewhere I would never know. My sister wanted that emptiness and freedom just as much as I did. But she knew it better than me. She had a Sunfish sailboat. I could only look out from the dock and watch. That was my life—*watching*.

I fell asleep on the kitchen table, and I awoke to a light nudge.

"James," she said, her left eyeball full of blood from a burst vessel. She looked scary and I shrunk back and fell off my chair. Her face was decorated with bruises, which had turned green and blue and yellow.

"You scared me," I laughed. "Is Daddy asleep?"

"He's asleep."

"How long was I asleep for?"

"Too long."

"Your eye."

"Come on," she said and helped me up. "I want to go out."

"Out where?"

"Out there."

"There's a storm. We can't. And Daddy said that—"

"I don't give a shit what Daddy said. I want to go out."

Crying, she kicked the back door open and pulled me into the barn with her.

"Jaclyn, what are we doing?"

"The gun."

"The gun?"

She tore apart the barn and found the gun underneath my father's precious car. Checking if it was loaded, she then tucked it in her pants and pulled me out of the barn and down to the dock.

"Stay right there," she said and untangled the rope from the wood post. A seagull was sitting on top of the post, and it looked down at Jaclyn. She tossed the gun into the sailboat and told me to get in.

"The storm," I protested, holding my hand out to feel the speed of the wind.

"Get in," she demanded. "Or I'm doing this alone."

"I don't want you to go alone."

"Then get in."

I hopped in with that kid hop. Hands in the air and that stiffness in the landing because my center of gravity was off. My bones were still growing and everything was awkward. The muscles weren't there either to cushion the landing. Kids moved like a stack of sticks thrown together. That lack of coordination.

"Watch the sail," my sister warned. She was captain now.

The sail caught the wind and we moved fast through the streams. Before we knew it, we scaled that horizon line I would normally admire from over there, where my father and mother existed. They didn't exist here, though. We were free here. The forces of nature would dictate us now. Away from the grip that stunted us and that Victorian house out there in its stillness and hatefulness and that numbness it brought to look at it and that not knowing if it would ever come back to hurt us. I cupped my hands to focus the vision and searched and searched and searched, and there it was, so isolated, my father in that living and breathing thing, sleeping so sound after he wrecked us for the day and my mother asleep after she yet again hit her daily breaking point. Each day was the end for her. That eternity, or the lack of it, she had and made us have. How off, over there, that Victorian house was—the Victorian stillness in it and those quiet demons it housed and the way it breathed in this stillness and stood so *there* in its dumbfounded presence and so very gone it was, cowering away as we distanced ourselves from it.

This house went away from us. We didn't go away from it. And it went off behind the trees as the coastline bent away from this living construction and our sailboat followed the wind and it became one eerie drift to freedom.

The shift in wind flung the sail around and my sister couldn't keep up with the sudden movements.

"James," she called to me through the rain and the wind. "It'll be calmer out there. Good thing you didn't change into dry clothes," she laughed.

I was very cold, and she could see I was. But she would have to ignore it. We had to get away.

"I'm very cold," I said, helplessly.

"I know. I'm sorry."

"Will it be warmer out there?"

"Yes. It'll be much warmer—and freer. We have everything ahead of us, Jamie James."

The rain steamed off the bridge from the wind obliterating it against the framework. We went under the bridge and felt enclosed by its dark underbelly. The hollow howling echoed under it and the rain followed us along with the wind.

"I feel like this storm is just going to get worse," I said.

"It'll be better out there."

"Will it . . . ?"

"It'll be much better out there."

Like a wooden figurehead carved into the bow of a ship, Jaclyn hung off the front looking to the possibilities of the Atlantic. She would talk to me without turning around. The wind and rain hit her hard, but she still didn't budge. She was the figurehead of this little Sunfish. Everything was out there.

There.

There.

There.

And she would lead and be at the forefront of *there*.

A gust threw us left and then another slapped us right. My father's spirit was out here fighting against us. I could feel him and the abuse. My sister kept still and focused, relentlessly living her dream. Not even Mother Nature could stop her. The thing she would be, would be out *there*.

"The wind," I screamed. "What do you want me to do?"

"Hold it as you are. We're going where we need to go."

Another gust. A larger gust. A vicious one blown from the mouth of that Victorian house, which was now so very gone and hidden by the bend of the coastline.

"You're doing great, Jamie James. Give it ten more minutes. Just ten more minutes."

It wouldn't be any better out there.

We both knew it.

This could only end.

The sail dipped the other direction and kissed the waves and then swung back up and kissed the waves on the other side. Then the wind pushed us forward even faster and another gust slowed us and tried to push us backward. I had no idea what I was doing and held the things I needed to hold. I was always needed for something with my sister. And I was needed here. I had worth here. I had a function and a purpose. She couldn't have done this on her own. It made me feel better to be of use. She had a way of making me feel that I really had a purpose.

. . .

"Liar," they chanted.

"Liar."

"Liar."

"Liar."

Professor Nelson liked this and let it go on for far too long. Then, when he felt like it was right on his clock, he sung out through his opera lungs: "Enough!"

"Enough," his voice boomed like powerful thunder, like Zeus or some other powerful Greek god. He was Zeus in his own mind.

"Enough of this," *Boom*!

"James is only a student," *Boom*!

"But he has a right to an opinion," *Boom*!

Zeus would put us right. He would show me sympathy, as all great leaders did. The sky-and-thunder god would guide us through these trying times. We were so unsure, and he was so all-knowing. He would tell us the truth. He would tell us what to do, how to feel, and what to think.

"I received this student's counsel," *Boom*!

"And he knows not what he talks about," *Boom*!

"Though I received his counsel," *Boom*!

"I want you all to say thank you to your fellow student, James Anglish," *Boom*!

"A thank you for being at my service," *Boom*!

The sky-and-thunder god had commanded his yipping hyenas to stand down and welcome me with praise.

"Thank you," one student said and kissed my cheek.

"Thank you," another said and kissed my shoulder.

"Thank you," the class said and bowed.

"Thank you is a grand gesture," Professor Nelson said, touching the tips of his fingers together. "Opinion, immature or not, is welcomed here."

His cheeks were still wet in some spots and those spots refracted the sallow lecture hall light. They reminded me of the cheeks of Thomas the Tank Engine. The rolling eyes and those pillow dough mounds and the heavy creases around the lips and the round face and the bent eyebrows moving up and down to express basic emotions: happy, sad, scared, confused.

"There will be no draft," he repeated.

"There will be no draft," the class chanted.

"There will be no draft."

"There will be no draft."

"There will be no draft."

"Now," he lectured on, "we will not be—"

BLUE ALERT.

Wrists vibrating.

Wrists illuminating.

The class got swept up in one group cry and Professor Nelson fell to the ground again and rolled around the flooring weeping. Matt followed along again, as he was trained to do.

BLUE ALERT.

Wrists vibrating.

Wrists illuminating.

More students began to spit for some reason and a few more convulsed. I could tell their convulsions were fake and they'd reenacted it to build from the drama of the real one.

BLUE ALERT.

Wrists vibrating.

Wrists illuminating.

After each alert, the delirium grew and grew and grew. Students soiled themselves and pulled the feces from their underwear and threw it at each other. The pupils in their eyes expanded and the once green and blue and brown and hazel turned to beady black. Like those eyes on a dead deer head hanging from the wall, they had no life in them as the madness took over.

BLUE ALERT.

Wrists vibrating.

Wrists illuminating.

This time the Blue Alert was a tornado watch. Most, if not all, weather alerts were classified as orange, not blue. It went from white, which was more of an update, to brown, which was more of a warning, to orange, which had the weather briefings, to gold, which had the crime briefings, to blue, which was the high priority—a national emergency. But reporting did tend to ambulance chase Blue Alerts.

U's meteorologists were a unionized crew that defined special interest. Their influence was immense, and my father couldn't even control them. If they wanted to attach bad weather to a draft and a potential world war, they could get it done and make you think the locusts, the wildfires, and the earthquakes are coming. They were coming for you—and just *you*—because everyone's actions, besides your own, had changed your world for the worse and had done this to *you*. Look at what has been done to your precious planet. You have to dodge the tornadoes now because of them. They raped and pillaged your mother, Mother Earth.

BLUE ALERT.

Wrists vibrating.

Wrists illuminating.

Such unbelievable levels of hissing and moaning and crying, and not one of the students, including the professor, knew what the alert was about. They wanted me to tell them, and they wanted Professor Nelson to stand up and command them to condemn me for the alert and then grace me with fake acceptance. In this culture of ours, blame had to be placed on someone. And that someone had to be within your group so you could feel the cleansing for yourself. An individual blamed somewhere else meant nothing. For a single action, there was one person from every group to blame. I was the pariah for this classroom now. And I would be the one to tell the information and be blamed for the information. And Professor Nelson would be the one to save me.

"Tornadoes," I announced, my wrist in the air.

"What?" Zeus boomed, still a turtle on its back.

"A tornado watch," I said.

Professor Nelson stood and Matt followed. The class calmed itself.

"Class," Zeus bestowed on us, his hands scanning across the chairs like he was parting the Red Sea, "not to worry . . . it's a tornado watch."

"James is to blame," a student cried.

"James is to blame," another cried.

"James is to blame," the class cried.

"James is to blame."

"James is to blame."

"James is to blame."

The man who started this chant was fined for littering more times than any other resident of New York State. People who littered were just as bad as sex offenders, and their offenses were publicly documented online. They had a litterer tracker. Do you have a litterer in your neighborhood? "Wow, Mr. Sumners seemed like such a nice guy," I said once after searching. "What a shame that is!"

Mr. Sumners ended up killing himself. He jumped off the GW Bridge like the rest of them. I forgot to tell you, but the GW Bridge was nicknamed Death Bridge. Many of the Suicidal Watchers would go there after someone had been accused and watch and cheer as the accused jumped. Kids went to Death Bridge with their parents. They did drugs together and incest became a very common thing. I forgot to mention that, I think. But it did. You really couldn't be too much of a parent anymore. Parents went from being the cool friend to the lover.

Anyway, I was very surprised that this man, who started the chanting, hadn't killed himself. He went to Death Bridge a lot to watch others put an end to it. His name was The Man because the public decided he didn't deserve a name. Ashamed of himself, he still managed to go to class and cheer on the suicides at Death Bridge. What a thing, really.

"I need sex," Zeus declared.

The students remained still, and a woman volunteered to sacrifice her body.

"Sex, please," he boomed.

"I need sex now," he boomed and boomed and boomed. "Sex. Sex. Sex."

She undressed and they went at it and the rest of us watched. It was terrifying how her body would get lost in the dough of his stomach. The Michelin Man and this tiny woman rolled around and moaned and cried and yelled at each other and slapped each other, together in one stinking ball of sweat. Matt tried to join, and the Michelin Man rose in his godly stature and loomed over this little man. He paused the sex to assert his authority over this student. That tiny woman was his tiny woman and no one else could have her, least of all Matt.

"Run off," Zeus cracked. *Boom*!

"Run off, little one," he said, in an even deeper voice. This is what a god sounded like.

"No," Matt defied. He would show this tiny woman, his unknown love.

"What?" Zeus rumbled.

"She's not yours."

Zeus walked over to a sword he brought back from somewhere in Scotland.

"Last warning," the thunder said, warning of its lightning.

"I love this woman," Matt cried. "I love her so. My little angel, you are. Oh, how I love thee."

This turned into a play. Matt and Professor Nelson would fall into their imaginary worlds and act it out in front of us. The entertainment would begin.

"Then I must kill thee," Zeus cracked. *Boom!*

He drove his sword straight through Matt and it came out the other side. The class was in a state of shock and the quiet settled in.

"I did warn thy fellow classmate," he spoke in some old type of English. "But that gent wast too fustian and that gent proudness result'd in his death. Those who dost dare me wilt kicketh the bucket."

Matt held the sword in his body and stammered on the stage until he fell to the ground, looking up at some light fixture.

"Thy light shine on me," he said, dying. "It's bright. And it shines on me. Goodbye, bright light," he continued, for the last time.

Zeus let him die and then went back to smothering his object of sex. The woman didn't seem to care that her admirer lost in the joust and the class went on watching and she rolled around with the professor in Matt's spreading pool of blood.

When Zeus finished, she went back to her seat and sat there naked and covered in Matt's blood. A few bouts of sex broke out around me and, before I knew it, the whole classroom was naked and involved in one big orgy.

"Stop," Zeus thundered. "I am finished—and so are you. It's time to learn now. For me to teach, and for you to learn."

In a hurry, my classmates found their clothes and got dressed and sat down.

"Animals," he said and grabbed Matt's head and pulled the sword out of his body. He then dragged him off the lecture stage. Matt was laying behind the presentation screen where the flag post was.

"Is everyone clothed?" he asked.

"Yes," one person answered.

"Yes," another answered.

"Yes," the class answered.

"That's impossible," he thundered. *Boom*!

Holding up a shirt, he began to shake from his building anger.

"When I lecture, students wear clothes. The sex is done. Who's renting this shirt?"

Silence.

"Who's renting this shirt?"

Silence.

His anger was rumbling, and building, and building, and building.

"One last chance!"

"It's mine," someone said behind me.

"It's yours?"

"It's an undershirt. I have my shirt on. I couldn't find it."

"You couldn't find it?"

"I'm sorry."

"I'm sorry," another said.

"I'm sorry," the class said.

"I'm sorry."

"I'm sorry."

"I'm sorry."

"What if another professor found this? What would they think of me?"

"I'm sorry."

"Would they think there was funny business going on?"

"I'm sorry."

"What would happen to my stellar reputation?"

"I'm sorry."

"Because of you."

"I'm sorry."

"Because you want to ruin me."

"I'm sorry."

"Because you want to cease to learn."

"I'm sorry."

"Because you are a *racist*."

The class shrunk back in horror and the student who had left his shirt on the lecture stage began to wail like a baby that has colic.

"You're a racist," Zeus proclaimed.

"A racist," the class echoed.

"A racist."

"A racist."

"A racist."

"And what is this?" he said and stretched out this shirt to read the print. "This is no undershirt. 'Mother Earth has no Planet B,' it says. What does that mean? You, the *racist environmentalist*—an oxymoron. Are you an oxymoron?"

"I don't know what I am," he answered, now on his knees.

"I will tell you what you are. You are the embodiment of White privilege. And your kind claim they are all environmentalists. It's too easy to be an environmentalist. It's your way of removing yourself from the people you suppress. Do you know Critical Race Theory?"

"I do not."

"You should."

"I'm sorry I do not."

"You should be sorry—because you are the byproduct of White supremacy feeding off our culture over time. You have the bug, and you don't even know you have it. You're a carrier of *racism*."

"I did not know I was infected," he cried.

"Don't get smart with me."

"I am being honest," he put his head between his knees. "I did not know I was infected."

"If you are being honest, we accept your apology."

"I am being honest," he cried. "I am."

"We forgive."

"Thank you," he laughed and cried and lifted his head, his face now red from gravity.

"As long as you're not an *elitist* like Fep Anglish."

The class looked at me with those deer eyes.

"James," Zeus roared. "Why don't you take Matt's body to the garbage."

It was sad to see Matt lay there limp next to the pile of trash bags. The bad weather was coming in, as it always did, and the sky was filling with burnt marshmallow clouds. They gathered to form those thunderheads and their flat bottoms made me feel trapped under one gigantic puffy roof. This was nature's way of containing the population in its padded room, above and all around us, protecting us from ourselves, while we screamed and cried and laughed and spit and became incontinent, trying to roll about and wiggle ourselves out of the straitjackets.

"The garbage man," Zeus laughed with that big laugh gods have.

I would try to do a fast walk to my seat before he would make me do another errand.

"Stop," his voice cracked and echoed. "Hold right there."

I was so close to the seat.

"We're not done with you and your elitist tendencies yet."

I turned around to receive *the shaming*.

"You're my dog today, James. I've picked my dog today. And you know why I picked my dog today?"

He sounded like my father. When the real abuse came in, it always hit home.

"Why?" I had to ask.

"Because you're a boy of privilege—and that's something you'll always have."

"I'm sorry I have privilege."

"Are you really sorry? Or—are you going through the motions?"

It took me too long to respond and the class began to laugh.

"Even the class knows it," he thundered.

The class laughed more because they knew Professor Nelson wanted them to. It proved his point further and gave him even more control. He was now bigger than Zeus in his own mind.

"He isn't sorry," they chanted.

"He isn't sorry."

"He isn't sorry."

"He isn't sorry."

"And why aren't the elite ever sorry?" this omnipresent, all-knowing beast asked the class, his hand to his ear to draw in more anger and groupthink.

"Their ivory towers," they chanted. "Cowards in towers."

"Cowards in towers."

"Cowards in towers."

"Cowards in towers."

"And why, from up there, do they look down on us and watch us suffer?"

"We do the work," they chanted. "And they get the perk."

"They get the perk."

"They get the perk."

"They get the perk."

"Everyone in this class seems to hate you, James."

I would take the shame.

"How do you feel, James?"

"I feel ashamed," I memorized. This had happened to me before.

"What do you feel ashamed of?"

"Of myself."

"Say it full."

"I, James Anglish, feel ashamed of myself."

"Fuller."

"I, James Anglish, feel ashamed of myself for being the son of Fep Anglish."

"The rest."

"I, James Anglish, feel ashamed of myself for being the son of Fep Anglish, the personification of *White elitism.*"

The last part was the hardest to say because my father wasn't White. But it wasn't about being White or Black, it was about acting White or acting Black. And, to Professor Nelson, my father acted White, the worst type of White, the whitest of the White. And because he was Black it made him even more of a fraud.

"Are you regretful you're the son?"

"*I am.*"

"I'm sorry for you, James."

"I'm sorry," my scripted lines would go on.

"I'm sorry," I would repeat three times more.

Then nature's thunder came in. It rattled the walls and the chandelier swayed from the tornadoes. The class became uneasy, and Professor Nelson hid behind the presentation screen.

"We're all going to die," he cried. "Run for your life. The tornadoes are going to kill us all."

The class went in all different directions and students clawed at the windows like there was a fire eating them alive inside. I sat in my seat and watched.

"It's Mother Earth," one student knelt and grabbed my legs, begging to me. "She doesn't want us poisoning her body anymore. We are the virus. Death to us. She wants us gone—vanquished."

He pushed my legs aside to give himself leverage to stand up. Nearly pushing me off my seat, he had an announcement to his fellow classmates. Sticky drool hung from his mouth and its texture had thickened from the mucus dripping into it from his nose. He was a rabid raccoon, and it was impossible to know what he'd do next.

"She wants us vanquished," he announced and cried and then laughed and then cried and then laughed. He ended on the laughter.

"No," the class cried, with a few anomalies of interspersed laughter. A gun went off and a woman dropped to the ground. It was such a quick drop that I thought she fell through the floor into some creepy dungeon chute Professor Nelson had created in some pointless frenzied panic.

"We must burn it down," he insisted, pulling the quivering God of Zeus out from hiding.

"We're all going to die," the God of Zeus cried and pleaded. "I *feel* so sad. I *feel* so scared. I *feel* so confused."

"Professor, we must burn it down before the weather takes us."

"But I'm so scared."

"Feel happy then."

"But I feel scared."

They both rolled their eyes back and shook and chanted something in Old English.

"Do you feel happy now?" he asked.

"I feel happy now."

"Will you help your students burn it down before the weather kills?" At first, he was reluctant—because he knew what this meant for him.

"Will you help us burn it down?" he asked again, begging.

"If not, the weather will kill," Zeus said to himself. It was like a little prayer or a motivating piece of reasoning he had to run through his mind.

"The weather will kill," the student insisted.

"It will kill," Zeus agreed. "Burn it down." Now he took command.

The class shook their heads and wiggled the saliva out of their howling mouths. A few more guns went off and a few more dropped to the ground. I watched for a little longer before I casually walked out. But, before that, I observed them try to light a fire.

There was no gasoline in the classroom. Professor Nelson broke a wooden chair into pieces by slamming it against the wall. He attempted to create fire by rubbing splintered pieces of wood together. No fire, just bloody hands.

Failing, Zeus investigated his bloody hands and then wiped them against his face so he looked like some Native American war leader. A war cry took over him and he ran about the classroom with that Michelin body of his taking on its own inertia in all different directions. As he ran, it looked as though he was physically falling apart. Both shoes came off, his shirt buttons exploded and bounced against the floor, his pants popped open with his belt dangling about like a wild gardening hose, and, before you knew it, he was completely naked and his doughy contours slingshot their weight in various angles. He bellowed like an opera singer and jumped through the window (four very long floor-to-ceiling flights) to his death. It made no sense to me that he went out the window to avoid the weather. Many followed his lead and the campus's grassy patch below was covered in blood and bones jutting out of bodies. They fell on top of each other like sandbags. Then a tornado came careening through and swept the bodies up and dumped them somewhere else, some bodies boomeranging back, and others tossed to some other off-campus location. The weather had a way of doing this to people. Professor Nelson was not the first professor to kill himself over bad weather. When a storm of this magnitude came through, New York would lose an eighth of its population to suicide. The Mop would clean up the bodies like litter left over from a parade.

But now I was worried for my life in this classroom of guns blazing. There was a full-on shootout, and a bullet sliced the air by my eardrum. That was enough for me. Better to take a chance outside. I fought my passiveness and darted out of the classroom and flung my deadweight body out the door and into Mother Nature's fury. From outside, I looked at the fourth-floor window and those gunfire sparks lighting up the broken glass and those screams coming through but still cushioned by the thunder.

CHAPTER EIGHTEEN

Hoo Hoo!

I walked down to Central Park and the ceiling of clouds above me packed together even tighter, those thunderheads becoming one gigantic thing up there. Mother Nature had formed her army above us, and this was her D-Day. This was her revenge for what we had done to her for centuries. The damage was done and not one electric car sliced up or down Central Park West in its quiet precision. But I could still make out a strange vehicle and I was surprised to hear what I heard. It was the sound of petrol and pumping pistons. I knew that sound well from my father's racetrack.

"What the hell," I said to myself in the middle of the road.

A tornado came through and spun itself into the park. The petrol-pumping car raced toward it. I stayed in the middle of the road.

The exhaust popped like a firecracker, and it moaned from its swift gearchange. It was a DeLorean made to look like the DeLorean time machine from *Back to the Future*. The car hit the brakes and spun around me to make a clunky full stop. A slight pause for drama and then the doors opened like seagull wings. A man, who looked like Doc Brown, fell out of the car wearing a white jumpsuit. His hair was white and wild.

"Marty," he said to me, "we have to go back to 1955. Get in the car. They're coming."

"Who's coming?" I asked, confused.

"No time now."

He dove back into the DeLorean in that clumsy and frantic mad scientist way and shut the gullwing door behind him. I went around the car and found myself swept up in his lunacy and I threw myself in, the panic somehow controlling my muscle memory. Before I had time to realize the mistake I made, the gullwing door closed, and Doc Brown slammed on the gas and raced down Central Park West until he hit eighty-eight mph. We were heading straight for a tornado.

"Great Scott!" he laughed and cried. "The Libyans!"

In this moment of shock, I managed to have enough guilt left in me to feel bad for this Doc Brown wannabe. The strangeness of the weather broke his will, and the fantasy took over and now he was Doc Brown, and I was Marty McFly. I played the part well without even knowing. I was confused like Marty McFly, and I had a readiness about me that made it believable.

"The tornado will bring us back to 1955," he drooled, and his left eye went lazy. He began to convulse like so many of them did from the exceedingly high pressure they put themselves under. It was sad, but the body would just give out. This was more of a stroke, I guessed.

Collapsing against the steering wheel, his foot remained firm against the gas. And we screamed down Central Park West at eighty-eight mph. And that tornado was ten blocks away, tumbling up the avenue right for us.

I opened the gullwing door and watched the pebbles in the concrete turn to silver streaks as the car ate the road. I thought about the friction of the concrete against my skin, the layers shredding off with third-degree burns like cheese rubbing against a cheese grater.

There was no time.

I had to jump.

I had to do it.

But could I?

The accelerative winds thrust from the tornado made the metal of the car creak. Never had I felt anything like it. Even from the cockpit, the strength of that tornado told me all I needed to know about Mother Nature.

No time now.

I had to do it.

Do it.

Or die.

Five hundred yards away—that tornado.

Four hundred yards away.

Three hundred yards.

Two hundred.

I had to jump now.

Do it.

Or die.

I had to jump now.

And . . .

I bounced around the concrete and my skin shredded off my shoulders, hips, and knees.

When I stopped flopping about, I lay there waiting to be taken by the tornado.

"Take me," I cried. "I can't anymore. Take me!"

I really couldn't anymore. The modern life was just too much. The energy needed to live beyond the destructive drama was unsustainable. If I couldn't do it (with what I'd been through) then no one else could. We all thought that way. Each one of us thought we had it the worst. Maybe we did. Maybe we didn't. But I did. I had it the worst, even though everyone else did, too. And Mother Nature would spare me, and she would push that tornado away and guide it through the park to do its damage somewhere else. I was too pathetic right now to kill.

But I lay on the road like a fetus. Head bent in toward the legs, I wouldn't leave the womb. I would never leave the womb. I had nothing left in me to make me want to grow. Adulthood had left before it arrived and I saw that DeLorean circle around the tornado in the air, the Doc Brown wannabe shooting out of the window like a cannonball, first taking a ride out its wind-tails and then landing on a tree, where he was impaled by a branch. His white jumpsuit turned red, and dark yellow urine dripped from his feet onto the puddles of upturned soil and uprooted grass.

My wrist sent an alert radiating through my body, and its automated monotone voice told me that the winds were 193 mph and would increase to close to 220 mph. The downforce was too strong for me to stand, and I crawled and the exposed bone from my knees dragged like ivory against the concrete. The pain it sent through me was so intense I could feel it in the roots of my teeth. My body was experiencing one big brain freeze and my soul was hardening over. I was becoming my own hell. And I would fight the pain until I got somewhere safer in the park.

I wasn't too far away from Doc Brown's dangling body. The ground was mud, and the wind threw it around and dumped it in piles like it had done with the bodies. Still unable to stand, I could hear way off somewhere that pitter-patter helicopter chopping, and that mammoth groan a ship makes when it's sinking while the weight of the water bends its framework.

With the rain and the wind, it was all a blur. I couldn't see the trees hanging above me and I could just see enough to make out Doc Brown swallowed up by another tornado. I felt the orbital twisting, but I was too far away for it to take hold of me.

"Anyone out there? I tried to call for help. "Anyone?"

. . .

"You're better at this than I am," my sister called. When the boat nearly flipped over twice, she still didn't look behind her. There was a confidence she had in me, and I wouldn't let her down. I spent my life letting my father down. And I wouldn't let my sister down. I would get her to the Atlantic. I would get her to freedom.

"We'll make it," I called to her.

"Of course, we will."

"And we'll live somewhere else."

"I know we will."

"Away from Daddy."

"You'll never see *that bastard* again."

What a thing for such a young girl to say. So damaged a statement, it was mature. Words that would only come out of a battered wife's mouth after she signed the divorce papers. This is who my mother always wanted to be but never could be. My sister was too strong.

The gusts seemed to come from behind now and their left hook punches and right hook punches lost strength. It was all pushing us forward. Mother Nature was on our side. She wanted us out there. We would be alone with her. With no water. No food. No change of clothes. Because angry kids don't think anything through. And I was becoming hypothermic.

"Jaclyn," I slurred. My breathing, slow and shallow and my energy, depleting. I was losing consciousness and the confusion came in. I lost control of the sailboat when we entered that great body of open water. The winds were now unstoppable, and Jaclyn finally turned around and took control. We flipped and the boat turtled, and a rope attached to the mast wrapped around my leg and kept me under. The water stabbed at my nerves and the shock settled fast. Bubbles above me from Jaclyn's flailing feet. I didn't want to give up, but it felt so good to. I was sinking deeper until the rope caught me . . .

I would let go of living. That Victorian house. Looking at me from its unseen eyes. Inhaling through the front door and exhaling through the back door. Breathing in unison with my father's breath within its ribcage walls. Expanding and compressing. Expanding and compressing. Expanding and compressing.

Expanding.

Lifting me up.

Out of something.

Into air.

Into that air.

"James," she cried. "Breathe!"

Mouth-to-mouth.

Pump. Pump. Pump.

Mouth-to-mouth.

Pump. Pump. Pump.

Mouth-to-mouth.

Pump. Pump. Pump.

"James!"

Mouth-to-mouth.

Pump. Pump. Pump.

Mouth-to-mouth.

Pump. Pump. Pump.

Mouth-to-mouth.

Pump. Pump. Pump.

"James!"

Water released from the lungs. The air absorbing back into the blood and the life beating on. A pulse, like a replenished generator. Beating on. On and on and on, to do nothing.

The city came in and out of view from the breaks in the fog and the whole blur of it all around me as the rain and wind tore at my eyes. I could keep them open only for seconds now. Jaclyn was above me and she was trying to warm me. Everything was so cold and the ocean beyond wasn't our friend. Mother Nature didn't want us, and Jaclyn couldn't protect me now. The sailboat was still afloat, and we followed the waves farther out into the fog and the gathering storm. The weather tore at us one way and just before we could give up, it would tear into us from another direction. I welcomed my father now. I wanted him over Mother Nature. I think Jaclyn did, too. Anything but this. *Anything.*

"I don't know what to do, James," Jaclyn gave in. She always knew what to do.

"I . . ." I tried to speak despite the hypothermia. The heat escaped my body so fast, and the wind and rain wisped it right out of me.

"The ocean . . . that storm . . . we need—"

Jaclyn screamed for help and waved her hands in the air and then dolphin-dipped underwater.

"Jaa . . ." I called.

"Jaaaaaa . . ." I called again.

She rose to the surface and cursed and cried and laughed and then cursed and cried and then panicked and called our father's name.

"Our Father," she said in soft notes, the storm all around us exploding, "who art in heaven, hallowed be thy name. Thy kingdom come . . . Thy will be done, on earth as it is in heaven. Give us this day our—"

I had that look children possess when they see something different.

This wasn't Jaclyn talking. This was scripted. This type of talk had been branded into her. She was totally giving up. And I knew it was over.

"Jaaaa . . . ." I tried once more.

"Daddy!" Jaclyn begged. "Please! Please! Please! I want to go home. I want to go home!"

A flicker off there somewhere.

A flicker right over there.

A flicker right above us.

Lightning knifing down at the ocean.

Knife.

Knife.

Knife.

Slicing through the air.

Stabbing it.

Slice.

Stab.

Slice.

Stab.

And the air responding as it came back together and roared and sent its anger along the craggy body of an infinite ocean.

This ocean ahead of us.

In back of us.

All around us.

Hours of floating until there was no hint of a coast.

The pulse slowing and the eventual release of every working system of my body. It felt so good to let go again and the process of letting go was the ultimate heaven. Seeing and feeling the problems that ruined you becoming nothing. Everything meaning nothing. The spirit of you unshackling itself from the burden of you.

"Let me . . ." I tried.

"James," she cried.

"Let me die," I got out.

"No. James. No."

"Please!" I pleaded desperately.

"James."

As she stretched her cold and stiff body downward to hand me my toy pipe, I had that look children possess when they see something different. I felt someone's hand against my neck.

"I don't think he's alive," a voice said.

Another hand touched my neck.

"There's a pulse. Faint. But there's a pulse."

"James?"

Echo. Echo. Echo. Gurgle. Gurgle. Gurgle. The sound seemed to travel underwater.

"James," the echo went, stretching my name endlessly.

That static cotton dryness in my mouth, mixed with stale ginger ale bubbling out of the pain. The taste of wet wood, or something like that. Like that wooden spoon from the Haagen-Dazs mini cups, with its harsh bark flavor strengthened by each lick. The ice cream now gone, though. I was left with that chocolate-stained dry bark.

"James." My name stretched on and on.

Echo. Echo. Echo. Gurgle. Gurgle. Gurgle.

"Pull him out."

"I can't."

He stretched his stiff body downwards to hand me my toy pipe.

"Why, Jaclyn?" I asked.

The Martian man, silhouetted by the sun, looked down at me.

"Why, Jaclyn?" I asked again.

The Martian man wouldn't answer.

"Why did you let him do that to you?"

Echo. Echo. Echo. Gurgle. Gurgle. Gurgle.

"He's breathing. He's speaking!"

"Why didn't you let me die?"

"He's saying something."

"Just pull him out."

"He's tangled in the ropes."

"Cut it."

"Get the knife."

Movement. Shuffling sounds.

"He's free."

"I'm free," I said.

The scarecrow patched lights dematerialized into finer images that opened into recognizable forms. I could see a defined man with a big beard.

"I got him," he said.

My body felt heavy and numb and light. And as he pulled me out, I felt like a spirit rising from the grave.

The weight of living, gone, once again, like it had before.

"Where's the chopper?" he yelled.

"It's coming!"

Jaclyn was next to him wrapped up in a blanket. She was pale and shaking.

Behind her, the truck-size intermodal containers were stacked on top of each other. This was a cargo ship.

"James," her fleeting voice said. "Look."

She pointed to the open ocean.

That openness.

That lack of anything ahead.

Those waves.

The blackness ahead. That hint of gold sun.

You could only look forward when there was nothing else but horizon.

Ahead, that horizon.

Ahead, those waves.

That endlessness.

"We almost made it," her words shook.

"There's more to be seen out there," she went on. "I'll go back, *alone.*"

• • •

The wind took my voice away from me. My soundwaves, along with everything else, got sucked up and tossed around in the sky. Then, through sudden breaks in this watercolor scenery, I could again see that ceiling of gathered thunderheads. An image of something was projected against them from some source below. This source appeared to be coming from Central Park.

"Hoo Hoo!" the Pillsbury Doughboy said in his high-pitched voice and giggled. He was projected against the flat bottom surface of these thunderhead clouds.

That white, squishy body. That classic chef hat and white neckerchief. Those beady blue eyes. That little smirk. How cute he was.

"Have anxiety?" he asked down to the creatures he was selling to. "Worried about a world war? Worried about the draft? Worried about another pandemic? I am. And you should be, too. That's why the Pillsbury Doughboy takes XENTAGUIN. Hoo Hoo!"

The "Hoo Hoo!" echoed throughout the city but the wind dulled it enough to blend it in with the thunder.

"Help," I called—this simple word dematerializing in the white noise howls of the wind.

"Anyone," I said. "Please."

That sound came back—the pitter-patter helicopter chopping and that mammoth groan. It was louder this time and not even the wind could howl it into its white-noise submission.

A few people ran by me toward it. They had flashlights and wore biohazard suits. The light from their flashlights zig-zagged along the ground as they ran in frantic pursuit.

"Help," I tried again. "I can't . . ."

"James!" one person screamed, his light pausing on my face.

"Yes!" I cried, unable to see through this light in my eyes.

"I've been looking for you!"

With another person's help, he picked me up, and put my left arm around his neck and my right arm around the other person's neck. They carried me to their destination and my feet dragged on the ground and I looked at my knees, and that exposed bone, and I felt sick from it. Throwing up on myself, the numbness settled in my core and my legs and arms were no longer a part of me. I was no longer a part of myself.

"Come on, James," the man's voice fought the wind. "Try to help yourself. We won't be able to carry you all this way. You're slipping. Grab on harder."

"I can't feel a thing," I answered.

"Try."

I got a better grip and curled my wrists around their necks so I wouldn't slip.

"That's better, James," he said. "Almost there."

The leaves and uprooted grass cut at us, and I had to close my eyes. The two men wore goggles and through the pink blood-illumination of my eyelids, I could see searing lights cast from that pitter-patter helicopter chopping and that mammoth groan. There was something almost dinosaur-like about the sounds and I tried to open my eyes to see this aerospace thing.

Its black candy cane exposed carbon fiber weave ran up the sides of the spacecraft and *U* was painted on the pointed wings.

This needle was prepping itself in its mechanical anger to stab the wall of thunderheads and free itself of Mother Earth's rage and hatred of man. The virus was finally leaving its host, the Earth's immune system taking command and winning.

CHAPTER NINETEEN

....

Exccal

The door opened and shut behind us and I opened my eyes in that lazy, gradual way. You could put music to everything I did, and I acted as if the camera were on me. For this dramatic scene, I would open my eyes as slowly as possible. In my mind's eye, I saw a drummer banging away to enhance the effort of what it was like for James Anglish to open his eyes.

Bing. Bong. Bing. Bong.

They open twenty-five percent.

Bing. Bong. Bing. Bong.

Fifty percent.

Bing. Bong. Bing. Bong.

Seventy-five percent.

Bing. Bong. Bing. Bong.

Wow, what a thing inside.

Inside, the carbon fiber weave came through the thin layer of white paint. You could see the contours of the weave pop in and out and it made the walls feel organic. It felt uneven, like someone's back, and it was warm like someone's back. There was something living in it. To the touch, there was a pulse. Not of the engine, but of something else. There was something else in it. I swear. I'm not crazy.

But, despite these weird observations, I knew this interior very well. Only the most exposed, unadorned, and raw was reserved for Fep Anglish. No comfort anywhere. Just crude carbon fiber. Even the seats were carbon fiber, not leather. The rest of U's fleet of spacecraft used leather and other comfortable and very opulent materials built in with unending user-friendliness. My father bought all these *comfort-crafts* and then gave them away to his board and a few other top-level U employees. You never wanted to leave these comfort-crafts. It's hard to explain how much money was really put into them. The leather used for the captain's chair was Shell Cordovan, a membrane between two layers of horse butt that had to be shaved down and hot stuffed and glazed. The process took over six months, from start to finish. Nothing machine made about it—everything handmade, over time. And that user-friendliness. Get in, press a button, buckle up, no turbulence under 300 mph gusts, then the movies, exercise, fine food, your own Michelin-star kitchen staff, then more fine food, more movies . . . and then, there you are, landing right on the surface of Mars. When you have the money, it's that easy to achieve science fiction.

"Get ready for takeoff," one of them told me.

The captain took off his biohazard suit and I was surprised to see that it was Rick.

"Why weren't you at school?" he asked. "You go to school, don't you?"

"I do, but—"

"You should've been in class. Your purpose is to learn."

"There was—"

"I don't want to hear it. I was searching all over the fucking place for you. And if I hadn't . . . listen, just sit down, and buckle in. I'll bandage your legs and arms when we're airborne and out of this atmosphere. Buckle up *now*—it's going to be extremely bumpy."

This was my father's personal spacecraft, and its trimmings were thrown away. The captain's chair was not made from Shell Cordovan. There was no start button. No turbulence control under 300 mph. No Michelin-star staff. No fine food. No movies. Nothing like Fogo Island. This spacecraft was stripped-out, center control–focused, void of aides and any assistance, uncomfortable as hell, exposed, raw, carbon fiber here and carbon fiber there, exposed framework; rattles and rivets and dripping glue and leaking oil, and smells of burning plastic and crudely perfect engine dynamics. Tribal, almost.

The prep for takeoff felt ritualistic, following the flight manual, page by page, paragraph by paragraph, line by line, and word by word. Like that car of my father's. That machine he tried to kill me with and managed to kill himself with.

Stripped down.

Eggshell light.

No unneeded electronics of any kind.

That delicate porcelain-plastic weightlessness superimposed with its stiff, seemingly Martian-made, aerospace strength.

"This manual," Rick yelled and tore the pages out in anger. "He had to make it hard on himself, didn't he?"

"We have to go," the other said, still in the biohazard suit. "There's no time."

"Where are the others?"

"They said they were coming. But we're gonna have to go. We have no choice, Rick. We have to go."

"The manual is impossible. Fep made it impossible. He's gonna kill us cause he's a freakin'—Take off the damn suit already. You're going to contaminate us with that suit. Take it off."

The suit slipped off and I recognized the man underneath it. I couldn't remember his name, but he was a member of my father's board. I think he was the oldest one and the most resistant toward my father. And my father hated him for it. He called him "The Bastard from the Past." I remembered that. Not his name. This good old child-brain of mine.

"Let me see it," the old man said and picked up the manual. "Is this English?"

"How does a manual have equations?" Rick laughed. "I mean, really!"

"This isn't English."

"I don't know what it is."

"Alright," the bastard said, his finger in the air to pause the moment. "Over there. Over there."

Rick followed him to the millions of buttons.

"That!" the bastard pointed.

"That?" Rick asked back to be sure. You could see him trembling.

"Yes."

"You want me to press it?"

"I mean . . ." the bastard now questioned himself.

"I'll press it," Rick decided.

"I'm pressing it," Rick said again.

"Yes," the bastard finally said.

Button pressed.

A sudden shift in tone of the engine sounds. Then a cavernous whale-cry of volcanic depth.

"That sounds like something," Rick said with joy.

"That does."

The bastard, now with more confidence, went back to the manual.

"I see now," he said. "Alright. Now, pull that."

Rick pulled the lever up and the heat from the engine leaked through the unevenly displaced rivets and the glue melted and dripped down on us. We were in this animal's open jaws, and it was salivating from the prospect of its first meal.

Then the door opened, and the wind looped in and tossed up anything unattached. The bastard chased around the manual.

"These goddamn guys," Rick growled. "Never late—but late now. Come on."

The whole board arrived. I could tell by those overly confident voices of theirs. And the way they wiggled their unathletic, self-serving bodies out of their biohazard suits to reveal their identities to me. And then to throw those suits down the trash chute, everything about what they did, so expendable.

"Help out with the damn manual," Rick demanded of the group he was now leading. "I don't understand a word of it."

They were a good team trying to figure it out. Funny how no one took notice of me or asked me to help. I was a goldfish in a bag. My mouth opens. And my mouth closes.

And more levers pulled, and switches flicked, and buttons pressed, and codes imputed onto the touchscreen.

"*Buckle up*," the spacecraft suddenly told us.

Rick claimed the captain's chair. And it wasn't like it was comfortable, the whole thing made of carbon fiber. The rest of the board sat in splintering wood seats and jittering plastic seats. The vibrations from the engine stretched the wood apart and loosened the bolts holding the seats to the floor. It was death in here. And my father loved it for that.

"*Winds, catastrophic*," the spacecraft said. "*Advise not to fly. Advise not to fly.*"

"Override," Rick barked.

Pause.

Rattling.

Splintering.

Shaking.

Jittering.

This loosening organic interior.

"*Are you sure you would like to override? Please say* 'override' *again, if you would like to override.*"

"Override!" they all demanded.

Pause.

Rattling.

Splintering.

Shaking.

Jittering.

This loosening organic interior.

"Why in the hell didn't we take our own spacecrafts," Rick bitched like a brat, his voice rattling and splintering and shaking and jittering.

"You know damn well," one of them answered.

"How is this piece of junk five times the price?" another asked.

"I have no idea," another answered.

"Because that Fep gave our spacecrafts away to his space exploration division."

"Rick, how'd he swing that?"

"Screw you, Hub," Rick laughed.

"Right from under us."

"Oscar, you had a lot under you."

"I am faithful."

"Faithful to every one of your mistresses."

"Fuck you."

"No, fuck you."

"*Airborne in . . .*" the spacecraft then announced, after completing its standard diagnostics.

"*Ten.*"

"*Nine.*"

"*Eight.*"

"*Seven.*"

"*Six.*"

"*Five.*"

"*Four.*"

"*Three.*"

"*Two.*"

"*One.*"

The face of the Earth fell back behind the smoke launched from the rocket engines. Between the g-forces and the turbulence, the drama of takeoff was biblical and apocalyptic. I was worried my neck would break. The tornadoes slammed us left and then right and then right and then left.

We punctured the ceiling of thunderheads, and the windows turned a blackish gray. Lightning flashed and the thunder of Mother Earth told us to leave and never come back. The roar managed to dwarf the sound of the rocket engines.

Then we were clear.

A sudden calm.

A smoothness through the highest clouds, those mesospheric marshmallows.

Straight into this clean, weightless, and frictionless beyond. And that silent and fading rocket trail so white against the approaching darkness of space. And the letters of *UNIVERSAL* circling around the belly of the dark blue ocean. The *U* coming toward us with its weightless massiveness, projected from those 35,000 projectors, somewhere down there.

"How about that," Hub said, developing a misplaced sense of confidence.

"Touching the face of God," Oscar commented.

Sam appeared paralyzed in his seat. "Soon we'll know what God is."

"I plan on living," Alex went on. "Only the dead know God."

"We are God," Nick laughed.

"All of us," Noll added.

"No, sons of God," Andrew added. "The seven Jesus babies."

They all laughed.

"Amen, brutha," Oscar said. "Amen to that."

"What the hell are we doing?" Noll laughed.

"No one knows," the rest of the guys answered.

"It doesn't feel like two hundred and fifty-five thousand miles per hour, does it?" Oscar marveled.

"It sure doesn't," Hub said. "More like fifty-five."

We looked out the spacecraft's windows and the lightbulb surface of the moon opened into our line of vision. One of the windows had ~~Sixto's Sugar Man~~ keyed into it. No one took notice of it besides me. They were all too distracted by that White Castle space station hamburger joint my father had famously completed a few years ago. He'd financed the whole thing himself just so the elite could have a White Castle in space. That way, before you got to the moon, you could stop and get a slider and a soft drink.

"White Castle," Nick marveled, the hot white light from the space station reflecting off the moist lenses of his wondrous owl-like eyes. The space station was so brightly lit. Like one of those Shell stations in the middle of nowhere blaring with energy against a black and barren night-cloaked countryside. He tried to peer out the window to further see this attraction. But he was still bolted in with seatbelts and stabilizers.

In contrast, Rick looked out the window and reflected on life. What a great thinker Rick was. And the rest of this crew would leave him alone to think. They would also leave me alone. But they did that because I wasn't worth talking to. The kid. The son. The teacup Chihuahua.

"Oh god," Alex screamed, "I'm such an idiot."

"What?" Nick asked.

"I tried to fart," Alex said. "But it didn't work out."

"You're a moron," Hub laughed.

"I think," Alex said, "I think I pushed a little too hard. I was trying to time it right."

"You gotta be kidding me," Oscar laughed.

"I'm not kidding you, Oz."

"We get stuck with this guy," Noll added.

For the first time, we felt a clean but persistent pull. It dragged us straight back into our fastened seats.

"Jesus," Andrew mumbled.

"We're approaching the five hundred grand mph mark," Hub said. "Space cowboys."

"Giddy-up, giddy-up, giddy-up," Noll added. "As our blackie Fep would say."

The boost wouldn't let up and Hub looked concerned. If Hub was worried about something, everyone got worried about it.

"Any day now," he said. That was his way of voicing possible doom without panicking.

"Any day," he said again.

The boost let up and everyone was relieved. The misplaced sense of confidence returned.

"That lingered," Nick commented.

"I need some goddamn scotch," Noll laughed.

"The one thing I miss is scotch," Alex said. "It makes you drink like a man and shit like a baby."

"Only drink scotch when the scotch is drinking you," Oscar said.

Laughs, laughs, laughs—laughing all around. The misplaced sense of confidence reaching a fever pitch.

"Like life," Sam said, "you water down scotch to enjoy its essence."

"Are we in a scotch commercial?" Nick asked.

"It's so bright," Andrew commented. "It's like a small sun—not a moon."

The light slanted in through the window and the domestic and shielded life of Earth felt so far away when this alien cosmic life began to grow on us. And it took form when that moon was at our fingertips.

A little half-lit light bulb we could click on and off. A bulb full of oceanic dust, the soil layered over craters.

I began to think about Apollo 11—what was running through Armstrong's mind when he landed on the moon. What a thing that must have been. Those centuries ago. And here we were.

"I think there's one more boost," Hub said. "That'll get us into seven figures."

"Two more," Nick corrected.

"Nick's right," Oscar agreed. "Once we get beyond the moon, we'll get shot well into the seven-figure mark."

"We'll turn to liquid," Noll commented.

"I know who's going to shit himself again," Hub laughed.

"When's the last boost?" Sam asked.

"Think it's fifty thousand miles or so beyond Pluto," Alex said. "Then we cruise."

"You're right," Hub said.

"Wow," Andrew laughed, "Hub's not on the money today."

"I sense an accent," Nick commented. "When you said: 'on the money.'"

"Did you?" Andrew asked.

"Say LaGuardia."

"Why?"

"Just say it."

"I hate being in the middle of jokes."

"No one hates that. Come on."

"LaGuardia."

"I see."

"See what?"

"You hear anyone say LaGuardia," Nick sermonized, "and you'll know where they're from—anywhere in the world. You get the bullshit right out of them, whether they're running from something or just pretending to be what they're not. You always know with LaGuardia."

"You're sayin' I'm a fraud? You say I'm runnin'?"

"Not in the slightest—because you're a real New Yorker."

"I'm an Italian Jew from Boston, you moron."

"You're either so Jewish you're Italian or you're so Italian you're Jewish. Right? Am I right? Is that how it goes?"

"Close enough."

"Anyway," Oscar interrupted, bringing the conversation back to where it started. "Maybe we gotta get ourselves a new captain."

"Go for it, guys," Rick laughed. "Take the pressure off me."

"No," Oscar went on, "we like the pressure on you. It's nice to know I can't get blamed for anything."

"Captain Hub," Noll laughed. "We're like monkeys going into space. Space monkeys. And you're the leader of us space monkeys."

"Not space cowboys?" Hub asked.

"Nope, space monkeys."

"Yeah," Noll said, "if we were space cowboys, we'd be making a pit stop at the moon."

• • •

The moon fell behind us in a different way than Earth had. Once that'd happened, the comfort of knowing the moon would always be in front of us was gone.

"I'm just waiting for it," Noll said, closing his eyes.

"Any second now," Hub answered, closing his eyes, too.

BOOM!

BOOM!

SWISH!

SWIOOSH!

POOF!

That boost turned into three angered jolts and then ended with a shuddering swish, swoosh, and poof akin to the light and clean brush of dragonfly wings by your ear. The engines calmed themselves down and the blankness around took control.

"Christ!" Nick yelled.

"That was hell," Alex said.

"One more, guys," Hub announced.

The Moon and the Earth were now specks amidst the millions of trillions of specks. Blackness and blankness were the vast oceans.

"We won't see Pluto," Hub said. "It's on the other side."

"What about Mars?" Andrew asked.

"Well beyond Mars now," Hub said. "I wonder . . ."

BOOM!

BOOM!

SWISH!

SWISH!

BOOM!

BOOM!

"Goddamn it," Alex yelled. "I wish they could have warned us a little more about these kicks. My neck. Jesus, my neck."

The confidence was eroding.

"My back," Noll said.

"My everything," Oscar groaned. "Jesus Christ, I guess we're done."

"That can't be the last of it," Hub commented. "There's no way we're beyond the orbit of Pluto."

"Three boosts, right?" Andrew asked.

"Should be," Hub answered.

"Should be?" Alex questioned.

"Yeah, should be. Unless there's something I missed. The engine is Exccal so it shouldn't need more than three boosts."

"Exccal?" Nick asked.

"Did any of you guys pay attention in that class?" Hub asked. "The one Fep made us do?"

No one responded.

"Read any of the books?"

No one responded.

"Did anything?"

No one responded.

"Exponential Acceleration—ring a bell?"

No one responded.

"Exccal is Exponential Acceleration. You know exponential growth?"

Some gestures of acknowledgment.

"When something grows exponentially."

He paused.

"Listen, it grows at a hell of a pace. Exccal works the same way. The speed or acceleration, or whatever you guys want to call it, doesn't just grow on itself—meaning that no matter how fast we're moving, this Exccal engine always thinks we're totally still. Not moving. No acceleration. No speed—at a total dead stop. Each time the boost kicks in, the new speed is raised to the power of the initial speed. Whether the initial speed is five miles per hour or a million, it doesn't make a difference. It'll be the power of whatever that initial speed is. In other words—and I'll say it again to your thick skulls—Exccal doesn't care what the speed from launch or boost is. An initial speed can be increased by a billion percent with the same output of energy as something that is increased by five percent. It's the epitome of efficiency."

You could tell the inner workings of Exccal were out of Hub's grasp. But, like all smart people, he could explain it in its most basic form. Unless he was bullshitting. Who knew? This crew wouldn't have known the difference.

"I always wanted to see Mars up close," Sam said to Rick, changing the subject. "I was looking forward to that. To living there, too. But Rick. Damn Rick. Making us the Christopher Columbus of some unknown planet light-years away. It's ridiculous."

I would continue to be silent to get all the answers. They wouldn't notice me. The board chattered so much the truths always came through, even if they were trying to keep it secret. I was a fly on the wall, and I kept quiet so they wouldn't swat me away.

BOOM!

BOOM!

SWISH!

SWISH!

BOOM!

BOOM!

CHAPTER TWENTY

Fight the Power

"That's the last of it," Hub said, the tone of his voice inconsistent and very worried.

"I'm losing faith in you, Hub," Noll responded.

"How in the hell fast are we going with your efficiency acceleration mumbo jumbo?" Alex asked, holding his stomach. "Because I feel like I'm feeling it."

"You guys feeling the speed?" Hub asked the group.

Everyone shook their heads.

"I can't even imagine how fast we're going," Hub wondered. "If Exccal is working, it's beyond comprehension."

"Beyond space monkey comprehension?" Oscar joked, grasping for that confidence. "Or beyond space cowboy comprehension?"

"Moving at the note of the universe." Hub commented.

"The note of the universe?" Sam asked.

"The speed of light, I mean."

Rick nodded because he liked the phrase.

"The note of the universe," Rick announced like a king. He would talk now and grace everyone with his presence and his grand words. "Hub, where did you hear that?"

"I made it up."

"You didn't make that up."

"I did. I made it up on the spot."

BOOM!

BOOM!

SWISH!

SWOOSH!

POOF!

SWISH!

BOOM!

BOOM!

"Hub," Grumpy called. "Seriously, what the hell is going on?"

Grumpy? Yes, I did say Grumpy.

Our speed managed to change our reality. The subconscious fought against the perceived. Like some ridiculous version of *Space Jam*.

"I don't know," Happy answered. "No idea."

"Can we stop it?" Bashful asked.

"Turn around?" Dopey added.

"We can't do anything. This is beyond our control."

Sneezy freed himself from his seatbelt.

"Put that back on," Happy screamed.

"I'm looking for an abort button."

The rest of the group sat back as Happy played alpha. "It's not the fucking movies."

"I know—*this* is more messed up."

"What the hell is happening?"

"Why are we characters from *Snow White and the Seven Dwarfs*? What the hell!"

Rick began to cry—*the king* began to cry.

"If another boost hits, you're dead. Buckle up."

"I'll take that chance."

"You'll be like a moving bullet in here. You can hurt us."

"I'll take that chance."

"There's no abort button."

"How do you know?"

"Because I'd be the one to know."

"I forgot, Hub, you're the big hotshot around here."

"I pay attention around here."

"And the rest of us are idiots."

Sneezy fiddled around with random switches.

"You're turning the light on and off."

"At least I'm trying."

"To kill us."

"To help."

"Sit the hell down."

SWISH!

SWOOSH!

POOF!

Sneezy fell to the ground in a frantic, unnatural fall.

"Hear that?" Happy yelled. "Get buckled in—now."

"Come on," Grumpy said. "Buckle up."

SWISH!

SWOOSH!

POOF!

"Buckle up," my father screamed.

"Get in your seat," my sister cried.

SWISH!

SWOOSH!

POOF!

Sneezy strapped himself in. He was pale and distant. He seemed to sink away somewhere. Not a word would come out of him.

• • •

"Hub," I yelled. "Hub, hear me?"

"Oscar," I yelled.

"Sam," I went on.

My echo: "Alex."

My echo: "Noll."

My echo: "Nick."

My echo: "Andrew."

"Rick!"

Reverberations.

Reverberations.

Reverberations.

"Hellooo?" a voice answered . . . echo . . . echo . . . echo.

"Hellooo?" another voice called out . . . echo . . . echo . . . echo.

"Hellooo?" yet another pleaded . . . echo . . . echo . . . echo.

I couldn't answer.

I tried.

But I couldn't.

The echoes then dissolved into a *brush* sound.

Forever, it seemed.

Brush.

The deep nothingness.

This long voyage into nowhere.

The board members floated lifelessly around the cabin and, out the window, I saw a small planet. It was white. There were no oceans. Nothing but white powder. I felt the deceleration tearing at my body and the rubber bodies bounced around the cabin.

"*Prepare for landing,*" the spacecraft said. "*Beginning initial descent. Estimated arrival—sixteen minutes. Atmosphere is thirty-three percent argon, thirty-three percent nitrogen, sixteen percent bromine, and eighteen percent iodine. Surface cannot support life. Spacesuit needed for exploration.*"

"What's the purpose of this flight?" I asked the spacecraft, begging for further guidance.

"*The purpose of this flight is . . .*"

Pause.

"What's the purpose of this flight?" I asked again, beginning to cry.

"*The purpose of this flight is . . .*"

Pause.

I began scream and shook the floating bodies for an answer.

Oh, god!

What's happened?

I put myself into a self-propelled panic, where my mind went around and around, with centrifugal force, and I cried and laughed and cried and laughed, around and around and around my mind went.

Then that alert came through.

The signal my wrist picked up was very faint and weak. But I could still hear it in my mind.

BLUE ALERT.

"BPU's special forces," it said, "captured and executed. Beashock Barnstormer's army invades Israel, burning down the White House and the Blue Planet United Capitol. Sentinelese forces unleash virus throughout the Middle East and portions of Europe. Naval forces heading to North America, carrying weaponized virus for lethal action. Citizens of the United States refuse to defend the BPU and call the draft 'sexist, racist, and xenophobic.' Protests and riots rattle New York, Los Angeles, and Miami. Americans decide to meet the Sentinelese with open arms. Reports of early arrivals in Miami and New York. Viewer discretion is advised."

The video came on and the image manifested in my mind. I was there. Right at the scene. At New York, with the reporter.

"As you can see," the reporter said from the GW Bridge, "the first line of Sentinelese forces has arrived right here on the Hudson."

The camera showed World War II battleships passing underneath the bridge. There were well over twenty of them.

"We have no idea how Beashock Barnstormer commandeered these ships, and we have no idea what to expect after they anchor. Where they anchor is also an unknown."

The camera zoomed in on a crowd of people hanging off the bridge. They were whistling and clapping.

Signs bobbled in the air reading: *BPU: Beat People Up!*

Other signs read: *We understand you!*

Some others read: *Open your arms. Don't open up arms.*

The reporter's face took too much focus now and he went on reporting in that mechanical way:

"The residents of New York seem to be elated by the supposed 'invasion.' Here's one New Yorker's view on the Sentinelese."

A man dressed like John Lennon hogged the camera with his hot breath and his girlfriend hung on his shoulder. She had temporary tattoos stamped across her face, glitter drizzled around her eyes, and a tall Uncle Sam hat on her head. Her boyfriend wore opaque circular sunglasses and a white sleeveless *NEW YORK CITY* shirt.

"They just want to be accepted," he said, like Jesus would. "They're like anyone else, you know. You gotta give a man a break when he wants a piece of bread."

"Give a man a break when he wants a piece of bread," his girlfriend chanted.

"Give a man a break when he wants a piece of bread," another chanted.

"Give a man a break when he wants a piece of bread," they all chanted.

"Give a man a break when he wants a piece of bread."

"Give a man a break when he wants a piece of bread."

"Give a man a break when he wants a piece of bread."

It changed into:

"Give them a break. And break some bread."

"Give them a break. And break some bread."

"Give them a break. And break some bread."

And on and on it went.

The reporter's wax face came too much into frame again.

"New Yorkers welcome the Sentinelese," he said, opening his arms with sudden emotion still in the confines of his professionalism. "And they believe the Sentinelese will welcome them, too."

The camera moved away from his face and zoomed in on a warship seeming to reverse its direction. Its broadside now faced the screaming crowd on the bridge and its artillery battery pointed up at the camera.

"They're saluting us," one person screamed.

"They're saluting us," another said.

"They're saluting us," the crowd said.

"They're saluting us," they chanted.

"They're saluting us."

"They're saluting us."

"They're saluting us."

Then a crack in the fabric of the air. The screen went blank, and the signal was lost. All the tech in my body went dead and the spacecraft entered the atmosphere of this white planet.

. . .

Jaclyn pointed to the open ocean.

That openness.

That lack of anything ahead.

Those waves.

The blackness ahead. That hint of sun.

You could only look forward when there was nothing else but horizon.

Ahead, that horizon.

Ahead, those waves.

That endlessness.

"We almost made it," her words shook.

"There's more to be seen out there," she went on. "I'll go back, *alone*."

. . .

"I don't think he's alive," a voice said.

"The *son*—is the son alive?" another asked.

"That's what I mean."

"Let me see."

A hand touched my neck.

"There's a pulse. Faint. But there's a pulse."

"Fep?"

"I'm pretty sure he's gone."

. . .

"What's the purpose of this flight?" I asked for the last time.

"*The purpose of this flight is . . .*"

Moments later, from some unknown location, John Williams' "Somewhere in My Memory" from *Home Alone* played.

It got louder and louder until it suddenly dropped and then trailed off into thin, very light notes dematerializing into this abyss.

Now, pure silence.

Until I heard, without cease, something entirely new. It burrowed itself into this purity and this calm: "Fight the power," I heard, in its infancy.

"Fight the power," it grew.

"Fight the power."

"Fight the power."

"Fight the Power" by Public Enemy played on, and it was time for me to let go . . .

"Clear!" I heard from beyond.

Rumbles off in the distance.

"He's gone," a voice said.